Better Together

SWEET HAVEN FARM
BOOK TWO

JESSIE GUSSMAN

Contents

Acknowledgments

Cover art by Julia Gussman
Editing by Heather Hayden
Narration by Jay Dyess
Author Services by CE Author Assistant

∼

Listen to the unabridged audio for FREE performed by Jay Dyess on the Say with Jay channel on YouTube. Get early access to all of Jay's recordings and listen to Jessie's books before they're available to the general public, plus get daily Bible readings by Jay and bonus scenes by becoming a Say with Jay channel member.

To my parents.
Dad power-walked us through the railroad tunnel, and Mom drove the getaway car. I was well into adulthood before I thought to wonder what normal families did for fun. I love you both. Thank you.

Special Thank-You's*:*
My husband spoils me beyond words. It's been a joy to share the journey with you.

My life has been enriched by my children. Thank you for making me laugh.

Every chapter in this book contains the impressions of my critique partner, Carlyn Jones. You point out the weaknesses in my writing with the graciousness and class of the Southern Lady you are. You have been a huge blessing in my life. Thank you.

Thank you so much to my beta readers and Critique Group: Ramla Zareen, Kimberly Dallaire, Tiara Giles, Lydia, Maryanne Fantalis, Negeen Papehn, Shoba Sadler.

Chapter One

"No way am I going in there." Harper Bright took a second look at the yawning black hole in the mountain in front of her and crossed her arms over her chest. She didn't need her doctorate degree to know this was a bad idea.

"Did you know this tunnel was on Hitler's charts during World War II? If he ever made it stateside, it was one of the places he planned to bomb." Wyatt Fernandez planted his feet and put his hands on his hips. His dimples flashed but he spoke in the tone of voice that said, "I hear you, but I'm ignoring you".

He used the same tone every time he dragged Harper on some crazy adventure or another.

She walked toward the openmouthed hole. Despite her family having owned the ground around the tunnel all her life, she hadn't known about this small spot in Central Pennsylvania being on Hitler's map.

The looming mountain that shot up around the ravenous cavity blocked the sunlight. Leafy green trees waved in the warm June breeze. Harper squinted up. "You know, someday, we really ought to start acting like the mature adults we are."

"Gimme a break, Harper. The only time you ever spend two

seconds not acting like an adult is when I strong arm you into it. Like now. This is going to be fun." Wyatt flashed that irresistible dimple and his brown eyes twinkled. Harper wasn't exactly short, but she still had to crane her neck to look at him as he walked beside her. His lanky frame had filled out in the decade since high school. Actually, now that she thought about it, he'd filled out very nicely. Broad chest, wide shoulders, and long, muscular legs. A flare of heat unfurled in her stomach. She straightened her spine. This was Wyatt. Her best friend.

They reached the orifice of the mountain. Cool air blew from its depths. It smelled heavy and sweet, like rotting soil. Their next steps took them inside. The hair on the back of Harper's neck poked straight out. She scooted closer to Wyatt.

"I'm not seeing the 'fun' part." Her voice echoed off the cavernous walls. Water dripped hollowly, echoing in the blackness.

Wyatt kept walking. "This isn't supposed to be fun. It's research. Do you want to find it or not?"

Harper bumped Wyatt's arm with her shoulder. "You know I do."

She wanted to see if the old stories were true, but couldn't help shivering as she looked around at the stone walls arching above. The farther in they walked, the darker it got. At this point, she could barely see Wyatt's outline. She pushed back the fear threatening to break loose in her head. It wasn't that walking in the tunnel was particularly dangerous. It was more the idea of the dark unknown and being trapped in a small space with an angry locomotive.

As if Wyatt could read her mind, he said, "There isn't any danger if a train would actually go through while we're in here. Although, I have heard that there could be a bit of air suction."

She planted her feet. "What?"

"Kidding." He pulled on her arm. "Come on."

She started walking again. Slowly. "What did you mean by air suction?" Wyatt had always been better with hard science. All she'd cared about was finding the family heirloom that her great-great grandmother had told her was hidden in the deepest depths.

Wyatt tapped her head with the hand that wasn't dragging her toward the tunnel. "Well, since you're the brain in this relationship..."

She swatted his hand and continued to drag her feet, even though she'd already decided to go along with his nutty scheme, the way she always did. After all, not only did she want to find the ring, but this could be the last time Wyatt and she went on an adventure together. She'd gotten the call yesterday that her tenure vote was scheduled for the end of summer. It was the one last thing she had to cross off the list of career goals she'd made the day she had graduated from high school.

"Quit it. You're smarter than me, and we both know it. I just happen to be able to stay in one place long enough to get a degree." It wasn't that she was so smart. She was simply willing to work hard. Plus, she liked to study. She'd enjoyed every second of the last ten years. Which led her to the vexatious question that had plagued her since the phone call: *what now?*

"Ouch." Wyatt placed a hand over his heart.

She shrugged. Too often she'd wondered that maybe what she'd been working toward all this time wasn't what she really wanted anymore. More likely she had become overly comfortable with achieving her goals, ticking each accomplishment off of her internal checklist. "It's true."

"Yeah, well, you had a nice, secure home all your life."

And he hadn't. Never really knowing or being wanted by his father, losing his mother in a tragic skiing accident, being sent to live with an uncle he barely knew. Of course, if he hadn't come to live with the man her mother eventually married, she would never have gotten to know him. She bit her lip. "I'm sorry."

"Hey, not a problem. I'll only rub it in if you change your mind and turn around."

They walked far enough into the tunnel that the light behind them faded, and Harper could no longer see the road under her feet. Dread balled and rolled in the pit of her stomach. She reached for Wyatt. Big and strong with rough calluses, his hand enfolded hers with an ease born of familiarity.

How could she have forgotten how easily Wyatt's touch could calm her? All the numerous phone conversations and thousands of text messages couldn't replicate the comfort of his touch. The miles between them had always multiplied Harper's anxiety. The pictures he sent hadn't helped. Standing at the top of some snow-covered mountain with only clouds and sky in the background, or his arms outstretched, moments before he leapt from a who-knows-how-high cliff with only a thin bundle—hopefully a parachute—strapped to his back. Of course, she wasn't sure which was worse, the pictures, or the times when she didn't hear from him for days. He always warned her when he might be adventuring out of service areas, but that was one instance when knowledge wasn't power, as her ragged, bloody nails could testify.

"Do you think we're halfway?" she asked.

"Why are you whispering?"

She shivered—she hadn't noticed she was whispering. "Just in case there's a bear hibernating in one of those alcoves you talked about."

"It's June."

"Maybe it's waking up late this year." Even to her ears it sounded asinine. Her cheeks heated. She looked over, but they were so deep in the mountain that she couldn't see a thing. The darkness hid her flush. Lifting her chin, she tried to focus on the stories she'd heard as a child. If they found what they were looking for, it would be worth facing her fear.

"I can't believe someone has actually hired you to teach college students." He squeezed her hand, and she didn't need a light to know he smiled beside her.

"I revert to my inner child when I'm scared spitless."

Wyatt activated his cell phone light. "There." He pointed it at the wall. Sure enough, just ahead an arched area was chiseled into the side of the mountain. "Maybe three feet deep, three feet long and," he looked up, "seven or so feet high. We'd both fit in there easy."

"Us and the serial killer that eludes the cops by hiding in here." She tugged on his hand. "Come on. Faster."

"Didn't you ever hear you gotta enjoy the journey?" Harper could hear the grin in Wyatt's voice, but he did speed up a notch. For her. Heck, this was child's play compared to the stuff he normally did.

But it was Wyatt, and she didn't have to pretend to be brave. "I'll enjoy it once we're out of here."

"It'll be over then." He chuckled. "Oh, except we have to walk back through."

She stopped so fast her feet probably left skid marks. But she wouldn't know since it was darker than sin, and she couldn't see a blasted thing except for the far tunnel opening which didn't seem to be getting any closer.

"We only have to go to the middle hidey hole. That's where it's supposed to be. No one said anything about walking through." Fear had turned her backbone into an icicle. "I know you're an adrenaline junkie, but I'm allergic to the stuff."

Wyatt snorted. "If it weren't for me, you'd be moldering under your books and lab rats. How many times have you left the state?"

"Three. And it was three too many. I like being home. I like moldering." She kept her eyes fastened to the circle of light on the ground from Wyatt's cell phone until he put it away.

"I like being home, too. But being home is sweeter after you've left it for a while." His thumb moved lightly over her knuckles.

A little of her tension eased. "I always assumed you had itchy feet like your mom."

"A little, I guess."

"If that's not it, why not come home? You know Fink and my mom would love to have you back helping out on the farm." She'd love to have him back, too. Gosh, she missed him. She hadn't realized how much.

Even though he'd been away more than home the last few years, she still considered him her best friend. They had always told each other everything.

Well, except anything that even hinted of romance. Growing up, she'd always been very aware that her mother had gotten pregnant with her at fourteen. Harper had determined not to go down the same path, closing herself off to the very idea of boys or boyfriends. Studying instead of dating. She supposed, at twenty-eight, it was probably okay to crack that protective shell.

"Come on, Pickles. We're almost half-way. The next hidey-hole is probably close." His deep voice rumbled above her.

She smiled at the nickname he had gifted her with years ago.

Light cut through the darkness parallel to the ground—the wrong angle for Wyatt's cell phone—just before he tensed beside her. The rumble in the air and the vibration under her feet confirmed what her brain had suspected. She turned to be sure. The entire mouth of the tunnel was blocked out by the massive shape of a train engine. Like a flesh-eating bacteria, magnified, with teeth bared, it bore down on them.

Acid shards cut through her trembling body. She barely felt Wyatt yanking on her arm. She couldn't get her feet to move. The engine powered closer like a black avalanche, chewing up the distance between them.

He swept her up in his arms and jogged the two steps to the nook, flattening himself against the side wall so his back was toward the train. The roar of the engine and the squeal of metal on steel reverberated throughout the stone walls. The vibration seemed to be alive, monstrous, so close and big and loud she could almost see it. She pulled her body into a ball and pressed against him. She wrapped her arms around his head, wanting to protect him, too.

Her breath came in short gasps. Panic rolled through her like a bowling ball heading toward the king pin.

She closed her eyes tight, until it was only Wyatt's solid, comforting warmth pressing into her and the deafening noise all around. He cradled her and bent over slightly. The tangy, heavy stench of diesel exhaust filled the air around them, burning Harper's nose.

Eventually the engine noise faded away and, although the train was still loud, the cars passing had a more rhythmic feel. Loud clack-clack, then fading out before coming back combined with the occasional earsplitting screech of metal on metal.

Wyatt's stubble rubbed her cheek. She closed her eyes and moved her cheek back over his. Her chest tingled. She froze and her eyes snapped open. This was Wyatt. Her best friend. She would not allow their friendship to be ruined because she all of a sudden had some wild ribbon of desire winding through her. No matter how delicious it was.

His breath warmed her ear as he said, "Now we know there's no air suction."

"I'm going to poison the next meal I make you," she hissed into his neck, only half-joking.

"I've heard that before." His heart beat steady and strong against her. The dratted man wasn't even scared.

The last of the cars went by. The noise faded.

She loosened her arms from around his head. She didn't know what she was trying to protect him from anyway.

It was probably time to remember she was a grown-up. A professor up for tenure vote at the end of the summer. But Wyatt's warmth and strength were alluring. She didn't want to pull away from the hardness of his chest or lose the comfort of his touch. But she couldn't let him stand here holding her forever.

"Okay, put me down." She lifted her head and smacked his shoulder lightly, pretending she hadn't been clutching him like two oxygen atoms on a hydrogen, and praying her knees wouldn't buckle when he complied.

She wiggled to prompt him to move, but a new sound echoed in the darkness and she froze. A hiss. Followed by a rattle.

"Holy crap." Her arms tightened around Wyatt's neck. "Is that what I think it is?"

"Yeah. Someone's practicing the maracas." She could feel his head tilt in the darkness. "They're pretty good."

Her teeth rattled together, but she snorted a laugh. "That's a rattlesnake. It sounds close."

"I don't think we need to worry. I thought it was a stick when I first stepped on it, but sticks don't typically wrap themselves around your leg."

Chills raced up Harper's spine. Her mouth opened, but it took a minute to make her voice work. "You're standing on the snake?"

"Yes, ma'am."

The sound like stones shaking in a tin can echoed throughout the tunnel again.

She ignored the note of sarcasm in his voice. "What are we going to do?"

"You're the one with the doctorate. How about I keep standing on the snake while you think?"

Her throat slammed shut. She struggled to swallow. "I study nutrition. In a lab. That's what the doctorate is for. Food."

"Branch out a little."

Despite Harper's all-encompassing fear, she smiled. "Okay." She took a deep breath. If he wasn't worried, if he thought it was funny, well, she could do humor, too. "I'm thinking about white sandy beaches, relaxing waves, warm sun..."

"Try again."

She grinned—still petrified, but Wyatt exuded calm. "Hey, that was helping."

He snorted.

Ideas were not exactly filling her mind. Her brain had diverted all her blood flow to the areas that made her want to pee and run at the same time. She went with the only plan she could think of. "How about I grab your cell phone out of your pocket. I'll shine the flashlight down at your feet..."

"Um, close your eyes while you do it, just in case..."

Harper twisted gingerly in his arms and felt for the phone attached to his belt, not wanting to make him lose his balance, although he seemed rock solid. Funny, because she still pictured Wyatt as a gangly teen instead of the unflappable man holding her in his arms and not even breathing hard. "Just in case what?"

Silence.

"Wyatt. Is there something you're not telling me?"

"Not really."

Not really? That meant there was something. What could be worse than a rattlesnake? "If there was a bear in this hidey hole, I'd have figured it out by now."

"I'm sure you would have, Pickles." He shifted ever so slightly. "Would you just shine the light down?"

She paused with the phone in her shaking hand. "What does 'not really' mean? You're standing on the snake, right?"

"One of them."

"Holy crap. Holy crap. Holy crap."

He gave her the password to his phone. She pulled up the flashlight app with shaking fingers. Something caught her eye in a crack in the stone behind Wyatt's head. Her racing heart jumped. She squinted to see more clearly. She'd forgotten the reason they were in the tunnel in the first place.

"Harper? Tell me you're not playing Candy Crush."

"Uh. No. Of course not." She juggled the phone to her other hand.

Once they got the snake figured out, she could examine the crack more closely. There was definitely something there. Faded blue fabric, maybe?

She shone the light at the ground, keeping her eyes trained on the wall. Now that she knew something was there, she could see the shadow that marked the spot.

Wyatt shuddered. "Eh, I was wrong."

"Thank God." Cool relief flooded her. Her fingers lifted and skimmed the smooth surface of the stone.

"There's three."

She tensed.

Then yelped.

She dropped his phone.

Wyatt jerked.

With her free hand, she slapped at the wall. A small object landed in her palm.

Chapter Two

Fate could certainly be strange at times. Wyatt finally had Harper in his arms, but he also had three rattlesnakes curled at his feet.

He would stand on a hundred rattlesnakes for the chance to have Harper in his arms, her warm breath teasing his neck, her hands gripping his shoulders, her sweet scent surrounding him.

The woman was oblivious. Still thought of him as a gangly, awkward, motherless boy she'd adopted as her brother. That hadn't changed in the last eight years.

As the phone fell, the snake on his left boot struck it. Wyatt didn't wait to see more. Pushing off with his right foot—the one on the snake —he leaped as far as he could, then jogged a few yards away. He didn't feel any sharp pricks indicating a bite. The snake that had been wrapped around his leg tightened its grip before it slipped off. Awfully nice of it, he had to admit. As he suspected, the snakes were probably sluggish from being in the cool tunnel. However, their venom would be just as, if not more, potent.

After he'd taken enough quick strides to be safely away, he stopped, adjusting Harper in his arms. He breathed in her scent—vanilla berries —and smiled at the contradiction. She was always so serious and mature, but her scent was utterly feminine and almost girlish. He closed his eyes, taking another deep breath, resisting the urge to snuggle his face into her soft brown hair.

"Are you okay?" he asked.

"Yeah. My stomach and heart don't feel like they're trying to escape through my cervical vertebrae anymore."

"Just relax. I'll set you down in a minute." The two tracks that ran east-west from New York City to Chicago merged into one to go through the tunnel. Computerized dispatching and GPS monitoring meant trains could be pretty darn close together. But Harper still clenched his shoulders in a death grip. They had a minute for her to relax before they turned around.

"What about your phone?" Harper asked against his neck. Every time her lips moved against his skin, shivers raced up and down his spine and the hair on his arms stood up. He couldn't let her find out. If she knew how madly in love with her he was, he'd lose the best friend he'd ever had.

He shifted before asking, "Did you just volunteer to go back for it?"

She snorted.

He couldn't contain his chuckle. "Yeah, that's what I thought. I'll come back for it later, with a flashlight and a stick."

"And a gun," she said fervently.

"It's illegal to kill rattlesnakes."

"You're kidding."

"Nope."

"That's nuts," she huffed. "They're dangerous. Someone could get hurt."

"Don't think that law was designed with the safety of the American citizen in mind."

She snorted again, and he smiled. Next week he would be heading off with friends to finally fulfill his late mother's dream of backpacking through the European Alps. It seemed an appropriate thing to do to commemorate the ten-year anniversary of her death. Then he was heading to Chile for a permanent position of managing his dad's ski resort—another thing his mother had wanted.

But he'd always hated the idea of leaving Harper. And the words "permanent position" made him loathe the idea even more.

Though after he'd been around for a few weeks, he'd hate the idea of staying, too. Harper never noticed him. Not the way he noticed her.

They weren't related by blood, since his uncle married her mother a few years ago. But Harper saw him as her stepbrother, or step-cousin, or some kind of family relation.

He didn't have any such illusions. She was the one he wanted. Had always wanted. Unfortunately, she was practically married to that university. First her bachelors, then her masters, then her doctorate. Now she wanted stinking tenure. By the time she got her nose out of her moldy old books and finally noticed him, he'd be lucky if he had any good teeth left.

So, it was probably for the best that he was leaving for Chile. Maybe the next time he was home, she'd open her eyes and see *him*. Of course, if things went the way his dad wanted, he'd be spending the rest of his life in Chile.

And, knowing his luck, she'd end up married to some cerebrotonic bore.

Her voice floated through the darkness. "You can set me down now. Your arms are probably numb."

"I'm fine."

But she squirmed, and he didn't want her to suspect that he still held her because he wanted to, not because he needed to. He lowered her.

Harper grabbed his hand. In the dark, he didn't even bother to hide his grin. That was the whole point of getting her to do crazy things like this with him—he got to hold her hand, and on this rare occasion, hold her. And she thought *he* was doing *her* the favor.

"Are you laughing?"

"At what, Pickles?" He pulled her toward the tracks. They could walk on them past the hidey hole. The snakes had fulfilled his thirst for adventure. For the next ten minutes or so, anyway. He guessed Harper had quenched her thirst for much, much longer.

"Your mind is so twisted, I couldn't even begin to guess," she said.

His grip tightened on her hand as his foot caught the small bed of gravel the train tracks rested on. "Watch your..."

Harper gave a sharp cry as she fell.

Chapter Three

Pain burned up from Harper's ankle to her knee. She bit back a moan.

She felt Wyatt drop to his knees beside her.

"Are you okay?" Concerned laced his voice.

"I think I twisted my ankle." She took a deep breath and blew out slowly. The pain settled into a dull thump, only occasionally shooting up her calf.

His arms slipped under her, and he lifted her. "I can't see a blessed thing in here. Can you move your toes?" He stepped over the rail and started walking down what she assumed was the center of the tracks. It really was as black as a closed coffin. She shook her head slightly. Bad analogy.

"Yes. I'm sure it's not broken. I think I can walk." She took another deep breath, this one contained a large dose of Wyatt's unique, comforting scent.

"I can go faster if I carry you. They arrest trespassers, you know."

Harper's chest seized. Of course. "Something else you neglected to mention before we decided to do this crazy thing." She thought of the small pouch she'd shoved in her pocket. Hopefully this would all be worth it. Still. "How long do you think it would take the railroad police to get here if the engineer saw us?"

It was hard to say for sure, but an arrest and trespassing charges on her record would probably affect her tenure vote. A little voice whispered maybe it was a good thing, but she pushed it aside. Of course tenure was what she wanted. Isn't that what she'd spent the last ten years working toward? And it was all within reach. She was happy, not restless.

"Thirty minutes if they come from the shop in Altoona," Wyatt answered her question. "I'm sorry I got you into this."

"Tomorrow we'll be laughing," Harper said, hoping it was true.

"Unless we're in jail."

She laughed into his shoulder. "I can always count on you to be honest."

"Hey, I've gotten you into a few tight spots, but I've never left you. That ought to count for something."

She tightened her grip on his neck. "It does. The only excitement I've ever had in my life has come from you. I'm sure at some point, maybe when I'm eighty, I'll appreciate it." This could be her last adventure. Wyatt would leave for Chile. She would stay, getting tenure. Both of them doing what they'd dreamed of. Somehow the thought depressed her. "Oh, I'm sure you'll appreciate it."

His voice dipped and lowered, all but whispering, sending odd quivers down her spine.

When they were younger, she and Wyatt had been partners in adventure. Equal. Wyatt might have been just as likely to push her into something as to help her out. Now, it seemed like he had matured. His protectiveness toward her made her feel...feminine. Even in the dark harshness of the tunnel, the emotion sifted through her body, shimmery and soft, burgeoning in her chest and making her skin tingle.

"Are you sure I'm not too heavy?" she said, laughing to cover the awareness that she should not be feeling toward her best friend.

"I can't even tell I'm carrying you."

Wonderful. He couldn't even tell he carried her, but it was all she could think about. "I hadn't realized that you had morphed into He-Man since your last visit to the farm."

All she needed was some light banter to remind her that Wyatt was her buddy, not her boyfriend.

"Superman." He corrected her.

"I assumed if you were Superman, you would have flown us out of here by now."

Wyatt's back shifted under her, like he'd shrugged his shoulders. "You'd better watch it, Pickles. Don't challenge my superpowers. I've got you in my clutches."

Water dripped nearby, echoing through the tunnel clearly. A cool breeze blew Wyatt's clean, soapy scent back across her face. She inhaled. She'd rather be in Wyatt's *clutches* than in anyone else's. The irony of her situation hit her.

By far the youngest professor on staff, Harper didn't usually have to fight herself to be decorous and sedate, as befit a college professor. Her current position, clinging to Wyatt's shoulders and bouncing with each step he took, trespassing on railroad property and sharing the cool, damp tunnel with at least three slithering reptiles, was not exactly dignified.

A familiar rattle sound joined the drip of the water, reverberating off the stone tunnel sides and ceiling, coming from nowhere and everywhere. Even though she knew *she* was perfectly safe, Harper still tensed, gripping Wyatt's shoulders. Maybe he wore boots, but he was still vulnerable. He tightened his hold on her, as though in reassurance.

"Left," Wyatt said, although she already knew the snakes were still on the wider side of the tunnel.

A beam shone past her head.

"Train," she yelled, even as she looked around Wyatt's shoulder to be sure.

Already in the tunnel, the locomotive blocked all the light from the far opening as it barreled down upon them. The thunderous sound filled the confined space, echoing along the walls, seeming to amplify with each bounce of sound waves.

Deja vu.

"We're going right," Wyatt said in a shout she barely heard as he turned his body that direction.

"Put me down," she hollered. She twisted as he moved. Because there was no road on that side of the tracks, the space between the tracks and the wall was much narrower. There was no way he'd be able to hold her and still fit between the train and stone wall.

The train loomed large in the darkness. They needed to get off the tracks. He released her legs. Squeezing an arm between their bodies and grabbing her around the waist, supporting her as she limped, he moved her off the tracks toward the right side. Away from the snakes.

Stumbling over the right rail, she cleared the tracks, hitting the stone wall almost immediately. Slightly behind her, she sensed Wyatt's presence, until he stumbled over the rail. He fell to the stones. Swinging back around she saw his legs were still over the rails. Just a few seconds and the train would be on them. Ignoring the pain in her ankle, she grabbed Wyatt's arm and yanked with strength aided by adrenaline. His knee caught on the rail. His body twisted.

With no time to coordinate movements, Harper kept her grip on his arm. Summoning every bit of muscle she could muster, she hauled back. Wyatt propelled himself forward at the same time. His body hit hers. He twisted and they fell together, pressing against the hard stone wall. The engine roared by. She pressed her face against the smooth, cool rock. Her heart punched her ribs, fast and hard.

The train thundered along, mere inches from her head. She should be petrified. And she was. But Wyatt's breath was hot on her ear, his body hard and warm against hers. Her hands clenched the solid muscles of his back and their legs tangled together. Awareness tangled up in her fast-beating heart, tripping it.

She squeezed her eyes tightly closed like that could somehow shut down the sensations she shouldn't be feeling. Not now. And most especially not with Wyatt.

~

HARPER LAY on her shabby chic sofa. Her foot was propped on two pillows. Wyatt's eyes caught hers and she scrunched up her nose. "I really don't think all this is necessary."

Wyatt clenched the glass of water in his hand. It hurt to see her hurting. "Humor me. I feel bad that it was my idea, and you're the one with a sprained ankle."

"Well, I've always wondered if the stories I'd been told as a child were true. Oh, that reminds me—" Harper dug in the front pocket of her jeans. She pulled out a musty little blue velvet pouch. Worn.

Wyatt's mouth fell open. "You got it? When did you get it?" He put a finger out and touched the faded fabric, then glanced into Harper's face. She smiled like she'd just cracked the code to win the lottery.

"While you were tripping on your alter-ego, the snake charmer, I continued to be focused on the task at hand..."

"Was that before or after you dropped my phone?"

"Minor detail." Harper waved her hand, and Wyatt bit back a grin. It hadn't seemed so minor at the time.

He twisted the glass in his hand. "So, while I was holding the snakes at bay, you found your long-lost family heirloom?"

Harper held the pouch by the strings. The smile faded from her face. "I don't know if that's what it is or not."

"So...are we going to look?" Wyatt set the ice water down and moved a stack of books so he could sit on her coffee table. For an organized person, Harper had books everywhere in her tiny efficiency apartment.

"I don't know if I want to know." Harper met his eyes and he recognized the uncertainty there.

"Why not?"

"I've been hearing those stories all my life. How my great-great-great-grandmother left her ducal husband in England to run away with an Irish sharecropper." Her fingers smoothed over the small pouch. "That's my history. I don't want it to change."

"But you want the truth. Plus, change doesn't equal bad."

Harper shrugged and dropped her eyes. Wyatt's heart dropped along with them. That was the second reason they could never be together. Not only did he not want to risk ruining their great friendship, but Harper was so grounded in her farm and family. She hated change. And for them to be together would rock her world in too many ways to list.

She stared at the pouch. "To have my world shifting around me just makes me feel...insecure."

Wyatt tried to lighten both their moods. "Does that mean we never find out what's in the pouch?"

Her lips tilted up and she held up the pouch. "Do you want to do the honors?"

"It's your family. I'm the snake-charmer."

"You were amazing with that, by the way." Harper looked up at him. His heart swelled at the sincere admiration in her gaze. If only he could turn that admiration into love.

He smiled to conceal his thoughts. "Thanks."

Harper grinned back at him. Then she loosened the strings on the pouch. "Here goes." She turned the pouch upside down. A thick gold band with a sparkling green emerald and intricate gold work dropped into her hand.

Wyatt whistled. "I'm not an expert on jewelry, but that thing isn't your run of the mill mall jewelry store ring. It looks heavy."

"It is." Harper picked up the ring and twisted it in different directions. "There's an inscription." She turned the ring and squinted. "Sweet Haven of Rest."

"I wonder what that means." He was curious, sure. But he was enjoying more the wonder on Harper's face.

"This is the ring! That's what my grandmother always told me it said." She turned glowing eyes on him. "My great-great-great-grandmother had that engraved after they got to America. I guess, even though she was married to a duke, her life wasn't that great in England. She expected things to be much better here on the farm. And, of course, she couldn't keep another man's wedding ring, and no one would believe that the poor Irishman she'd run off with would have given her something so grand, so she had to get rid of it." Harper shook her head. "Can you imagine what she left? Safety, security, her husband..."

"All for love." Wyatt wished the old woman was here today to give Harper a lesson on the power of love.

Harper turned the ring over, looking at it from all sides. "I can't imagine crossing an ocean and going to an unknown land would have been worth it. I think this ring is evidence she wasn't sure either."

"I think the fact that the ring was still in the tunnel is evidence that it was."

"Why?"

"If she wasn't happy, wouldn't she have gone back and gotten the ring?"

"Maybe she forgot about it."

"That's my point. Look at that thing. It's not something that's going to slip your mind. Especially if you're unhappy and miserable."

Harper's brows drew down. "Good point."

"Your grandmother chose love." Wyatt nodded to the green fields outside the small living room window, indicating the farm that she and her Irishman worked together. "It was the right choice."

Harper snorted. "All except that small detail about her still being married to her husband in England."

"True. She never married your great-great-great-grandfather?"

"Nope. That's one good thing about moving across the ocean where no one knows you. They just pretended they'd always been married. No one ever questioned it."

"The tunnel was a good hiding spot."

"Yes." She twisted on the pillow. "Thanks for suggesting we go look for it. It was definitely worth the twisted ankle."

"And the snakes."

"Uh…"

"You wouldn't have the ring."

"Okay. You're right. And the snakes."

From the kitchen counter, Harper's phone rang.

Wyatt jumped up and brought it to her. "It's your mom."

"That's odd. She usually calls in the evening." A pinch of worry caught in Harper's chest as she swiped the screen. "Hello?"

"Harper. Honey."

"Mom, what's wrong?"

"Sweetheart, I don't want to worry you." A statement like that always caused worry. Harper twisted the heavy gold band she still held, then she slid it on her finger. Heavy and cool, it somehow felt reassuring, too.

"What is it?"

"It's Fink. He didn't feel well yesterday. Then he collapsed last night. I'm calling from the hospital."

Harper sat up. She gripped the phone tighter. She hated travelling. She hated leaving home, but family was more important. "I'll catch a plane and be right out. I'll take care of the boys."

"No. Grandma and Grandpap have them. Everything's fine right now with the boys." Ellie paused. "Actually, a cousin I'd never met is staying with them, too. She's helping with the boys."

Harper felt guilty for the relief that cascaded through her. She really didn't want to fly to Arizona. She didn't want to fly anywhere. "What about Fink? What about you?"

Her mother sighed. "He's stable. But they think it's sepsis. They've started antibiotics, but they're going to culture it because they think it might be resistant."

Harper gasped. "MRSA?"

Her mother paused. "Possibly," she whispered.

"Mom, I can't let you do this by yourself. I'll catch a flight..."

"No. That's what I was calling for. I didn't want to worry you. But, the last thing Fink said before he passed out was about getting the pumpkins planted. I assured him that you and Wyatt—did Wyatt get in?"

"Yes. Last night." She met Wyatt's gaze, noted the furrow above his nose, and gave a little smile. He lifted his brows in question and she put a finger up.

"Oh, good." Ellie sighed with relief.

"He's planning on heading out early next week."

"Oh." Her mom's voice sounded weak, tired. "I don't have much time here. The doctor is supposed to come out and talk to me any minute. Do you think that you can find someone to help with the farm?" Voices in the background babbled incoherently, then her mom came back on. "I need to go. I'll call you later. Just, if you can take care of the farm...."

"We've got it, mom."

"Thanks, honey."

Harper slid her phone from her ear. She met Wyatt's concerned look. "Fink's in the hospital. Sepsis. Maybe MRSA. The boys are fine. I told her we'd find someone to take care of the farm."

"Is Fink...?"

"She said he was stable. She seemed more upset that Fink was worried about getting the pumpkins planted than worried that he was going to...die."

"I see." Wyatt stood. He shoved his hands in his front pockets and walked the short distance to the front door, staring out the window. "He could be in the hospital for weeks."

"And you're leaving."

He glanced over his shoulder. "Don't you have a research position that is starting?"

"Yeah." It was a full-time position, plus reading and paperwork in the evenings. She most certainly wouldn't have time to have the farm ready for fall customers. Unless she gave the position up. But she couldn't. Her tenure vote was at the end of the summer. If she backed out of the research position, no one would think she deserved tenure. It just wasn't done.

Harper sat up and swung her foot to the coffee table, although her head was now throbbing harder than her ankle.

Sepsis. MRSA. That was serious stuff. Surely her mother was beside herself with worry. She wanted to rush out. But that's not what her mother had asked her to do.

"Mom wanted us to either take care of the farm, especially getting the pumpkins planted, or to see if we can get someone to help out, since we both have things we need to do."

Wyatt turned from the door and studied her for a moment, with as serious as an expression as he'd ever used. He rubbed a hand over his face. "As much as Fink and Ellie have done for me, I hate to let them down."

"Yeah." Harper fingered the ring. This farm represented generations of her family. "I'm going to hobble up to the house. Mom has a list of emergency contacts and some other numbers in her desk. I can get started on trying to find someone."

Immediately, Wyatt was beside her, holding her hand. "We'll get someone lined up to take over. Then I'll get the pumpkins planted."

"And I'll get a list made up of all the things that will need done in the next...month? Do you think it will be that long?" The weight of responsibility settled heavily on her shoulders. She couldn't let her mom down. Wyatt squeezed her hand and she gave him a grateful look. He'd never let her down.

"Hard to tell. I don't think it would be out of line to make plans for that long. He'll probably be weak when he gets home. And your mom has the three boys to look after."

"That's true. I think Bill Sinclair down the road borrowed their skid loader last fall to clean out his barn after his broke. We'll try him first."

Wyatt smacked a hand on his leg. "Yeah. Neighbors are always eager to help each other. We'll have people beating the doors down to help."

~

THREE HOURS later Wyatt pushed the red "off" button on the farm house phone. He placed both hands on the desk and flexed his shoulders.

"No luck?" Harper asked from the desk chair, without much hope on her face.

Wyatt straightened and ran a finger down over the curve of the roll top desk. "No. They have family coming in from Wilkes-Barre. They said they could come over and water our flowers. Feed the cat."

Harper rolled her eyes. "Funny how many of our neighbors don't know we don't have a cat."

"Everyone has a cat."

"We should get one. I've talked to about sixteen people who are willing to come feed one for us."

"And zero who are willing to trim Christmas trees or spray apples or set up sprinklers to water pumpkins for the next six weeks." His eye caught on the corner of an old envelope sticking up along the edge of the lower part of the desk. Like it had fallen through the crack. He teased it up.

Harper held up a little green book. "I've called every person on Mom's Christmas card list who lives in the state."

"Plus that one who lives on the Maryland line." He almost had the envelope free. It was off-white with a stamp design he recognized from his senior year of high school.

Harper rolled her eyes. "Yeah. Two hours one way isn't that far to drive for family."

"Can't blame her for not wanting to make that drive. Not with her triplets being only four weeks old."

"Yeah. Remind me to tell mom she said thanks for the bottle warmers. I didn't even know we had a relative with triplets."

Wyatt tapped the envelope against the desk and tried to imagine Harper with triplets. "Hope they don't run in the family."

"What do you care?" Harper laughed at him.

Wyatt put his hand to his ear, mimicking someone talking on the phone and spoke in sotto voice. "Wyatt, come rescue me from my kids. They take after my great-great-grandmother who fled England. These munchkins are fast."

"Very funny." Harper fingered the book again. "What do you have there?"

"It looked like it got caught between the cracks. The postmark on it is ten years old."

Harper tilted her head, reading the fuzzy print. "That's from the Pennsylvania Department of Permits and Licensing. Surely if Mom or Fink needed it they would have noticed it missing by now." Harper narrowed her eyes. "Should we check?"

Wyatt shrugged. This could have been something they misplaced years ago. He opened it and scanned the letter inside.

"What?" Harper asked, peering over the edge.

"It looks like Fink applied for a permit to develop the mountain. This is the approval letter." He held up the other paper, which was a bluish color with gold lettering. "This is the permit."

"That's odd. I don't remember hearing anything about that."

"Me either." Wyatt stuffed everything back in the envelope.

"That's ten years old. Obviously, nothing ever came of it."

Wyatt placed the letter on the desk next to the side he'd pulled it from.

Harper tapped the little green book on the desk. "You're sure you called everyone in Pennsylvania?"

Wyatt nodded. "All except that Avery Conrad. She's the first name in the book, but I've never heard of her and she lives in Philly. That's like five hours away."

Harper sighed. "Too far."

He hated seeing her so dejected, and he couldn't stand that she was worrying about the farm. "Well, one neighbor didn't answer. I'll try him again."

Harper's phone rang and she grabbed it off the desk. "It's my mom," she said before she answered.

Wyatt pulled his own phone back out and stepped away. By the time he finished talking with the neighbor, who couldn't help because his mom had just been diagnosed with cancer and they were starting treatments in Pittsburgh, Harper was already off the phone with her mom and was digging through the desk.

He walked over beside her. "Everything okay?"

"Yeah. She wanted the insurance info. Apparently, they've switched insurers and she has the wrong card in her wallet. She's too worked up to remember the name of the new insurance company." Harper shuffled some papers around, then dug through a stack she pulled from the second drawer on the right. "It's in a business sized envelope just like this..." Her voice trailed off as she read the bright pink sticky note attached to the envelope on top.

"What?" Wyatt bent over and squinted at the familiar scrawl on the sticky note.

Taxes have tripled.
Will pay with money from selling pumpkins.

The return address on the envelope was the County Assessment Office. His chest tightened.

Harper tapped her finger on the note. "That explains why Fink's last words to Mom were about the pumpkins being planted."

"Yeah. It's kind of important to pay taxes." Wyatt put a hand on the desk and leaned on it. "I agree that this really isn't any of our business, but...do you think there's more like that?"

"More tax bills?"

"More bills that are depending on farm income to get paid."

"I know Mom was making as many decorations as she could. But I thought it was more that she was thrilled to finally have the boys in school and to have time. Maybe they need the money."

Wyatt tapped his finger on the desk. "Fink wouldn't have been worried about it otherwise, but we need to find that insurance info."

Harper met his look with a frank one of her own. "Right. Sounds like either the farm needs to generate money, or we'll lose it." She touched the ring on her finger, then seemed to shake herself. "Oh, Mom said that Avery Conrad is a professor and a distant cousin of Fink's. She might be willing to come out for the summer."

"Give me her number. I'll give her a call."

"Sure." Harper flipped through the green book, found the page and read the number off to Wyatt. He dialed. No point in waiting. They hadn't accomplished a single thing all afternoon.

A voice answered after the second ring. "Hello?"

"Hello. This is Wyatt Fernandez. I'm Calvin Finkenbinder's nephew.

A small pause, during which Wyatt hooked a hand around the back of his neck. He'd feel like an idiot if this woman didn't even know who Fink and Ellie were. She spoke. "Oh, you mean Fink, he's like my third cousin or something? He married Ellie-something, right?"

"Yes, that's him. I'm sorry to cold call you like this, but he's having a bit of a hard time, and I thought you might be able to help. Ellie said you're a professor?"

"Yes. At Penn U. I teach music theory."

Uh oh. Not looking good. At least she'd have the summer off.

"I also play the tuba in the Philadelphia Orchestra. Maybe you've seen us play, but they're off until fall. Are you calling about tuba lessons? Because I don't give lessons in the summer. Students are too unpredictable. Going on vacation or swimming or they want to sleep in. Every day half the students cancel and how am I supposed to make any plans—"

"Excuse me." Geez. Wyatt interrupted just to give the lady a chance to breathe. The logical part of his brain said to get off the phone, but he'd practiced his spiel so much over the last three hours, that it tumbled out of his mouth without thought. "Fink is in the hospital and they're looking for someone to help on the farm."

The other end of the phone fell completely silent. Then, "I'd have to bring my Abyssinian cat. It's neutered of course." She went on about the cat and its medications and the timing and the special requirements that it needed that precluded being able to board it at a kennel. Wyatt wasn't exactly timing it, but it seemed like at least fifteen minutes before she stopped for air and he was able to tell her he'd text her the address.

She agreed to come out Monday and hung up. He stood unmoving with the phone still at his ear.

"Wyatt. Wyatt? What's wrong?"

His hand dropped slowly from his ear. "I think I just solved our no-cat problem."

Harper started to smile. Apparently, the look on his face made her rethink that decision. "I was kidding about needing a cat."

"She's coming."

Harper's eyes lit up, but she tilted her head. "Why did you just say that like she's next-of-kin to the chainsaw murderer?"

"I'm not sure we need to worry about her running a chain saw."

"But she can use hedge trimmers, right? Does she know much about farming? Can she spray the sweetcorn?"

Wyatt looked at his phone, like it had somehow conjured all of this up. "She plays the tuba."

Harper's eyebrows flew up. "The tuba?"

"She has an Abyssinian."

"And...that's a hairdo that requires multiple bottles of hairspray, similar to a beehive?"

"It's a cat."

"You're scaring me, Wyatt."

"I'm a little shell-shocked myself. She, um, talked a lot." He tried to look on the bright side. "But she'll be here Monday."

Chapter Four

That evening Harper and Wyatt sat on the porch swing together. Wyatt swung gently with his foot. Peepers from the pond filled the night air with song. The springs creaked rhythmically.

Harper leaned her head against the swing headboard, her phone in her hand. She hadn't called her mother, not wanting to bother her if she was talking to doctors or nurses about Fink's care. But she hadn't set it down.

She glanced at Wyatt out of the corner of her eye. He'd been quiet after their disappointing afternoon. Of course, she'd been quiet and preoccupied, too, because of Fink and her mother. That was probably what was on Wyatt's mind, too.

She put her hand on his leg. Immediately, she remembered the hardness of his body and the prickling sensations she'd had in the tunnel. Those complications weren't exactly welcome right now, or ever. But snatching her hand back would only make everything more awkward. She patted his leg instead, like a mother patting a child's head.

"What are you thinking about?" she asked.

The muscles under her hand tensed. He blew out a breath and they relaxed. "It's been ten years since my mother died."

Harper snapped her gaze to his face. "I hadn't realized."

"I was going to the Alps because that's something she always wanted to do. I thought to do it in her memory." His head rolled to the side and she caught his gaze in the hazy evening light. "I had even thought I might talk you into going with me."

Her eyes flew open and her heart spiked in her chest. "If I didn't have that research position..." Who was she kidding? She didn't want to travel to Arizona to see her sick stepfather. She had even less desire to take a trip to Europe just for kicks and giggles, let alone to climb a mountain. But for Wyatt...

"Nah, it's okay. I knew you probably wouldn't go. I just sometimes get these crazy ideas."

"You don't have to tell me about your crazy ideas," Harper said, then regretted it. She held her hand up. She wasn't planning on wearing the ring constantly, but she had put it on earlier and hadn't taken it off. Maybe she'd rent a safe deposit box, although it seemed like a waste to put something so beautiful and precious away. The emerald caught the light of the moon and muted sparkles winked on her finger.

A piece of her history, there on her hand.

The connection to her ancestor, and to the farm she loved, made her smile. "I wanted to thank you again for making me go today. I wouldn't be wearing this right now if it weren't for you." She patted his leg again, ignoring the hardness and the way touching him made her heart flutter. "I wish you had something like this from your mother."

"I don't have anything tangible. But I have her dreams here." He put his balled fist over his heart. "She wanted to see the Alps. But, more than anything, she wanted my dad and me to get along. She always said he wouldn't change; it was up to me."

His hand came down and covered hers where it rested on his leg. Guilt puddled in Harper's heart. Selfishly, she'd not wanted Wyatt to go to Chile. But Wyatt needed to go if only to preserve his mother's memory, just as much as she needed to do what it had taken her all day to decide.

"I found another envelope after you left," she said softly.

"You dug around in their desk some more?" Surprised laced Wyatt's voice.

She smiled to herself. Wyatt knew she was such a prude she'd never root through someone else's stuff. "No. Mom texted me and asked me to take a picture of the passcodes she had written and stuck in an envelope. I did that, but I found something else." She turned her hand and her fingers laced with Wyatt's.

He waited.

"They have every afternoon from mid-September to mid-November reserved for school field trips." The discovery had cause a thick cape of blackness to wrap around her heart. All that revenue would vanish along with any hope of paying the taxes and keeping the farm.

"Wow."

"Yeah. Thousands of dollars they stand to lose if there are no pumpkins, corn, squash, gourds, corn, hay...." Her voice trailed off. So much work to do.

"Well, I've been thinking—" Wyatt began, but she cut him off.

"I have, too. I've worked hard for tenure. Years. Looking back, though, it feels like nothing, because I loved what I was doing so much. But lately..." She sighed. She wouldn't admit this to anyone but Wyatt. "Honestly, over the past few weeks, I've been so close to finally getting what I want, but I'm not even sure I really want it anymore. I think I do. Still, this afternoon, as I thought about which is more important to me —the farm or getting tenure—it took about two seconds to decide. My family. This farm. I can't separate the two."

Wyatt squeezed her hand. He shook his head. "That's kind of what I've been thinking. Yeah, I wanted to go backpacking over the Alps for my mom—I can't even remember what she looked like anymore and that bothers me. I'm losing her."

Harper bit the inside of her cheek at the sadness in his voice. All she could do was squeeze his hand, but it didn't feel like enough.

Wyatt squeezed back, and his voice lightened. "But I'm going to Chile and that has to be enough. The first thing I did when I got my phone out of the tunnel this evening was to call my friends and tell them to go on without me."

She straightened and looked at him. "You didn't!"

"Yeah. I'm going to stay at the farm. I'll take care of things. Uncle Fink took me in after Mom died. It's the least I can do."

"Too late, Wyatt. I already called Dr. Hitten, the supervisor on my project, and told him I was out."

"Call him back. I've got this."

"It's my family. My farm."

Wyatt swallowed. He lifted their joined hands and studied them for a moment.

Her own throat grew tight.

He whispered, "Don't you know that it's mine, too?"

Harper's mouth hung open. She couldn't think to close it.

"You're my family." He dropped their hands and gave the swing an extra hard push with his foot.

"I'm sorry. You belong here. Just as much as I do. But I never thought that this was your problem. What about your mom? What about the anniversary of her death?"

"I loved my mom. And I miss her. But she's not the woman I thought she was if she'd rather I run around the Alps having a grand time while the family farm crashes and burns. I'm not the person I want to be if I could do that." The swing's chains creaked, blending with the sound of the peepers from the pond and the rustling of leaves.

Harper sighed. "That's how I feel. My position at the university is nothing if I don't have this farm as my base."

"What I can't decide is what to do about Avery."

What did she have to do with anything? Harper turned to look at Wyatt. He had a mock serious look on his face. He was trying to break the tension, because he never could be serious for long. Harper laughed. "It sounded like she wanted to come here."

He lifted a shoulder. "Plus, she's family."

"Most importantly," Harper said with a lifted brow, "she has a cat."

WYATT PULLED up the neighbor's drive and parked the old farm pickup next to their house. After using hot pads to carry the pan of lasagna Harper had made that afternoon while he started planting the pumpkins, he stepped up on the immaculate porch and pushed the doorbell with his elbow.

There was no curtain on the door, and he watched through the window as Gator Franks strode down the hall. The barrel of a rifle stuck up diagonally past his head. Ammo belts crossed his chest. A handgun was strapped to his hip on top of his fatigues.

The door opened.

"Wyatt." The man nodded without smiling. But his eyes went to the pan of food, and he breathed deeply through his nose.

"Target practice?" Wyatt nodded at the guns and ammo.

Quiet and driven, Gator had been a great friend to Wyatt the first year he'd moved here. He nodded once. "Spent the morning surrounded by white lab coats. Needed to destress."

Probably the stress was more because it wasn't easy for anyone to see their mother fighting for her life. But Wyatt didn't say anything. Gator wasn't exactly known for being in touch with his sensitive side.

A shaggy, mangy looking cat twined around Gator's ankles, then walked its front paws up to Gator's knee. A big, rough hand reached down and gave the cat a rub between the ears.

"Still picking up strays." Gator had never particularly struck Wyatt as a cat person, but he'd always spent the money he made fixing things around the farm on vet bills.

Gator glanced down at the aluminum foil covered casserole. "That Italian?"

"Lasagna. It's edible."

He cracked a smile. "After smoked groundhog, it's my favorite. How much of it did you eat on the way here?"

Wyatt returned the grin. "Mine's at home. Harper made me deliver yours before she'd let me eat."

"Good girl. Smart." Gator propped his shoulder against the door.

"Harper said you were only in for a few days."

"That's right."

"She wanted me to reassure you that the town is looking after your mom while you're gone." It had to be hard to have a job in Montana when his mother was sick in Pennsylvania.

"Thanks." Gator met his gaze briefly. His eye twitched. The only show of emotion.

A brunette head peeked around his shoulder. "Wyatt Fernandez. I haven't seen you in months."

Except for the dark circles around her eyes and maybe a little missing weight, Mrs. Franks looked the same as she had since high school. He would never have guessed she had cancer.

"Yeah. I'm in for the summer."

Gator put a heavily muscled arm around his mother's shoulders. Her housecoat was buttoned up tight, but she still crossed her arms over her stomach like she was cold.

He squeezed her to him, like he could warm her up. "Promised you were gonna stay in bed," he said, his voice sounding like casings in a tumbler, with an underlying tenderness.

"But we have company, son."

If Gator wanted his mother in bed, Wyatt didn't want to keep her up. "I can't stay. Fink and Ellie and the kids are gone. I've got to get back to Harper. We've got some things to take care of."

Mrs. Franks allowed Gator to pull her closer, but she didn't back away from the door. "She's been buried in the books, I suppose. I haven't seen her since I retired. She was close to tenure then. Does she have it yet?" Mrs. Franks asked.

"Not yet." The smell of tomatoes and spices suddenly turned his stomach.

"Let's not keep him from his supper, Mom." Gator reached a hand out to take the pan.

"It's hot," Wyatt said, although he hadn't gotten past Mrs. Frank's comment about Harper's tenure. Everyone knew it was what she'd been working for all her life. He shook his head. "Don't worry about giving the pan back."

"Thank you," Mrs. Franks said.

"'Preciate it," Gator echoed.

Wyatt met his eyes for a second before he turned. He saw something in them that he'd never seen before. Fear.

Wyatt walked down the steps. His heart bled for Gator, not sure if it was better to lose one's mother quickly, as he had, or slowly, with a slim chance the whole time that maybe he wouldn't lose her at all.

He shook the morbid thoughts away. But that made room for the same thought that had run on repeat through his head all night to settle. If the farm meant so much to Harper that she'd give up everything she'd worked for at the university to stay home and save it, she'd never allow herself to fall in love with him and move to Chile. And, more importantly, it would be wrong of him to expect her to.

Chapter Five

Monday morning, Harper had just gotten off the office phone with Gary's Chemical about spraying the peach trees, when a car pulled in the driveway. During the fall, it wasn't unusual for the lot to be full, but this time of year, since people didn't typically want to buy pumpkins and Christmas trees in June, they weren't open.

Before she opened the door, she texted Wyatt, who was on the tractor planting sweet corn, letting him know lunch was ready. Her ankle still pained her, but even if it hadn't, she was thankful that he'd not asked her to go with him.

The beige sedan motored slowly past the office and on toward the house. Although nondescript, she recognized the car. An odd tangle of anxiety and dismay settled in her stomach. She set the tray on the banister.

What was Professor Jeff Hitten doing here? As the head of the nutrition department, he was technically her boss. She couldn't think of anything she'd done wrong. She put a hand to her hair. Same ponytail she always wore, but he wouldn't be used to seeing her in jeans and a tee shirt. It bothered her to look less than professional, even though she was at home and had no reason to expect company. Her stomach tightened. He was less than ten years older than her, and was considered by other interns to be quite good looking, but he always made her feel young and slightly inept.

She hurried down the porch steps. The professor had already gotten out of his car. Despite the humidity, his dress slacks were neatly pressed with a perfect crease. His collared shirt looked crisp, and the man himself was pale and cool despite the heat.

"Professor." Harper closed the gap between them with her hand out. "So nice to see you."

He took her hand in his, which was white and soft. After glancing at the porch, he said, "I'm sorry. Is this a bad time?"

"Not at all. My step-cousin, Wyatt, will be here shortly for lunch. You can join us if you'd like."

"There's no need. I was away at a conference and just found out today that you backed out of our research project. Shelly Blair told me, but she didn't know why. I wanted to make sure everything was okay."

Reading nothing but concern in his brown eyes, Harper relaxed. "I'm fine. My step dad is in the hospital and I'm needed here on the farm."

Professor Hitten nodded, his lips pressed together. "I wish you would have said something to me first. The project this summer has potential to impact the way people think about nutrition in a big way." He sighed, clasping and unclasping his hands in front of him. "I'm in charge of the team. I can get you back on the roster."

Harper bit the insides of her cheeks. Across the yard, Wyatt drove the tractor into view. He'd given up his trip; how could she consider ditching him now? Plus, was tenure what she really wanted? She'd worked so long and so hard, and she'd enjoyed every second. Once she had tenure, what then? Her life stretched before her. Sure, she'd have the farm. Wyatt would see to that this summer. But what else? Her mom, her stepdad, her brothers. There was more, she was sure of it. For the first time in her life, the thought of the farm and her family did not completely satisfy Harper, and a tiny spot of restlessness chipped at her chest.

Still, it was unheard of to cancel a tenure vote. And if a professor didn't get voted tenure, it was understood they would find another position. At a different university. Harper's chest heaved. There were no other universities within easy driving distance, and she didn't want to move. She had to get tenure. But a professor's ability to get grants, do research and be published was a huge part of tenure. Now, all the board would see when they looked at her was someone who had taken the entire summer off, ditched a plum research opportunity, and hadn't published a paper in months.

But she couldn't leave Wyatt.

She lifted her chin. "I'm sorry, Professor. I've already told my family they can count on me. As much as I wish I could do the project this summer, I just can't."

"Are you sure?"

Not completely sure her face wasn't turning green, Harper nodded. Beyond the sickness, though, a small part of her loosened like a large, heavy chain had been unhooked and released.

The professor lowered his voice. "I like you Harper. You're serious and driven. But you know I can't cancel that vote. And if you back out of this research opportunity, you know they probably aren't going to vote for you."

Yes. She knew.

Professor Hitten adjusted his tie. "Is there anything I can do to make you consider changing your mind?"

"No. I'm sorry. I have to do what I said I would."

Professor Hitten gave her a long look. Then his expression changed as Wyatt walked up and stopped beside her, close but not touching.

He held his hand out. "Wyatt Fernandez."

"Professor Hitten." The professor's eyes narrowed, but he shook Wyatt's hand.

"He's my cousin." Some internal urge forced those words out of Harper's lips.

The professor's face relaxed.

"Step-cousin," Wyatt said. He finished shaking the Professor's hand and shifted closer to Harper.

Again the Professor's eyes narrowed, but she didn't care, enjoying the warmth and the feeling of security that Wyatt offered.

Professor Hitten cleared his throat. "If you change your mind before next week, let me know."

Harper nodded, her insides congealing like bacon grease as the professor climbed back into his car.

Wyatt stuck his hands in his front pockets. "Did he come to give you detention?"

Harper's lips twitched up. Somehow Wyatt could always get her to grin. "Nope."

He sobered. "It was about the research position, wasn't it?"

"Yeah."

"Do it."

She sighed as Professor Hitten's car pulled out of the lot. "No."

"I can handle the farm, Pickles."

"Would you leave me here alone to go on your Europe trip?"

"Of course not."

A few flecks of faded white paint fell from where her hand held the banister to the flower pot, already filled with soil and waiting for the geraniums her mother planted in it every year. She turned from looking at the empty brown fields and met his serious gaze. "I feel the same way."

One side of his mouth pulled back. "I didn't figure I could talk you into it, but I hate to see you miss out."

"Ditto." She shrugged, but she couldn't quite get her mouth to turn up.

Wyatt put his arm around her. "If you're going to keep looking glum, I'm gonna track that guy down and tell him you changed your mind.'

Although tempted to tell him about the tenure that she wasn't going to get, Harper decided to keep her mouth shut about it. He couldn't do anything, and she hated whiners.

"I'm a little bummed, but I'm going to be fine."

"Come on. We'll finish up early today. Tomorrow, I challenge you to a Christmas tree trimming race."

This time she did laugh. "You always win, but your trees look like they survived a typhoon."

Wyatt clasped a hand to his heart. "That hurts."

"It's true."

"I don't rub in the fact that your trees often look like they have a tassel at the top since you're too short."

"Vertically challenged." She put a hand on her hip. "Like you are somehow responsible for how tall you are."

"God favored me." He smirked at her.

"So God punished me by making me short?"

"You said it."

"You implied it!"

"No. I said your trees always look like they have a big ball at the top. You're the one who got all huffy and started yakking about being short."

"That's because you're acting like me not being able to reach the top of the tree because of a factor out of my control is the same as you mutilating yours simply because you lack the skill to properly trim an evergreen into a perfect Christmas tree shape."

"Hold up there, Pickles. This boy is not lacking skill."

"Then I guess you'll have to prove it tomorrow."

"Seven a.m. Sharp." He stuck his hand out. "Unless you chicken out."

She grabbed his hand. "This chick don't run."

"Obviously, you need to study up on your English as well."

"I was kidding. It was a turn of phrase…" Harper closed her mouth. She'd been enjoying her argument, no, *discussion*, with Wyatt so much, she'd forgotten all about her conversation with Professor Hitten and the almost certain loss of tenure. Which was surely what Wyatt had intended.

Her heart flipped like a burger on a grill. She could almost hear the sizzle. Shaking her head, she pulled away and turned toward the house. Now that the more-than-friends thoughts had entered her head, her whole body went haywire at the oddest times.

To cover up her odd reaction, she said, "Last one in the house does the dishes," and started running.

Chapter Six

"They look like they grew up drunk." Wyatt set his hedge trimmers down beside the first row of Scotch pine and pulled his gloves out of his back pocket while scanning the cloud-free, early morning sky. The sun sparkled on the clear water of the pond which lay in the dip, two hundred yards away. "Maybe that's how they got their name. Short for Scotch Whisky."

Wyatt had spent enough time on the farm to know they grew fast and, because of their deep tap root, were drought resistant, which made them a favorite of growers. But compared to a Douglas fir or a balsam fir, Scotch pines looked more like untamed octopuses than the proper cone-shaped Christmas tree. Maybe that's why they were his favorite, too.

"It originated in Europe. Probably grows well in Scotland." Harper's eyes swept over him. Lines appeared between her brows. "Where are your safety goggles?"

"We're trimming trees, not welding." He stopped at the end of the first row, admiring how different she looked in her long-sleeved shirt, jeans and work boots. Not studious. Not today.

"Welding?" She paused before walking to the next row.

The grass brushed the tops of her boots, and he made a mental note that it needed to be mowed. Snakes loved to hide in it, and he didn't want Harper getting bitten. "You know, with a rod about yay long." Wyatt stretched his gloved hands out.

"I know what welding is," Harper said. "I just...never mind." She shook her head, then adjusted her goggles and pulled her gloves on.

He started his hedge trimmer. Harper started hers. He pulled the trigger playfully, making revving sounds.

Harper rolled her eyes. He waggled his eyebrows at her.

She gave him her serious, I'm-gonna-whip-your-donkey look.

He loved that look.

Holding up three fingers, he waited for her nod. He put one finger down. *Two.* Then another. *One.* Waiting a beat, he fisted his hand, *zero*, before squeezing the throttle and starting on the tree in front of him. In the row beside him, Harper did the same.

How many times had they done this together? The last few summers he'd been off roaming the world, but before that, Harper and he had spent a lot of time trimming trees. They'd even raced before. And Harper was right—he did tend to sacrifice shape for speed. Well, not today. Today his trees were going to be perfect, and he was still going to beat her.

The scent of pine filled the air along with needles and small branches that flew from the blades of their trimmers. Like riding a bike, the proper angle and diagonal motion came back as easily as breathing. The buzz of the trimmers drowned out any other sounds, making his vision shrink to just the tree in front of him. Although he never lost the awareness of Harper behind or beside him.

He kind of wished they weren't racing, because he loved watching the serious look on her face. The way her eyes sized up the tree, the way she handled her trimmers with skill, and her feminine grace despite her jeans and boots.

A cloud passed over the sun and without its heat the day turned cooler. Ominous, almost.

He moved to the next tree, glancing at Harper, still one tree behind him. Taking a quick look at the rest of the row, he estimated that they weren't quite halfway. Plenty of time for her to catch up. He widened his stance and willed himself to move faster. She could beat him at this, easily. Always could. His problem was simply that he got bored and distracted. His problem in tree trimming, his problem in life.

Well, he'd given up his Europe trip for the summer. He'd struggled with the decision, but once it was made, he'd been fine with it. Especially seeing that Harper had made her own hard decision. That decision, however, had cemented in his mind that Harper would never belong to him. He'd always known that the farm meant a lot to her. So, if he was going to fulfill his mother's dream and his dad's desire, he had to be in Chile. There was no compromise.

He'd told his buddies earlier this spring that his wandering days were behind him. He hadn't planned to say that. But as the words were coming out of his mouth, he realized that it was true: he was ready to settle down and grow roots.

Problem was, his dad wanted those roots in Chile, and he'd always wanted his dad's approval. Craved it. He didn't even know why. It wasn't like his dad had ever wanted him before.

Now that he was an adult, with experience and talent, his dad had begged him to move to Chile. Wyatt wanted to say no. Just desserts and all that. But there was something inside of every kid who wanted his parents to be proud of him. Wanted to please his parents. Plus, back when he was a kid, his dream had been to run the resort. He'd never gotten over that.

Even though his mom had died ten years ago, he knew it would make her happy for him to work with his dad. She might have been a farm girl from Iowa, but she'd dragged him all over the world, sometimes as a free-lance journalist, sometimes on the arm of some rich man or another, sometimes she worked her way—entertainment on a cruise ship, scuba instructor in Australia, even a zookeeper's assistant in San Francisco.

Eventually she'd gone back to Chile, to his dad, claiming she was settling down. That she wanted her son to know his father. Wanted her little boy to be just like his dad. Then she was killed in an avalanche, and Wyatt's dad didn't have the slightest idea of what to do with him. So he bought him a plane ticket to Pennsylvania, where Uncle Fink, his mother's brother, lived.

Where Harper lived.

He snipped one more bulging area before moving onto the next tree. Maybe he should be grateful to his dad. After all, if his dad had kept him, he would never have met Harper. Of course, being in love with a woman who only saw a clumsy kid, and maybe a sense of humor, wasn't exactly easy.

The buzzing of his hedge clippers became louder. It sounded angry. He'd checked the oil, sharpened the blades, what could be the problem?

He glimpsed a huge, brown-paper-like ball—a hornet's nest inside a branch of the tree he was trimming. Harper jerked on his shoulder as hot pain ignited in his cheek and hand.

"Run, you cracker head," Harper shouted. She yanked on his arm again.

Dropping his clippers, he pushed her shoulder, altering her direction. "To the pond," he yelled. He shoved her forward.

They sprinted toward the pond. A black cloud of the angry insects buzzed above Harper's head. He didn't see any on the back of her light shirt. Pain burned in his own shoulders where he'd been stung through the thin shirt material. His cheek stiffened as though he had a wad of cement in it and his hand stung.

Still running at full tilt, Harper reached in her back pocket and took out her phone, dropping it in the grass. That was a good idea. Wyatt unhooked his from his belt, getting a finger stung in the process, and dropped his as well.

They had almost reached the pond. He'd swum in it several times over the past decade with Harper, although neither of them really liked to, since the bottom was soggy mud and a film of algae covered it most of the summer. Not now, thankfully. Too early in the season.

As they flew down the last steep hill, he yelled, "Shallow dive."

The pond was only four to six feet deep; a steep dive would be dangerous.

"Swim under the surface to the willow on the other side," he shouted as they careened wildly down the hill. The branches hung gracefully over the water. They might offer some protection from the furious hornets.

She jerked her head in acknowledgement without breaking stride. Although she did slant him a microsecond look that said things like this happened uncommonly often when she was with him. She looked forward and didn't catch his answering grin and shrug. Just as well. The innocent look probably didn't come off well when a person was flat-out sprinting away from a swarm of angry hornets.

They reached the edge of the pond, still sprinting. The buzz of hornets filled the air. Their black bodies careened around his head. He took a deep breath and jumped a fraction of a second after she did, watching her. She hit with the shallow angle she needed to and he splashed in right beside her.

The cold water shocked his system, and he allowed the power behind his jump to glide his body forward while he took several seconds to adjust to the completely new environment. Although he couldn't see much in the murky water, he could just make out Harper's leg beside him. Her work boots must have been getting waterlogged, because her body looked like a ship going down. His own feet were being dragged to the bottom.

The pond wasn't deep enough to worry about drowning, so he didn't work to take the boots off. Rather, he allowed his legs to drop and push in a slow motion run against the bottom of the pond, staying under, still heading toward the willow. Harper did the same.

She flipped, rolling in the water until her back was down. With his lungs burning, Wyatt copied her motion, allowing only his nose and mouth to come out of the water, blowing like a whale, then sinking back down, turning and heading in the direction of the willows.

Harper grabbed his arm. Her ponytail floated in wispy strands around her head. Her cheeks were puffed out from holding her breath. She pointed slightly to the right, correcting his course. He didn't think he was that far off, but was hardly in a position to argue with her.

It turned out she was right. They broke for air the second time directly under the overhanging branches.

"This is not my fault," he panted.

"No one blamed you for anything. Although if you are defending yourself before anyone has accused you, it sure makes you look guilty." Harper puffed, pushing her hair out of her green eyes.

"You definitely don't look like a professor now."

"Staying alive took precedence over being dignified." Harper peered through the hanging branches. "There's a cloud of hornets hovering over the water."

"I see." A cloud was an apt description. "They don't look like they're giving up."

"Angry and stubborn. The absolute worst characteristics a hornet can have." Her teeth started to chatter. Harper never could handle the cold water.

"Intelligence would be bad, too."

She snorted. "Yeah, they'd have found us by now."

"Gotta look on the bright side, Pickles."

"I just ruined a two-hundred-dollar pair of work boots, I've got pond scum in my hair and hornet stings on my back, and you're telling me there's a bright side?"

"Sure, you get to hang out with me."

"This is not hanging out."

"Good point. We're gonna lurk in the murk. We'll start a new trend. Too bad we can't take a selfie."

"Yeah, that would definitely make it worse if my phone were lurking in the murk with me."

"Positive thinking, phrased as a negative. Even if you do look like a drowned ostrich."

"Ostrich?"

"Your neck's looking kind of long today." Slender. Graceful.

"When you're not around, nothing like this ever happens to me." Her teeth were chattering so hard, he was afraid she might be in danger of hypothermia.

"No wonder you're always so happy to see me."

"I'm happy to see you because for some odd reason I like you."

"You're cold. Come here." He moved toward her in the shallow water, putting one knee down on the pond bottom and planting his other foot, making a seat with his leg for Harper to sit on.

She floated toward him, dodging the hanging branches, and sat on his leg. He pulled her closer to his chest. Her entire body shook with chills.

"I'm sorry." The words came out on a croak and he cleared his throat.

"It's not your fault. You know I was teasing."

"I know. But it does seem like I make you miserable."

"You make me laugh." She smiled over her shoulder. "Wow. Your cheek is swollen like a balloon." She brought a hand out of the water to touch it gently. The cold on his face contrasted nicely against his tight, hot skin. If only he could close his eyes and allow her to cradle his cheek in her hand. He pushed the thought away.

"Hurts."

"I don't recall you being allergic to hornet stings." Lines crinkled her forehead.

"Me either."

Her lip pulled back. "Did you get stung anywhere else?"

He held up the finger that had gotten stung when he pulled his phone out. It was swollen.

"Being in the cold water must be helping that," Harper said. "Anywhere else?"

"A couple on my back, my arm. It's my face that hurts, though. Maybe I got more than one there."

She squinted at his face. "Looks like maybe the stinger is still in there."

"What about you?"

"If I'm stung, my adrenaline hasn't subsided enough to allow me to feel it yet." She chuckled softly. "I haven't run like that in years. I might not be stung, but I'm going to be sore tomorrow and completely worthless." She chuckled again, not as softly this time.

His heart sang at the sight of her smile, even if her chattering teeth made her face look like it was vibrating. Maybe she liked adventure more than she let on.

"You're gonna chip a tooth."

"Lots of people live without all their teeth."

"You'll never catch a husband if you chatter your teeth off."

"That's fine. I don't exactly have the husband-catching net or hook or whatever equipment it takes to snag a guy."

Oh yes, she did. At least for him. She'd never even had to try, but she'd had him hooked almost since the first time he'd seen her. "I think the way to a man's heart is supposed to be through his stomach."

"Well, my doctorate's in nutrition. That should give me an edge."

"Or not," Wyatt said.

"What's that supposed to mean?" she hissed. Luckily, the hornets had started to dissipate.

"There's the way you got your nickname."

"Those pickles were good."

"I'd hope so. You gave a jar of pickles to everyone for Christmas. And when I say everyone, I mean you were passing them out on the street. The grocery store stocker, the preschool janitor, complete strangers. It was my first Christmas with you all, and I'd never met anyone who gifted people with pickles."

Harper huffed. "That year our cucumbers produced like rabbits on fertility drugs. What was I supposed to do? Let them go to waste?"

"Might have thought about it."

"Ha. My Scotch-Irish ancestors come back from the grave and cut the toes off little girls who waste things."

Wyatt adjusted Harper closer to him. Her shivering had him worried. "And you stopped believing that story when you stopped believing in Santa Claus."

"My mom didn't do Santa Claus or the Easter Bunny, but I know all about ancestors with knives." Harper smiled playfully and Wyatt's gaze caressed the laugh lines around her eyes and the way her mouth crinkled up.

"Wow, and I thought I had a rough childhood."

"Scarred me for life. That's why I have to cook to get to a man's heart." Harper snuggled in closer.

"I think each successive degree diminished your cooking abilities. At this point you'd probably try to explain to your potential husband that steamed bugs raise your good cholesterol and improve overall heart health."

Harper nodded. "They actually do."

"Yep, Pickles. You need your teeth. The cooking ain't gonna do it for ya."

"Very funny, Wyatt. Plus, I don't know why you're trying to marry me off. You just lost your chance with Rayna and Sugar. You sent them off to Europe with that handsome Rex."

They were connected on social media, so of course she knew who his travelling companions were going to be, although he didn't think Harper had ever met Rayna or Sugar in person. "You think Rex is handsome?"

"If you're into the whole chiseled jaw and sculpted muscle look."

Wyatt rubbed his jaw. "So you dig me, huh?"

She snorted, which came out with a kind of grunty clack. "I thought it was the bee sting making your cheek swell. Now I realize it's your ego leaking out of your brain. I'd get that checked if I were you."

"You wound me."

"You're gorgeous, Wyatt. Everyone knows it. I don't know why you're fishing for a compliment from me. I'm just the bestie. I'd still think you were great even if you were as ugly as a tire fence."

His chest heaved. Harper had called him gorgeous. He clamped his mouth shut over the words that wanted to come out—to return the compliment, tell her she was beautiful, that he'd hoped to take her to the Alps with him, that she was the only one he wanted with him as he commemorated his mother's death. He tried to keep his reaction hidden, and said casually, "You think I'm great? Better than Rex?"

She nodded. "Even with your face swollen and pond scum stuck in your teeth."

"I have pond scum in my teeth?" He really didn't give a flip what he had in his teeth, but if it made Harper laugh, or eased her mind, he'd play along.

"Some kind of blackish-green goop. Makes you look a little like a swamp monster."

"Man, if only I'd have known that thirty minutes ago, I could have scared those hornets away by smiling at them." He glanced between the willow branches toward the dissipating cloud of hornets.

"That's great. I can't wait to be warm again."

"Here, let me up. I'll get out on this side and see if they notice."

"No," she wailed playfully. "I don't want to lose your heat."

"A small sacrifice now will mean heat and warmth sooner." He imitated her most scholarly tone, although he really didn't want to let her go. But her chattering teeth concerned him.

"Would you stop being the voice of reason?" She shifted so he could straighten. "I'm not used to it coming from your lips."

He tapped her nose then pointed to the hornets. "Watch for them to swarm us again. Be ready to duck under the water."

"I'm ready."

He gave her a last look, praying the hornets were gone and they could get out. Her lips were blue, her face pure white, and her shivering not as violent, which he knew was not a good sign.

He pushed through the water, dodging the willow and carefully pulling himself up out of the pond. He stood, then took a few steps to the side so he could see around the tree.

No hornets.

He turned back. Harper was already pulling herself out of the water. He bent to help.

HARPER REACHED for Wyatt's offered hand. She was shivering so hard, she missed it the first time. She'd be fine, though. Shivering was good.

It was Wyatt's face that bothered her.

She'd studied allergies and knew enough that his swollen face made her nervous. The rational side of her brain said if he was going to have a fatal reaction to the hornet stings, it would have happened by now. But there was still the danger of his airway being swollen shut. And there was also that outlier reaction. The one that didn't follow the rules.

Wyatt could die. For the last twenty minutes, she had been trying not to panic.

He couldn't know she felt that way. She didn't even want him to know she was worried about his face. She pressed her lips together.

Sliding up the steep bank of slippery mud, Harper held tight to Wyatt's hand.

"Do you think you can walk to the house?" Wyatt asked.

With the deep crease in his forehead, and the pinched skin around his eyes, she didn't have the heart to pretend to be worse off than she was.

"I can." As stubborn as he was, she wouldn't be able to get him to the hospital. Maybe he didn't really need to go. Probably he didn't need to go. But the idea of losing Wyatt froze her insides more solid than the cold water ever could.

At least the swelling on his face didn't seem to be getting any bigger.

"I'd like to avoid the tree with the hornets' nest in it." By at least six miles.

"Yeah." Wyatt grunted. "I like adventure. But I've had enough for an afternoon."

"For a lifetime."

"Oh, no. Not that long."

She laughed. Wyatt's arm came around her shoulders to keep her close, warm her up. A little twist of panic stirred in her chest at the thought that he might find out about these new feelings she had for him. She had to play it cool.

She loved him as a friend, but it was impossible to deny that there was more going on. For her.

If it was "friend" love, she wouldn't have been tempted to put her lips on his neck. To trace the strong line of his jaw. To lean against the hardness of his chest. Although she would probably still be every bit as tempted to knock him over the head with a hard, blunt object and drag his body to the ER. Of course, killing him kind of defeated the purpose of an ER visit.

They didn't say much as they searched the grass for their phones, then made a long, looping detour around the tree with the nest and closed the distance to the house. Harper didn't trust herself to speak. There was nothing like surviving a dangerous situation with her handsome friend to loosen her lips about her true feelings.

She couldn't let him know. So she kept her lips clamped shut, which also kept her teeth from chattering out of her head, and trudged stoically to her apartment.

He removed his arm from around her shoulders to open the door. "I'm all wet and hate to come in. Will you be okay?"

She nodded, her fingers going to the buttons on her shirt. Only she was shivering so badly, she couldn't grip them.

"Um, maybe not?" She scrunched her face and glanced at Wyatt, expecting him to have some smart-butted comment to direct at her. Instead his eyes were wide open, his jaw hung down, and his facial expression looked similar to the way she would expect if she'd suggested he sacrifice his firstborn to the corn god.

Was she that repulsive to him? Seriously, it wasn't like he loathed her. They were best friends.

"Never mind. I'll just rip it off." She tried to get her shaking hands to catch hold of the collar.

Wyatt coughed. "No, I..." His voice came out two octaves too high. Harper would have laughed if she wasn't so close to crying. So much for thinking he might return her feelings.

He cleared his throat, and reached for her hand. "I can help."

"I wouldn't want to stress you out or anything," Harper muttered, resisting a little as he grabbed her wrist.

"I can make the sacrifice."

She kept her eyes on the floor. His fingers grazed the skin at her wrists.

"Let's do these first," Wyatt murmured.

Not wanting to admit that made sense, she kept her face turned down. Her stomach did a slow roll as he slipped the button through the hole.

"Give me your other hand." His voice sounded low. Almost tender.

Harper complied, trying to pretend her breath hadn't grown faster, and that his near-rejection hadn't hurt.

He cradled her wrist in his hand, and this time she watched as his blunt thumbs skimmed over her skin then worked the button through the hole.

Her small apartment seemed to compress, the air heavy, the silence thick. Her lungs shook, causing her inhale to shudder. Her heart beat so loud her cheeks flushed as she imagined he could hear it. And could know exactly what he was doing to her.

"Come closer so I can get the rest of them."

She swallowed, but didn't look up. "You don't have to."

He tugged on her hand and she moved in front of him, waiting.

"I'm sorry, Harper."

Gosh, did he have to make it worse by apologizing? She shook her head. He couldn't help it that he hadn't wanted to touch his friend like this. She wouldn't want to undress any of her colleagues at work. "It's not your fault."

"I'll, uh, close my eyes." His voice sounded like sandpaper lined his throat.

"It's okay," she whispered. "I have a shirt on under this one."

His fingers hovered under her chin, like he was going to say something else. He touched the button. "I can close them anyway."

Heat smoldered through her shirt. She wanted to whimper, to throw herself into his arms, to demand that he stop treating her like his sister, but she gritted her teeth, fisting her hands at her sides. "Just hurry."

He seemed to gulp. His hands slid down to the next button. His fingers worked it free. Her shirt slid open, revealing more of her white cami.

She watched as though it were happening to someone else. Wyatt's hands on her shirt, brown and tan against the blue outer shirt, the white inner one. The hair on his arms curled crisp and dark. So tempted to touch it, she shoved her hands in her back pockets.

Her front brushed his arm.

He jerked.

Her heart stuttered. The room seemed to shrink. His breath skimmed across her skin.

"Hold still," he growled.

She froze. The last button slipped out. Wyatt didn't move. She glanced at his face, ready to apologize. His neck was red, his cheeks flushed, and shiny pearls of sweat glittered on his forehead.

Her heart thumped as they stared into each other's eyes.

He spun on his heel and plunged out the door. He didn't look back as he powered through the yard and disappeared into the farmhouse.

Harper released her breath. She spread her hands out in front of her and looked down. Steady as a rock. Wyatt might not stop running from her until he hit the next continent, but at least her shivering had stopped.

Chapter Seven

After the idiot he'd made of himself, Wyatt had been tempted to hide in the house until tomorrow, but he had to make sure Harper was okay. From where he stood in her kitchen, he could hear the water in the bathroom running, so she'd at least made it that far.

He wasn't sure what he should do, how he should act. After pondering it for the time it had taken to shower and change, he decided to just act the way he normally did. Maybe Harper would brush off his foolish attraction to her as another one of his eccentricities. Maybe.

He rubbed a hand along the side of his face. It still throbbed, but the pain wasn't sharp or burning like it had been. Same for his shoulders and hand. If Harper didn't catch pneumonia, and if she hadn't guessed the strength of his feelings for her, the day could be considered a success.

His phone rang and he unhooked it from his belt, looking at the screen. His dad. A shot of nervous tension pushed through his body. "Hello?"

"Hey, son. Are you in Europe yet?"

"Well, about that." Crap. He'd told his dad he couldn't help at the resort during the busy season this year—their winter was the Northern Hemisphere summer—because of the prior commitment to hiking. He hadn't bothered to mention his mom or her death. His dad wasn't sentimental and probably didn't even remember or care.

"Is there a problem? Do you need money?"

Wyatt blew out a breath. His dad constantly offered him money. And he'd taken him up on it, too, especially when he was younger. Adventuring around the world wasn't cheap. Maybe that's part of the reason he felt like he owed his dad now.

"No. No problem, exactly. And I don't need money."

"But you're not in Europe?"

"No."

"That's great. We're swamped. I could really use you."

"So, um. You probably didn't hear that Uncle Fink has been in the hospital."

"How would I have heard that?"

Of course, he wouldn't have. His dad was only interested in information that pertained to his resort.

Wyatt rubbed the side of his nose. "Well, they needed someone to work on the farm."

"I needed someone to work at the resort. We're so short-handed, people are leaving and heading over to Carl's place, where they can get some actual instruction on the slopes." His dad's voice had raised a few decibels.

Guilt slithered through his stomach and bit at his chest. His dad might not have wanted him after his mom died, but he'd financed all his adventures. Fink had accepted him and provided a home for him, but money on the farm, even supplemented with the small school principal's salary, had always been tight.

His grip tightened on his phone, like holding it harder would negate the fact that now they both needed his help. And he didn't know what to do.

Wyatt wasn't afraid of his dad, but he seemed to forever come up short. Like now.

"You're saying..." His dad's voice had grown ominously softer. "That you stayed to help your uncle in Pennsylvania rather than coming down here and helping your father?"

He wanted to say that his uncle had taken him in when he had needed a home. That his uncle had housed him without complaint. His uncle hadn't worried about how it would affect his lifestyle. That throwing money at your son didn't prove your love. But those words weren't ones a man could say to his father.

The silence stretched.

Finally, his dad spoke, still low and obviously angry. "There is absolutely nothing keeping you in the states or on that farm. If you're interested in this business, you'd better get your butt down here."

Wyatt crossed his arms as though to protect himself from the harsh reality of the truth his dad had just spoken. There really was nothing keeping him in the states. Nothing except loyalty to his uncle for taking him in when his mother died, and Harper. His original plan had been to try to convince her to go to Europe with him. He wanted to spend a last summer with Harper before he left for good. He could hardly tell his dad that. Unless...

"My fiancée is here and I didn't want to leave her."

Silence on the line.

The seconds ticked by. Wyatt closed his eyes. What had he just said? Why? Maybe it was the longing of his heart, but that longing had just popped out of his mouth in the form of a lie to his father. He should do something to fix it. Admit that he'd just lied. That there was no fiancée. Harper would never be his fiancée.

His mouth stayed closed.

"You're engaged?"

His dad actually sounded hopeful. Less angry.

Wyatt closed his eyes and put his forehead against the cool glass of the window. "Yes."

"That's fabulous. I want to meet her."

"Yeah. You'll love her, Dad." Wyatt felt like he was having an out-of-body experience. His mouth kept moving, kept saying these things he wanted so badly to be true he could taste it. But they weren't.

Lies. His mouth kept forming lies. And his brain kept allowing it.

"I'm sending you plane tickets for next weekend. Bring her down. I deserve to meet her, at least."

Wyatt rubbed a hand over his head. "Ah, I'm not sure next weekend works."

"Why not?"

Wyatt wracked his brain for a convincing lie about something they had to do this weekend. Which was exactly the problem with lies. Once he told one, he had to keep telling them. Only the first lie he'd told had come from his heart. This one required creativity.

"We're swamped on the farm. It's going to be at least a month before I'd have any time, and even then…"

"I'll give you a month there, then I want to see this fiancée. I'm emailing you the ticket info. Get your butt down here, show me the girl, let me charm her into wanting to live here, and I might forgive you for throwing me over for your uncle. How long are you stuck there for, anyway? When can I expect you here for good?" As always, his dad's manner was brusque with no time for nonsense or dithering.

Wyatt struggled to shift gears. Had he agreed to take his fiancée to Chile? "I'm not sure. I'm going to have to talk to my fiancée about that." After he found a fiancée. Or he could just tell his dad the truth. But the odd feeling of not having control of the situation continued.

"When's the wedding?"

"I'm not sure."

"She is planning on moving here with you, correct?"

Not in this life. "I'm not sure."

"Fine. I just want to be a part of your life, son. I want to meet this woman." Amazingly, his dad's voice softened. "I'm sure she's amazing, and I want her to feel comfortable here and know that she's welcome."

His dad was used to getting his way. It was a handy characteristic for a resort owner. For any business owner, really. He could make things happen.

But it wasn't so handy when one was on the receiving end.

"I've got this, Dad."

"See that you do." There was a pause. "I'll have Sophia get the tickets—" he paused, probably while looking at a calendar, "—and plan on picking you up from the airport Friday, August twelfth. I'll have you fly back out on Monday. Unless you want to stay?" He sounded so hopeful, Wyatt could hardly stand the pressure of the guilt in his chest.

"No. We'll need to leave."

His dad paused. "Okay, then. See you next month."

"See ya."

Wyatt let his hand drop away from his ear. He pushed the red button, then rested his whole cheek on the cool, soothing glass, allowing his body to sag.

"Wyatt?" He jerked up and spun around. Harper stood in the hall doorway. Her hair was wet, but combed. She wore a green tee shirt and a pair of cutoffs. Her feet were bare. "Was that your dad? Are you flying to Chile?"

Chapter Eight

Harper's legs didn't seem to be able to move. Not since the word fiancée had come out of Wyatt's mouth. When was he going to tell her about his fiancée? Her entire chest felt empty and hollow, white. Why did it bother her so much that Wyatt had a fiancée?

Only because she hadn't met her. And because her best friend hadn't told her something so important. Not because she was upset that Wyatt was getting married. Not at all.

Yeah. Right.

"Um, Harper. Why don't you sit down? There's something I need to tell you."

She obeyed, moving like a robot. She'd just realized she had feelings for him, and now to find out that he was engaged?

His eyes narrowed on her. "I'll make some tea to warm you up."

Her eyes followed him as he moved around her small kitchen. His broad shoulders filled out the plain white tee shirt. The muscles in his back rippled under it enticingly. His jeans weren't tight, but he filled them out just right. And his bare feet somehow gave her heart palpitations. Casual in her house. Like he let his guard down for her.

Which was the actual thing. Wyatt was fun. And funny. He worked hard, but wasn't afraid to goof off. The only person in the world who could make her laugh at any time, guaranteed. He knew her, actually *knew* her. And he liked her anyway. Gosh, she hadn't realized how much she appreciated Wyatt not seeming interested in girls at all. She was happy with the way things were, and she assumed he was, too. In hindsight, she should have realized that not everyone was happy to sail smoothly through life, avoiding change.

From a young age, she had known that it was safer to stay home. Since her dad died to be exact. She'd been young, but not too young to hear the adults in her life saying that her dad should have been happy to work on the farm. That wanting to provide a bigger, better life for his family had caused him to take the road construction job where he'd been in the accident that had killed him.

Change scared her. It reminded her of the brevity of life and brought back all those feelings of fear and insecurity she'd tried to hide from her mother once she realized her daddy was never coming back. That dead meant gone. Then, of course, like any normal child, she'd become fixated on what might happen if the same thing happened to her mother. She'd spent years waking up crying.

She hated change, hated risk, hated anything that threatened to rock the solid, secure little world she'd built around herself. But Wyatt thrived on it.

She tucked her legs under herself and adjusted the blanket on her lap. Change was a part of life, she knew that. And she would face this unexpected and, frankly, unwelcomed change head on.

A clatter from the kitchen indicated a dropped spoon. Wyatt was never clumsy. And he was never slow. Obviously, he had to be dreading having this discussion with her.

Well, she'd make it easy for him. After all, their friendship was the most important thing. He had no idea that she'd started to develop feelings that went beyond that boundary, and she had no intention of telling him now. She might be losing him in some ways, but she couldn't bear to lose her best friend.

And she would love his fiancée. She would. If necessary, she would force herself to. And she wouldn't be jealous. She would be kind. She would treat the woman like a sister. She would be happy she caught a man as wonderful as Wyatt. She would not be upset Wyatt would be making another girl laugh, dragging someone else along on his adventures. Harper choked back a snort. Whatever girl Wyatt chose, he probably wasn't going to have to drag her on adventures. She'd probably drag him.

She glanced at the kitchen where Wyatt stood with his head and shoulders above the short bar. He put sugar in her tea. His spoon clicked against the mug as he stirred before snapping the lid back on the sugar container.

She should have noticed him before. But she'd been too busy shoving her nose in her books, trying to keep life from changing at all. She hadn't wanted their friendship to change. Even now, she would never open her mouth. Having him as a friend was far better than making things awkward between them or losing him completely.

He carried their tea cups over, and she smiled up at him, hoping her dismay did not show on her face.

"Are you getting warm?" he asked.

She nodded. "Thanks."

The teacup shook a little as he set it on the coffee table, and his perpetual smile was missing. He perched on the edge of the chair across from her, setting his own cup down without drinking any. Resting his arms on his spread knees, he gripped his hands together.

A spot of nerves pinched her stomach. She had to make this easy for him.

"I heard what you said."

"I thought maybe you did." He grimaced. "I'm sorry. I really didn't mean for it to come out like that."

"It's fine. I'm actually really excited." Okay, so that wasn't true, but she really wanted it to be. "This is great."

Wyatt didn't say anything. His mouth hung open and his eyes were wide. "You're seriously okay with it?"

"Well, yeah. Of course. Why wouldn't I be?" She was not going to ruin his happiness just because of the pain that crushed her own chest. She tried to pretend her lungs didn't feel as inflexible as tin cans.

"I just..." He ran a hand over his face, then tilted his head. "I...I thought you'd be a little more upset."

She scrunched her face up in her best how-could-you-think-that look. "No way!" She smiled. Hugely. Her cheeks felt brittle. "We've always supported each other one hundred percent. I'm your backup. You can depend on me. We've been best friends since we met. Just because you didn't tell me..." She shrugged like it was no big deal. Hopefully he was believing her act.

"I didn't know." He lifted his hands up, a look, half-happiness, half-unbelief, on his face.

She blinked. What? "You didn't know?"

"No, not until just now." A full-on grin stole over his face. He shook his head. "I didn't really think you'd be okay with it."

"How could you not know that you're engaged?" she asked incredulously, all pretense gone.

"Because I wasn't. Until just a few minutes ago."

"I thought you were talking to your dad."

"I was."

"And you told him you were engaged."

His smile disappeared. "Yeah. I did." He rubbed the back of his neck. "And of course, right away, he wants to meet her."

"Of course he does."

"I'm so glad you understand."

"So you haven't asked yet?"

"You're going to make me ask?"

He told his dad he was engaged, but he hadn't asked the girl yet? "I think that's only right." Hello.

"Are you messing with me?" he asked incredulously. "That's weird."

"I'm not messing with you. It's just common sense. If you want a girl to be your fiancée, you have to ask her to marry you first."

"So, we couldn't just pretend?" Wyatt had gone white.

"You don't want to get married?" She tried to keep the relief out of her voice, but she was afraid she wasn't very successful.

"I do. I really do. I just wasn't sure how it would work."

"Usually you get a license. Then find a preacher..."

"Shut up, Pickles."

"Seriously Wyatt. You can't announce an engagement to your dad before you've at least asked the girl."

"I wasn't expecting to announce it. He just backed me into a corner, giving me a guilt trip because I was here helping Uncle Fink when he wants me down there."

She waved a hand in the air trying to show her nonchalance. "That's fine. You just need to work it out with her."

"I'm trying."

"No, you're not. Get off your butt and ask her." There. Twenty years from now, his kids could thank her.

Wyatt stood. Part of her heart tore. She swallowed and picked up her tea cup. Wyatt must have noticed her distress, much as she tried to hide it, because he came over and knelt on one knee beside the couch.

"Harper?"

Wow. It was serious if he was using her real name.

"Yeah?"

"Would you please go to Chile with me as my fake fiancée?"

HARPER'S MOUTH DROPPED. So did her tea cup. Hot liquid splattered everywhere. She yelped and jumped.

Wyatt snatched the blanket, yanking it off her to keep the tea from soaking through. Her forward momentum pushed her into his chest. Already off balance in the awkward one-knee kneeling position, her weight threw him back and to the side. He grabbed her as he fell, hoping to keep her from hitting the sharp corners of the coffee table.

They landed on the floor, tangled in a tea-soaked blanket. Harper lay half on his chest, her wet hair brushing his arm and her big gray eyes blinking in his face.

He grunted. "That wasn't the reaction I was expecting."

She snorted. "That wasn't the question I was expecting."

"Holy cow, Pickles. You used to be normal. Now you've turned into a girl."

"I've been a girl all my life, Ding Dong."

"But you don't act like one. I don't have to guess what you're thinking. I don't have to tiptoe around you. I don't have to put myself through contortions to right some perceived wrong I didn't even know I committed." He closed his eyes. Her weight pressed on his chest, in a good way. "At least I didn't used to."

She tweaked his nose with her finger. The scent of berries and vanilla tripped in his brain, and it was all he could do to not put his arms around her and settle her closer.

"I just didn't understand. You have a fiancée that your dad wants to meet. But she can't go, so you want me to fill in. Even though you know that I hate travelling and..."

"No."

"Yes, I do."

"Stop, Pickles. Obviously, you didn't hear as much of my conversation as I thought you did."

"Tell me."

"My dad was giving me a hard time about being here with Uncle Fink instead of being down there helping him. So I lied to him. Told him I wanted to stay here to be with my fiancée." He still couldn't believe he'd done that. He grabbed a handful of Harper's hair, on the pretense of moving it off his shoulder. "You should let this down more often."

She blinked, and he mentally kicked himself. It was bad enough he was asking her to pretend to be his fiancée, he was really going to scare her away if he didn't get a hold of himself.

"Really?"

"Sure. When it's wet like this, it's almost a weapon, flapping around, slapping my face. Next time your tea cup attacks you and I'm trying to save you, you should at least refrain from trying to knock me unconscious with your hair." He pushed it aside because the desire to wrap it around his fingers and bring it to his nose was almost overwhelming.

"Maybe you should refrain from shocking me with crazy questions."

He sighed. "I would think you'd expect it from me by now."

"You're right. But that one was just bizarre, even for you."

"So you never did answer me."

Her eyes dropped and she looked away. It was her I-don't-want-to-do-this-and-you-can't-make-me look.

Yeah, that was the reaction he'd been expecting. Now, he needed to try to convince her. So he piled it on. "You have my back. You're my best friend. You support me one hundred percent."

Harper put both fingers in her ears, resting her chest on his. "Blah, blah, blah. I can't hear a thing."

He circled her wrists with his hands, surprised at the delicacy of her bones. Tugging gently, he pulled her fingers out of her ears. "Grow up, Dr. Pickles."

"You are the only person in the world who would ever say that to me."

He lifted a brow. Her neck turned red. He grinned. He was the only person who would ever see Harper do anything like put her fingers in her ears and say blah, blah, blah. But he had to tease her. "I'm the only one who tells you the truth."

"The only time it's true is when I'm with you."

"You're stalling."

"I know." She bit her lip, then, to his complete shock, she laid her head on his chest. He quit breathing, although his heart beat like a runaway locomotive. "You know I'd do anything for you. But I'm scared. Chile is so far away. We'll have to fly. There's mountains. People die in those mountains." Her voice dropped to a whisper. "My dad didn't need to go the whole way to Chile to die."

He forgot to try to keep her from knowing the truth about his feelings. His hands let go of her wrists and he put one on her head, stroking her cold hair, the other on her back. Fought to keep it still.

"I'm not going to let you die, Harper."

"I know. But you can't control everything. The airplane could crash into another plane in the sky…"

He fought the quirking of his lips. "Has that ever happened?"

"The Titanic only sank once."

"There are no icebergs in the sky."

"I know. But anything could happen. We could get stranded in the Andes. Or crash in Mexico. I don't want to leave my home, the farm." Her head came up. "I can't leave the farm! Sorry, I'd love to go, but I can't leave the farm."

"It's for four days. A month from now. You can leave."

There was a knock on the door.

Harper glanced up, then ducked and groaned. "I supposed it's too late to hide?" Harper asked.

"I'm pretty sure she saw us."

She bit her lip and shifted her body. "I've never seen that person before." She scrunched even lower. "How are we going to explain what we're doing?"

His lips kicked up. "We could tell her we're engaged." If they told enough people, maybe it would become true.

"That's great. But it's going to be awkward when we get unengaged."

"If the plane crashes in the Andes, we won't have to worry about it."

"So now you're giving me the upside of a plane crash?"

"Just trying to help you think positively."

The woman knocked again.

Harper rolled off Wyatt. He ached to pull her back to him. The only thing better than sparring with Harper was touching her while he was doing it. He stood, then helped Harper untangle her legs from the blanket and pulled her up.

He met her gaze, concerned but smiling, then turned and led the short distance to the door.

IT WAS the tuba that gave it away. Or maybe the cat.

White-blond hair framed big blue eyes that blinked as Harper opened the door. Everything about the woman was tiny and slender, but her pointy chin, tilted just slightly up, hinted at an iron will.

The woman's chest meowed. Or rather, the little animal with a green ribbon in its hair meowed from its position inside the carrier strapped to the woman's front. A big, black tuba case sat at her feet. It was about a quarter of the height of the woman. How did she carry it? Or play it?

Harper held her hand out. "You have to be Avery."

"Quite correct," the woman said pleasantly.

"I'm Harper, and this is your distant cousin, Wyatt."

Harper bit back a smile when Wyatt took the tiny hand with two fingers and shook it like it was a china vase.

Avery looked around. "There didn't seem to be anyone at the house, so is this where I stay?"

"We'll set you up with a room at the house."

Wyatt reached for the tuba. The woman beat him to it.

"Sorry. I don't let anyone touch the tuba. I even buy a seat for it when I fly." She patted her little cat's head and picked the tuba up as though it were a child's lunch box. "I'm a vegetarian and I don't do gluten, dairy, or night shades."

Harper stared at Avery.

"I just wanted to get that out there," she said with a friendly smile that softened her words. "Sometimes people get offended when I don't eat bread or tomatoes. Although it's the carnivores that get the most upset."

"I actually have a couple of degrees in nutrition, so I know the benefits of those choices. But how about we just put you in charge of cooking and we'll eat whatever you make."

Avery gave a decisive nod. "That would be best, I'm sure, because it will save us all grief later on, and I know a lot of great recipes anyway, although if your degree is in nutrition, I'd really like to discuss the subject with you at length, because had I not gone into music, I would have most certainly studied nutrition..."

She continued on while Harper and Wyatt exchanged looks. Wyatt cleared his throat.

Avery paused and Wyatt said, "Think I'll just head on down to the shed and get the gourd seeds in the planter."

"I'll be down as soon as I get Avery settled." Harper ignored his smirk as she stepped off the porch beside Avery. Fink certainly had interesting relatives.

Chapter Nine

Wyatt sat at the corner of the counter in Danny's Diner, using his straw to stir his ice water, watching the lemon swirl in graceful circles halfway down the glass. Harper hadn't wanted to come.

It might have a little something to do with Avery, although the woman had said she was tired from traveling and was turning in early.

Still, it discouraged him that Harper had turned down his invitation for dinner. He hadn't exactly asked her out on a date, but close. And she'd said no. Didn't bode well for his chances.

Someone bumped his shoulder, then plopped into the stool beside him. He glanced over. Rusty.

"Hey, man."

"It's not too often I catch you without a smile." Rusty waved at the waitress and ordered a drink.

Wyatt straightened and tried to pull the corners of his mouth up. Rusty was right; it wasn't often that he acted this morose. In fact, he usually only felt like this before he left Harper to head out on some adventure.

"That better?" He pointed a forced smile in Rusty's direction.

"Looks fake."

Wyatt snorted and went back to stirring his glass.

"What's the problem, man?"

Should he get Rusty's advice? Rusty wouldn't lie. But what kind of advice would he end up getting from a guy that Wyatt had never even seen with a woman? There just wasn't anyone else to whom he could turn. Sure, he had tons of buds who'd drop everything to climb a mountain with him or go spelunking. And most of those guys were good with the ladies. But the girls they hung with weren't like Harper. The things he did that would impress a "normal" woman got a big yawn out of Harper.

He waited until Rusty finished ordering his burger and fries.

"If I wanted to catch a girl's attention, what should I do?"

Rusty ripped open the paper on his straw. "We're talking about Harper?"

Wyatt went back to focusing on his glass. So much for being hypothetical. "Might be."

"So why don't you just tell her? Seems like the direct route would be the best with her."

"That could ruin our friendship."

Rusty ran a hand over his jaw, nodding. "Thought you said you were leaving to go to Chile before fall?"

He traced the condensation on the glass with one finger. "I am."

Rusty leaned back, offended. "I'm not helping you. What, you think Harper is a summer fling kind of girl?"

He jerked his head around. "No! I want her to go with me."

"To Chile?"

"Yeah. I have to go. My dad's expecting me. I pretty much told him I'd move down with the idea of taking over management eventually." He let out a breath and turned back toward the bar, taking hold of his glass and turning it on the smooth surface of the counter.

"And you think Harper's gonna move to Chile?"

The incredulous way Rusty asked the question made Wyatt realize how foolish his whole idea was.

"She's never going to move to Chile. Holy cow, it was all her parents could do to get her to go with them to see Niagara Falls."

That trip was a lifesaver now. Otherwise, Harper wouldn't have had a passport. "I know. You're right."

Carla sashayed up to the bar and set Wyatt's meal and Rusty's burger and fries down with loud clinks. She pulled a bottle of vinegar out from under her arm and set it in front of Rusty's plate. "You always ask for it. Figured I'd just bring it to you. You boys need anything else?"

"Nah. Thanks darlin'." Rusty waved her away.

Wyatt gave a shake of his head. She snapped her gum and hustled off.

Rusty dumped vinegar over his fries.

Wyatt watched with some revulsion. "Those things are going to be soggy."

"They're better that way."

The pungent odor of the vinegar burned his nose. "If you say so..."

Rusty picked up a dripping fry and squished it into his mouth. Wyatt wrinkled his nose and turned back to his water.

Rusty swallowed, then said, "So, either you need to stay here, settle down...which wouldn't hurt you a bit. Or you need to lay off the idea of having Harper."

Wyatt bristled. "Maybe she would love me enough to go to Chile with me." He wished it were that simple.

"And maybe she'll grow fins and a tail."

Good point.

Rusty held a dripping fry over his plate. "Seriously, man, she might go to Chile with you. But some people don't have the wandering gene. Just like you need your danger and excitement, Harper needs the security of her family, friends, and hometown. She's a great girl, but she wasn't born to run."

"Chile could become home to her."

"And a penguin could live in Death Valley."

"That's a little strong."

"It's a true comparison."

Wyatt smashed down the top roll of the roast beef sandwich. Mayonnaise oozed out in white blobs. Maybe he wasn't being fair to Harper. Rather than worrying about how to attract her, maybe he should concentrate on how to get over her.

As though Rusty heard his thoughts, he said, "You and Harper were made for each other. But you need to settle here, not drag her halfway across the globe."

"I can't."

"Did you promise your dad?"

"I did." There was more, but he wasn't going to try to explain to Rusty the feelings he had towards his dad and how his mother's death and memory complicated everything. He didn't even really want to and wasn't sure he could.

They ate in silence for a while and the words rolled over in his head. He wanted to prove to his dad he was trustworthy and capable. Maybe make his dad regret not wanting him. His chest tightened the way it always did when he remembered standing in the lodge kitchen after his mother's death. Like his grief wasn't enough, his dad had flatly stated that his Uncle Fink in Pennsylvania had agreed to allow Wyatt to live with him. To finish school in the states. It wasn't that Wyatt had loved his dad or the resort and hadn't wanted to leave. It was the sting of not being wanted by his own father. That sting had burned all his life.

How that translated to this burning desire to please his dad, he had no idea. But, yeah, something inside of him craved for his dad to be proud of him. Something else craved his mother's happiness, even though she was long gone. She'd wanted him to get along with his dad.

Rusty looked at him questioningly. "Wouldn't he understand that you want to stay here? Isn't there someone else who could take your place?"

Wyatt pushed his glass away. "He needs me there. The whole thing is going to be mine someday. Yeah, the agreement was verbal, but it's what has to happen." Maybe his dad's rejection should have made Wyatt desire to reject his father in the same hurtful way. But it had the opposite effect. There was almost nothing he wouldn't do to make his dad proud.

HARPER TIDIED the last of her books in her tiny university office. She really wanted to go with Wyatt to eat, but it was just a friend thing, and she wasn't sure how much longer she could keep up the pretense. The button scenario had been hard, but being tangled up with him on the floor had shaken her. She hadn't expected to have to fight so many different sensations.

So, she'd come to her office. Finals had been over for a month, but she'd been expecting to be back in the office because of research and hadn't made it back in to put the last of her things away. Avery had gone to bed early, so tonight had seemed like a good night.

She was teaching the same courses this year as the last two, so there was no real preparation. Although she tried as hard as everyone else to stay up on the latest data—and in nutrition the data constantly changed —she also tried to use the same books for several years, to help keep costs down for her students.

She looked around the small office one more time, smiling at the picture she had sitting on her desk of Wyatt and her three half-brothers. Wyatt lay on the floor, the boys sprawled out over and behind him. Kent, the youngest brother, sat on Wyatt's chest. The day she took the picture, Wyatt had just come home from trekking in the Amazon rainforest. He'd been without service for weeks and had been without a phone for almost as long, when a bridge had collapsed and he and his two companions had fallen in the swollen creek below. They'd all made it, but it ruined his phone. The family hadn't heard from him until he showed up at the farm, brimming with tales of adventure.

Although he'd told her he'd be in and out of service, she'd been worried sick when she hadn't heard anything for three whole weeks. As usual, though, she hadn't been able to stay angry and had snapped that picture not long after he arrived. It was one of her favorites. She sighed, part of her wishing that Wyatt could just stay home, part of her knowing that he wouldn't be who he was if he did. All of her was baffled by these new feelings simmering in her heart. Nutrition was her specialty, not psychology.

"Harper. I'm glad I caught you."

She whirled around. "Dr. Hitten."

"Jeff."

"Yes, of course. Jeff." She glanced at her watch. "It's late. I wasn't expecting anyone else to be here."

He shifted the stack of books and papers he held in his hand. "I've been getting things geared up for the research project. Has your situation changed? We could really use your help."

"No. I'm needed on the farm."

Jeff nodded. He pushed his glasses farther up his nose. Harper realized as she stared at him that people probably considered him handsome. He always seemed to have an abundance of undergrads hanging around. She'd assumed they were jockeying for position, but maybe they just wanted to be around the handsome, smart professor.

Her gaze skimmed over him. She couldn't remember seeing him in anything but a dress shirt and pants, usually covered with a lab coat. He never did anything to accentuate his physique, but now that she looked, he seemed fit under those loose-fitting clothes. His shoulders weren't as broad as Wyatt's, but his stomach was flat, his chin square, and his eyes honest and compassionate.

Dr. Hitten would be perfect for her. They'd never run out of things to talk about. He was already tenured, she soon to be. He wasn't going anywhere and she didn't want to. She thought he might be a little interested in her. Why couldn't she fall for a guy like him, instead of...

Her brain blinked red warning lights. She hadn't fallen for Wyatt. Had she?

"You were looking for me?" Harper asked, breaking the silence and banishing her unwelcomed thoughts.

He cleared his throat. "Yes. Actually I was. We've been asked to collaborate with the psychology department on a different project that starts this fall."

"That's wonderful news."

"It is. And I already told them that we'd do it. However, there is a pile of paperwork that needs to be sorted and graphed. It's the kind of thing I'd usually have a doctoral candidate working on, although it's more complicated than it typically is because of the collaboration." He lifted a hand. "I thought you might be willing to do the work. It would look good for the upcoming tenure vote."

This could fix everything. She should be happy and excited about the opportunity. Only...she wasn't. And she couldn't figure out why. But after all the work she'd put into getting tenure, it grated her to not accept this opportunity. Forcing her lips into a smile, she said, "I'd love to. Thanks so much for offering this to me. I hadn't been allowing myself to think about the tenure vote, because I was sure there was no hope for me."

"You have a good reputation around here as a hard worker and a team player. That should help you. That, and if you get paperwork for this new project together and organized, should help things work out in your favor." Jeff leaned against the doorframe. "I have to warn you, though, there's some research involved. It's complicated stuff. It's going to take a lot of time."

"I have to work during the day, but I'll have all evening to spend on this." Working on it should help keep her from thinking about Wyatt. Maybe Avery would be interested in helping.

"Good. If anyone can get it done, you can." He gave a short nod. "The psych department is going to email me the info they have. Plus there are some books and papers. I'll get everything together and you can drop by my office tomorrow to pick up the physical stuff. I'll forward the electronic info to you, so you can get started ASAP."

Harper nodded. This was a great opportunity. Maybe everything wasn't lost like she had supposed. She didn't know why she wasn't more excited. Once she got the stuff, the fun and thrill would probably hit her.

"I'll get on it as soon as you get it to me."

"That's a plan." One side of his lip lifted in a smile before he pushed off the door jamb and walked away.

Harper took one last look at the picture of Wyatt and the boys on her desk before she flipped the lights out and locked the door behind her.

Chapter Ten

Harper twisted the handle of the spigot. Water sprayed out over the pumpkin plants landing with satisfying thumps on the large, flat leaves. Yellow blossoms peeked out from under the green canopy. Unfortunately, with the current dry conditions, the plants needed a drink, or they'd end up with fist sized pumpkins this fall.

Harper's phone buzzed in her pocket. She reached for it. "Hey, Mom."

"Harper, honey. How are you?"

"I'm great, Mom. How's Fink?"

"They just moved him out of the ICU this morning."

"That's great news." She ducked and ran a few steps to get out of the sprinkler's way.

"Yeah. But they told us not to be in a rush. He'll need a lot of time to heal. They're talking about sending him to in-patient rehab." Her mom sighed. "We could be out here weeks yet."

"Do you need me? You know I'll come."

"I know, honey." Her mom sighed again. "But really, I'm fine. Jillian is doing great with the boys. Did I tell you she was in the circus?"

Harper stopped in the act of bending down to move the hose. "No. Seriously? I bet the boys love that."

"Yeah, they love her. I think they'll miss her more than their grandparents when we finally leave."

Harper snorted. "Well, it'd be hard to top a circus performer." Especially for her three little brothers.

"Jillian is a great girl."

"I'm glad that is working out for you at least. Is Fink keeping his chin up?"

"He memorizes the doctors' instruction pamphlets and follows them to the letter."

Harper swung the hose over the end vine so she could stretch the sprinkler a little farther. "Bet that drives you crazy."

"It does. Especially when the pamphlets contradict each other."

Harper bit back a laugh. At least Fink hadn't had a major personality change.

"The doctors are starting to wise up. They've given him several rather long pamphlets on good eating and the benefits of exercise. I think that's just to keep him occupied. If he's memorizing pamphlets he's not harassing them about anything else." Her mom laughed.

"At least you can laugh about it."

"Oh, that's Fink walking down the hall, and he's not supposed to be out of bed. I'd better go."

"Talk to you later, Mom."

Chapter Eleven

Wyatt carried a box filled with everything they needed to stake out the corn maze, following Harper to the edge of the seven-acre patch. The corn was slightly over ankle high. The perfect height in which to work. They walked along the edge of the field, past the pumpkins, which were vining out nicely.

"Usually the entrance is about right here, isn't it?" Harper stopped and looked around.

"I think it's a little farther on," Wyatt said. Not that he wanted to carry the heavy box any farther.

"Here, let me hold that while you eyeball it up. I know there's a way you always do it that gets us just as good as if I measured it." Harper turned and took the box from him.

"Watch it. The knife's in there."

Harper snorted, but handled the box gingerly. Like the knife would jump out and bite her.

Wyatt grinned to himself as he turned back and lined up their position with the fire pit twenty-five yards away. Parents liked to be able to sit by the fire and talk while watching their kids race down to the corn maze.

"Right here," he said, taking the box back. "You can kind of see the trail from last year." The path got worn down in the fall, but over the spring and summer the grass grew, hiding it.

"Okay, this is where we're going to start, then." Harper set the box down.

Wyatt reached into his back pocket and pulled out the maze they'd gridded out on a spread sheet. He unrolled it and adjusted it for where they stood. An unfamiliar sense of sadness settled around him. If he went to Chile, this could be the last time Harper and he ever made the maze together.

"You remember our first maze?" he asked casually.

Harper reached down and pulled several small stakes from the box along with the hammer. The sun glinted off her hair which was pulled straight back and stuck in a ponytail. She squinted up at him. "Of course. It was pretty simple."

He shook the paper he held. "It's gotten a lot more complicated over the years."

Harper grunted, then looked across the field of baby corn to where the huge old oak tree stood in almost perfect symmetry in the middle of the field like a guard. Several picnic tables, covered with tarps, were under it. One part of the maze would lead to the tables. "Life has gotten more complicated," she said with a slightly wishful tone in her voice. "It seems fitting that our maze does, too."

He pulled the bailer twine out and waited while she pounded a stake in. She nodded at the big oak tree. "That's my favorite tree in the whole world."

Wyatt looked at the old oak as he tied the end of the bailer twine onto the first stake. "You say that every year."

"It's true." She finished pounding the next stake. "How old do you think it is?"

"Couple hundred years?" He looked back over the area they'd finished. The maze was shaping up nicely.

Harper kept working as she spoke. "I was just thinking, it was here when my great-great-grandmother arrived, when she hid that ring."

"And it'll be here when your great-great-grandchildren make the corn maze." His heart pinched. Her children. Not his. His kids would be in Chile. "Do you think our kids will get together?" Man, he was feeling maudlin. Which was not like him at all. But the question was out there, hanging in the thick summer air.

Harper looked up at him. A glimmer shimmered in her eye. She smiled it away and lifted her chin. "Of course."

He'd been neglecting his duty, which was to lighten things up as they worked. "You know, I think this maze would work a lot better if we backed that part off about ten feet and cut the corner here…"

"You always do this!" Harper exclaimed. She stood, hands on hips, but the corners of her lips tilted up.

"Well, yeah. Life is about improvising." He smiled, turning his dimple toward her. Sure enough, her eyes dropped to it before she shook her head.

"Life is about following the script." She pointed at the paper with her finger. "We took the time to write that thing out. We know we're going to end up with something great if we follow it." She pulled out another stake and pounded it in.

"We could end up with something better if we don't."

"Or, we could end up with a corn maze that goes nowhere. Again."

He ignored the jab. "We won't know unless we try." He wound the twine around the stake and used the knife to cut it off.

"We will know if we follow the script." She stood.

He grabbed her shoulders. "How many years have we done this?"

She shrugged. "Ten, maybe?"

"How many years have we done it my way?"

"Half?"

"And how many of those have been successful?"

She pursed her lips. "Define successful?"

"People liked the maze."

"All of them," she said, despite the mulish set to her chin.

"Even when it didn't turn out quite the way we thought it was going to, people still liked it. It still worked. Just not in the way we had planned."

"Okay, Wyatt. You're right. I like this design. I kind of have my heart set on it. But it could be better."

"It could. If we do this…" He explained the idea he'd just gotten about a "secret" passageway that connected the two main legs of the far side of the maze. "And I think the teen boys especially will really get a kick out of that."

"You're probably right. And they're the age group that are the hardest to entertain and keep out of trouble."

"Yep." Wyatt looked over the field. They were about half done with the staking. It wouldn't require too much effort to change.

"Okay. So that means we need to move this stake back..." Harper grabbed the knife and twisted to slice the twine from the stake behind her, but she tripped, her arms windmilled and she bent to catch her balance. She took two big steps and fell with the twine wrapped around her ankle. Bright red blood flowed down her arm. He dropped his hammer and stake and rushed to her, dropping to his knees in the dirt. "Crap, Harper. Are you okay?"

She laughed. "I'm just embarrassed. I'm always so clumsy."

He took the knife from beside her where it had fallen and tossed it away. "No, I'd say what you just did took talent. How did you manage to slice your shoulder?" He pulled his tee shirt off and folded it quickly before pressing it against her shoulder.

She winced and glanced down. "I don't know. I'm just glad it wasn't my face." She grimaced. "Oh, it didn't hurt, but it's starting to."

He lifted his shirt. Her skin gaped and blood started flowing immediately. "That's definitely going to need stitches."

"Great."

"Hey, guys." Avery came floating down through the grass. "I've finished stacking the apple crates, and I'm here to help." She stopped short. "Oh, my goodness!" Her horrified gaze flew from Harper to Wyatt and back to Harper. She took a deep breath and all the color disappeared from her face. "I don't do well with blood. I don't do well at all. One time—" She swayed.

Wyatt took one step toward her, getting ready to catch her when she fainted.

"Turn around," Harper commanded from her position on the ground, interrupting Avery's monologue.

Avery spun away immediately. "I want to help. It's just that blood makes me dizzy."

"You can still help with the corn, but hold on just a second. I'll get

Harper and her blood to the ER to get her stitched up." Wyatt winced. The inside of his chest would not feel like a helicopter was landing on his pancreas if it were his shoulder that was bleeding. He hated it when Harper was hurt. He gritted his teeth and put Harper's hand over his tee shirt. "Press hard." He picked her up, then turned to Avery. "You can pull the corn out between the ropes. Make sure to get the roots."

Avery turned slightly, but did not look in the direction of the blood. She patted the ever-present cat in the carrier on her chest and bit her lip. "You mean, like touch the dirt?"

Harper shifted in his arms. "There are gloves in the laundry room at the house. You might want to go grab a pair."

Wyatt eyed Avery's long, pink fingernails and white hands. "That's a good idea."

"Okay. I can do that. And I'll get all the corn pulled out and is there anything else I can do?" she asked breathlessly.

"Not all the corn, Avery. Just the stalks between the ropes."

She nodded and started back toward the house. "Got it. The stalks between the ropes. I'll have it all done before you get back."

Harper and he grinned at each other. He was definitely disappointed they wouldn't get to see Avery pulling corn. Unlike anyone in any country he'd ever met, Avery seemed like a bit of a featherbrain, but over the past few days that she'd been on the farm, she'd proven herself a willing worker. She'd get that corn pulled out, and she'd do it without getting a spot of dirt on herself. Or her cat. He'd bet his best pair of skis on it. The look on Harper's face said she knew it as well. At least the pain grimace had disappeared. He'd thank Avery later for being a great distraction.

Chapter Twelve

Harper twisted her fingers in her lap. She could hardly believe a whole month had flown by. A full month of working with Wyatt.

The seating area where they waited for their flight to be called had filled with people, talking and laughing, but Wyatt had been uncharacteristically quiet. Was he as nervous as she?

She slanted a glance at him.

Nah.

Casually dressed in jeans and a tee, he slouched slightly, with his ankle propped on his knee, thumbing through a magazine.

He glanced up and caught her staring. His brow lifted.

Flattening her lips, she shook her head slightly and looked away.

Beside her he shifted, putting his leg down and leaning toward her. "What?"

How could she say she was nervous, scared, and homesick and they hadn't even left the country?

She cleared her throat. "Maybe we should practice acting like we're engaged." Immediately, she ducked her head to hide the widening of her eyes. *Where* had that come from?

Wyatt chuckled. "Nice try."

She jerked her head around. "What?"

"You're nervous. Probably scared. I bet you're homesick already, too. In order to keep yourself from running out of this airport, you're trying to distract yourself."

Wow. The man knew her better than she knew herself. She nodded, half embarrassed that he'd known, half relieved.

"Look around, Harper," he said in a low voice.

Her eyes wandered around the room.

"How about that couple over there?" He nodded at the far corner where a couple in their early twenties snuggled together, the woman's bare leg thrown over the man's, their heads together. She whispered, then smiled coyly. They laughed and kissed. His hand came up and ran through her hair...

"No," Harper croaked. "I'm not sitting in your lap."

"That's good, since I don't particularly want you there. My legs would fall asleep." Wyatt's eyes crinkled.

Harper crossed her arms over her chest. "If we're engaged, you should want me on your lap."

"If we're engaged, you should want to be there," Wyatt said reasonably.

She grunted. "Not at the airport."

"Why not?"

She looked around, then lowered her voice even farther. "Because people might think..."

Wyatt winked. "What? That we like each other? I think that's the point."

Okay. She could totally see herself sitting on Wyatt's lap, fingering through his hair, whispering in his ear. But he was her *best friend*. She absolutely could not entertain those thoughts. "It's a little much, and I think with our inexperience, we'd never pull it off."

"What are you saying? That I'd drop you? I think I can manage to keep something as large as you on my lap."

A voice came on the loudspeaker. They stood with everyone else and shuffled forward as general boarding was announced for their flight.

"I'm large?"

"I just meant, you know..."

"Yeah?" She fought to keep her grin in check as Wyatt tried to wrestle his foot out of his mouth.

His hands motioned in the air. "Like a mouse would be hard to keep on your lap. You, not so much."

Time to let him off the hook.

"What about them?" Harper indicated an older couple to their left. The woman read a book. The man's head drooped toward his chest, and it looked like he was sleeping. They didn't even realize the plane was boarding.

"That's not too different than what we're doing right now." He shrugged. "This should be easy."

She couldn't imagine ever looking that bored with Wyatt. "Well, maybe they're not such good role models. Looks like they've been married for sixty years."

"I don't care if I've been married sixty years or not, I'm gonna be having fun with my wife."

Just like she figured. Life with Wyatt would be a lot of things, but not boring. But thinking about life with Wyatt was pointless. Pointlessness had never been something she allowed in her head or life, and she wasn't about to start.

She followed Wyatt to their assigned seats on the plane, subtly checking out the other passengers, but no one else looked like they were engaged, or even in love. Not the couple with two small children—they looked stressed. Not even the couples who sat together. Most of them were on their phones, ignoring each other. A few shoved carry-ons into the overhead compartments, but none of them acted like a couple in love should. Maybe she had romanticized ideas of how love should work.

Pointing her chin at the two closest couples who were already settled in their seats, phones out, thumbs moving over the screens, she said, "Maybe we're talking too much. It looks like if you're a couple, you're supposed to ignore your other half."

"I don't think I want to be part of a relationship like that. Maybe we need counseling." Wyatt finished stowing his bag and dropped into his seat.

"Counseling?"

"Yeah. So we can learn how to interact with each other in a healthy way. Obviously, the couples around us are not positive examples." He grinned at her.

She rolled her eyes. "I think we can fake it."

He placed his arm, palm up between them. "I think engaged couples would hold hands."

She stared at his hand. Large. Long fingers. Calloused.

Her breath quickened. Surely not from holding his hand. She'd held Wyatt's hand plenty of times. Every time he'd gotten her into some scrape or talked her into his latest adventure.

But that was before. Before she realized she didn't look at him like a brother. She swallowed, cognizant that she'd waited way too long to bring her own hand up. She did so now, sliding her palm over his, matching her smaller, softer palm to his.

Wyatt stilled. Possibly because she hesitated. Or possibly because the touch and friction had electrified his hand and arm as much as it had hers. She could hardly think so.

She forced herself to breathe again, but it was wobbly. His fingers slowly curled, sliding between hers and enfolding her hand in his. Her heart trembled. Heat radiated out from her chest.

Folding her own fingers, she marveled at how their hands fit together. At how elemental they looked. At how easy it was to succumb to the idea that holding Wyatt's hand seemed natural. Somehow sensuous, yet comfortable.

Her hand tingled, but it was her heart, which beat softly with a warm and fluttery *thump-thump*, which concerned her. Of all the people in the world, there was no one she'd rather be with than Wyatt. She couldn't feel like this with him. She couldn't fall in love with him. But she couldn't pull her hand away, either.

Still, she had to put some distance between them. He could read her like a neon sign. And the last thing she wanted was to scare her best friend with the un-friendly feelings ripping through her chest right now.

"This is good practice, I think," she whispered.

He jolted, like her words had surprised him, or maybe reminded him of why they were holding hands to begin with.

He laughed. A little shaky. "Holding hands isn't hard. We do it as children. Anyone can do it."

"That's right." She slapped a big, carefree smile on her face before tilting her head up to look at him. "We've got this." Lifting their hands, she gave them a shake as though to prove it. But also to shake out the burgeoning sensations threatening the perfect friendship she had with this man.

~

"We definitely look engaged now." Wyatt twisted their hands over, stopping short. "What's this?" He touched the ring she wore with his free hand.

"I thought I should have an engagement ring."

"Crap. I never thought of it."

Her face tilted down and he couldn't see her expression to be able to tell whether she was upset or not.

She twisted the ring with her free hand. "Yeah, well, it's a good thing you get to practice on me. The next time you ask a girl to marry you, you'd better have one of those."

"I'll keep that in mind." The only girl he'd ever wanted to marry was sitting right beside him and had provided her own engagement ring. Man, sometimes he was a blunder brain. "That's the one from the tunnel."

"Yeah. It's a little thicker than I would have chosen, but I love the emerald."

He touched the ring now. It suited Harper. Elegant, not fancy. "If I were picking a ring out for you, I would have chosen something just like this."

He pressed his lips together. Although true, he hadn't planned to say it.

But she didn't seem to notice. "It's almost exactly what I would have wanted. I haven't really ever thought too much about getting married, but as soon as we saw it, I did kind of have the idea of using this ring as an engagement ring."

Things were getting a little too heavy for him. Unable to face the gray swirl of emotions in his chest, knowing she didn't return them, he said, "So you're not easy, but you're cheap?"

As expected, she laughed. "I guess that's a compliment. But now that you're an engaged man, you really need to up your game."

"Meaning the jewelry buying or compliments?"

"If this were a real engagement, both. But for the purposes of convincing your dad that you actually want to marry me, you might want to dig beyond easy and cheap."

"Eh, I'll just tell him you're rich."

"Seriously?"

He shrugged.

"What's this charade for if all it takes is money?"

"He's tried to talk me into the whole finding a girl with money before, and I wasn't going for it. I might have said something along the lines of money not buying happiness and all that sap."

"Great. Now I have to pretend to be rich." She glowered at him. He knew as well as anyone that she'd gone through school on scholarships and loans, and that her side job as a farmer wasn't exactly high-end. "And I also have to convince him that I'm going to make you happier than money."

"No pressure, Pickles." Wyatt couldn't tell her how much he had riding on this. Not in terms of financial gain or anything like that. But he'd struggled for too long to lose face with his dad. Guilt nagged in the back of his mind. His mother wanted him to get along with his dad, but somehow he didn't think she would have approved of lying to him.

"That's pressure! If they see through this, your whole reputation with your dad is down the drain. I know how much that means to you."

Maybe Harper did see. She'd be the only person in the world to understand how much he longed for the support and respect of his dad.

He tried to downplay it. "If it doesn't work, it's not like they're going to kick me out." He shrugged. "But I really do appreciate you being willing to do this for me." He squeezed her hand. "I owe you."

She smiled and shook her head.

He'd started the conversation when she'd been all nervous sitting in the airport. Now he'd be willing to bet she hadn't even noticed that the plane had been in the air for almost an hour. Only ten more to go. They were scheduled to touch down in Chile at 6 a.m. on Friday. If he knew his dad and stepmom, they had a jam-packed long weekend planned.

"Since we're engaged, you can lay your head on my shoulder and get some sleep," he said to Harper, noting the man next to the window was already sleeping.

"I'd do that even if we weren't engaged. Unless your real fiancée was here."

"I'm not going to have a fiancée that wouldn't be okay with that."

She laid her head on his shoulder and mumbled, "I wouldn't be okay with that."

Chapter Thirteen

Harper craned her neck as Wyatt slowed the rental car, easing into the plowed lot beside a large, yellow-orange log lodge. Although it wasn't as big as some of the glamorous hotels they'd passed down the steep, winding road, it sprawled out, almost like an eagle in flight. Two wings flanked a large middle with massive windows winking in the sunlight.

"This is where your dad and stepmom live?"

Wyatt studied the structure. "Yeah. There are about fifty rooms on either side of the house. The family has a private kitchen and rooms in the basement level. Dad's office is down there, too."

"Wow, it's huge." She couldn't believe that Wyatt had lived in such splendor. It made her little farm look dirt poor in comparison.

"It's small compared to most of the resorts in the Andes."

"I know. But over the years, when you've talked about it, I always pictured it in my mind as a little shack at the bottom of a big mountain, with skiers running around all over the place." She nodded in the direction of the lifts, where the white snow was dotted with people in brightly colored jackets. "I was right about the skiers." The way the house was set, there was probably a great view of the mountains from the back.

"There's a lot more to do here than ski."

"I can't believe you never described it better." She should have asked. Maybe he just assumed she knew because of the few pictures she'd seen on the internet. She'd never imagined anything this grand. Rich.

True, it paled in comparison to some of the monstrous hotels they passed. "This looks very exclusive." The nervous buzz that had been humming in her stomach all morning cranked up a few notches.

"They get some rich ticks here. Olympic caliber skiers. Brazilian jewel heiresses. The skiing is good, but the real draw is probably the hot pools that you can only reach by ski or snowmobile."

"Hot pools? Like you swim in?"

"Yeah, it's cool. To be in your swimsuit in the water, surrounded by snow. It's really amazing under a full moon at night."

It sounded romantic, too. She shoved the thought aside, not wanting to picture Wyatt with anyone else. Especially here.

Wyatt pointed at the mountain looming over them to the east. "That's an active volcano. That's why the hot pools."

"I would think this would be wildly popular."

"It is, to some extent. Dad's got the lodge and a huge hunk of the mountain, so he makes money on letting rooms, meals, and also the skiing and snowmobile trails. There's horseback riding down the road, plus all the hotels. He sells passes to those people, too."

They parked and walked up the cleared stone walk to the door. From the snow to the massive windows to the gold trim on the doorframe, everything seemed to glisten in the bright noon sun.

"I guess I should have been holding your hand." He opened the door for her.

"You pulled my luggage instead."

Wyatt had brought only a shoulder bag, claiming that he had clothes in his room here. Harper had packed the suitcase, and she was glad now that she'd brought more clothes than she ever thought she'd need. This didn't look like the type of place where one lounged around in jammie pants and a tee shirt all weekend.

The ball of nerves in her stomach exploded into a riot. The muscles in her back ached from the tension. She should have been the one to think of holding Wyatt's hand. She had agreed to play his fiancée. But she'd been obsessing about the luxury and money on full display. In shock because it finally hit her. Wyatt's family was rich. Which meant, of course, that Wyatt was rich.

She hadn't quite gotten her head around that yet. Yeah, she knew he travelled the world. That he'd done things normal people didn't do. That it cost money to parasail and bungee jump and climb mountains. She knew that in her head, she just hadn't realized the implications. To her, Wyatt was a sweet little motherless boy.

Okay, not so little. In need of a friend. In need of her. But, looking around at all this, well, he really didn't need her.

She stepped inside. Massive vaulted ceilings flew up around her. Sunlight streamed in the solid walls of windows. They could see clear through to the mountains beyond. Large, comfortable looking chairs and massive couches were artistically arranged. A few people milled about. Several sat reading. Some had food and drinks at a table and played a board game. The low hum of conversation buzzed around. Something that smelled like vegetable soup and homemade bread mixed with the homey scent of cut wood.

A middle-aged woman in a black and white maid outfit bustled around running a sweeper. She glanced up as they came in and did a double take. A smile wreathed her face as she expertly shut the sweeper off, locking the handle, and hurried over to them, her arms spread wide.

"Wyatt!"

"Abuelita," Wyatt said, wrapping his arms around the woman, who murmured in Spanish. Wyatt answered in the same language.

Harper couldn't understand what either of them said, but she could tell that Wyatt spoke slower. She hid a smile. His Spanish, which he'd admitted he'd never been good with, was rusty.

Wyatt had talked some about his abuelita when he'd first come to the states to live with Fink. If Harper remembered correctly, she wasn't his real grandmother, no relation at all, actually, but had travelled some with his mother, taking care of him.

Keeping his arm around the short, round woman, he turned to Harper. "Abuelita, this is Harper."

Harper started to hold her hand out, but after a warm glance at

Wyatt, the woman enfolded her in a soft, loving embrace, scented with lemon and pine, that suddenly made Harper very homesick.

"I've heard so much about you over the years," she said.

"Wyatt's spoken very fondly of you, as well, Abuelita." The unfamiliar word trundled awkwardly off her tongue, but Wyatt had never called her by any other name, and he hadn't introduced one now.

She turned to Wyatt, speaking in rapid Spanish. Wyatt grinned, shaking his head.

He answered in English. "My Spanish was never very good, and it's pretty rusty now. Plus, Harper's brilliant," he smirked at Harper, "but I could never get her to speak fluently."

"I understand a few words, but not enough to have a conversation."

"That's fine," Abuelita said. "People speak all kinds of languages here, but English is often the one most people know." She gave Wyatt a squeeze. "I'm just so happy to have my little boy back. Are you staying?"

"We're leaving Monday. Didn't Dad tell you I was coming?"

Her lips pulled back. "He said you were coming, not how long you were staying." Her eyes almost disappeared in folds of skin as she smiled. "I am so glad my Wyatt finally decided to settle down with a good woman. So many girls chase after him here. He is popular, no?" She chuckled. "But he is not interested in those silly girls. He has someone else in his head and," she patted her chest, "his heart."

Wyatt shifted. His cheeks became ruddy. Harper wasn't sure what to think. Abuelita seemed to be saying Wyatt had pined for...*her*. She cast a speculative look at Wyatt. He avoided her gaze.

"Where's Dad?" he asked.

Abuelita pulled her phone out and checked the time. "He is probably getting ready to begin instruction with the group of beginner skiers. He said you might help."

Wyatt snorted. His face seemed to say that it was typical of his dad to expect him to jump in. Harper was sure he didn't mind—she knew he loved being here—except...

"Don't worry about me. I'll follow you around until I get tired of it. Then I can entertain myself."

A muscle jumped in Wyatt's cheek. "It's just so typical of my dad. He wants to meet my fiancée, but wouldn't change his plans to do so."

Abuelita turned sympathetic eyes on Wyatt. "He is planning a big dinner tomorrow night. He is very excited."

Wyatt raised a brow.

"Do you want to rest? Are you hungry?" Abuelita asked them.

"I can always eat." Wyatt grinned.

Harper reached down for her shoulder bag. "I'll put my stuff away while you grab something, if someone will tell me where to go."

Abuelita nodded. "I washed everything and aired your room out. I will show you down. Wyatt knows where the kitchen is."

"I'll take her," Wyatt said, grabbing the suitcase.

Harper blinked. Did he not want her to be alone with Abuelita? It certainly wasn't like Wyatt to be so short. Then she realized...was there only one room? She hadn't even given it a thought.

After leading her through the great room and left down a short hall, pulling the suitcase, Wyatt picked it up and led her down a staircase that made a right turn halfway down.

"There's a lot of storage space, our private kitchen, living room, and the family's bedrooms are all down here. During the busy season, especially, the upstairs is open to guests, but this is always off limits."

"Are you okay?"

He kept walking. "Sure. Why?"

"You're not acting like yourself."

"I'm fine."

They came down into a large open area, with a wet bar at one end, and a kitchenette. Several couches angled around a large screen TV. Walking through that area, Wyatt entered the hall and walked past three doors on the right before opening the next.

Harper stepped in, puzzled. Wyatt never hid things from her.

A large bed, maybe queen-sized, took up most of the room. Along one wall sat a dresser. Two doors, a closet and a bathroom possibly, flanked it. High windows lined the far wall. Done up in navy and red, the room felt dark, and when Wyatt stepped in behind her, small.

He hit the light switch, and the overhead light/ceiling fan turned on. "I'm sorry. I should have thought they would expect us to share a room."

There was a narrow walkway between the right side of the bed and the wall. Harper gestured toward it. "I suppose I can sleep there."

"No. This is my fault. I'll sleep on the floor."

"We're going to be here two nights. I'll sleep there one night, you sleep there the other."

"I said I'd sleep on the floor."

"Are we seriously fighting about who gets to sleep on the floor?" Harper dropped her bag and set a hand on her hip.

"We are. And this is one fight I'm winning." Wyatt grinned, but it didn't really reach his eyes.

And that's when it hit Harper. "You thought he'd be waiting to see you."

He grunted and looked away.

Harper's heart ached for him. She closed the few steps between them and encircled his waist, laying her head on his chest.

WYATT ONLY HESITATED A SECOND. Despite his complicated feelings about his dad, Harper had figured it out. Or at least as much as anyone could. He put his arms around her and pulled her close, relishing her soft warmness and the cool comfort she offered. Breathing deeply of her berries and vanilla scent, he allowed himself to pretend for just a second that their engagement was real. That hugging Harper was his right. And if it were true, then what his dad did or didn't do wouldn't matter.

Wyatt pulled himself back from the fantasy and made himself loosen his hold, patting Harper's back like she was his friend and not his fiancée.

His dad was busy. Wyatt didn't really expect him to put his life on hold to meet his fiancée. But as hard as his dad had pushed for him to bring her down to meet him...

"I don't think he really cared about meeting my fiancée. I think he just wanted me down here to help him."

She leaned her head back and looked up at him without letting go. "I think you're right. But isn't that how your dad has always been?"

Disappointment descended like gray clouds in his mind. "Yeah."

"He's probably not going to change. So, you're just going to have to love him the way he is."

Resentment balled in his chest. "I know you're right. There's just a part of me that says if he loved me, he'd act a certain way."

"Sure. I think we all think that to a certain extent. But some people, especially driven, successful people, have trouble pulling themselves from their work and expressing their feelings."

Wyatt didn't think of himself as especially driven or successful, but maybe he'd inherited some of his dad's issues. After all, he was holding the one woman in the world that meant everything to him, and she didn't know it. And he couldn't tell her. Not now. He squeezed a little tighter instead.

She laid her head back on his chest. "But you don't have to change to be what he wants, either." Her hands slid up, then back down his back.

He shivered. Her touch was...different. Maybe Harper felt more than friendship for him. He allowed his hands to drift up her back. His heart thumped in his chest so hard and loud she had to hear it. He swallowed. His thumb touched the back of her neck and he slid it across her skin.

She moved her head, and he froze, his breath seizing in his lungs.

"Wyatt?" Her eyes had darkened with something stronger than friendship. But what that emotion was, he couldn't tell.

Her tongue touched the corner of her lip. His eyes clung to it like butter on bread. Suddenly, he couldn't get enough air. Limbs that had been young and strong only moments before now trembled. His hand fisted in the back of her hair. Her eyes widened briefly, then darkened with something even more potent. He could only hope it was desire. Whatever it was, it pulled him in. He couldn't stop the lowering of his head. Her arms tightened around him. He pressed her more firmly to him, feeling her curves blend into the hardness of his body. The hair on his arms stood up. He breathed her air. Her name feathered past his tingling lips. "Harper."

"Oh, I'm sorry."

Wyatt turned his head. Abuelita stood at the open doorway, a tray filled with fruit and chopped vegetables in her hand.

Harper gasped and jerked. Wyatt dropped his hands. Her hair slid out of his unclenched fist. The emptiness burned, matching the burn of disappointment in his chest. He had been one second away from kissing Harper. She avoided his gaze, studying the tray Abuelita held instead. But two spots of color marked her cheeks. If only he knew what she was thinking. If only she were as disappointed as he.

The room was as silent as a tomb and the seconds were ticking by.

One side of his mouth kicked up and he winked at Abuelita. "Hey, no problem. You can barge in anytime as long as you have food."

Harper moved back. Wyatt allowed her to put some distance between them.

"You better shut the door if you are going to be carrying on like that." Abuelita shuffled in and placed the plate on the bed. There was nowhere else to set it.

Wyatt laughed. "We weren't carrying on 'like that.' I was just hugging my girl." If only she really were his girl.

Abuelita pulled two bottles of water from her apron and set them beside the plate. "There is plenty of food in the kitchen. You know you can help yourself." She turned and began walking out, but paused at the door. "You remember what time meals are?"

"Twelve and six. Breakfast is buffet served from six to nine."

"Just checking. I don't want you to starve while you are here."

"If there's food, I can find it." Harper laughed softly. The sound soothed the prickly heat in his chest. She wouldn't be laughing if she were upset.

Abuelita looked out into the hall before she spoke again. "Kayla is here."

Harper stiffened.

"Thanks for the warning," Wyatt said.

Abuelita pressed her lips together. After a few silent seconds, she left.

"Kayla?" Harper asked softly.

"My stepsister. Sophia's daughter."

"You never talk about Sophia. I'd kind of forgotten you even had a stepmother."

He shrugged. "Not much to say. I don't know her that well. She and dad got together after mom died and I was in Pennsylvania."

"And Kayla is their daughter?" "No. Sophia had Kayla before she met my dad."

"Is there some kind of issue there? Abuelita's tone seemed like a warning."

He rubbed a hand over his head. He should have known Harper would feel the tension in the air when Kayla was mentioned. "I guess Sophia might try to push Kayla into the picture. Abuelita has hinted at it a few times, but Dad's made no secret that he's leaving the lodge to me."

"I can understand why Sophia would want her daughter included. This place has to be worth a fortune." Harper gestured with her hand, indicating the entire resort.

"It is. And it runs in the black, way in the black, every year."

She grabbed a carrot stick from the tray. "Then what's not to love?"

He held up a hand, following her over. "I'm coming down to stay. Once Uncle Fink is better, I've committed to being here."

"But you don't want to."

He took one of the ice-cold waters Abuelita had brought down, twisting the cap and taking a long swig before speaking. "You know my mom wandered around a lot. I mean, we were here more than anywhere else, but it's not like we lived here. This doesn't feel like home to me anymore than anywhere else in the world." For some reason, he couldn't admit to her that her farm was the only place he'd ever lived that felt like home. He'd never even set foot on it until he was seventeen.

Harper picked up another carrot stick. "So you might as well be here versus anywhere else?"

"Yeah, I guess." If he couldn't be with her, one place was as good as any other. And he'd already committed to being here.

She punched him lightly on the shoulder. "Don't sound so enthusiastic."

He gave her a little grin. "I suppose I love the idea of working with my dad. And I really do like being an instructor, working with people, even the business side of everything isn't something I mind. But I can't shake the feeling that Dad only wants me because of what I can give."

"And you want him to love you for yourself?"

He sat on the bed, his shoulders slumped. "I want him to be proud of me. I want him to look at me and see something worthwhile. More than a worker in his empire. Is that too much to ask?"

"You want him to be your dad first, your employer second?"

"I knew there was a reason I put up with you." He stood and laughed to break the seriousness that had descended on them. Harper knew him. She had him pegged better than anyone he'd ever known. Maybe he was just never satisfied because he wanted her to see him as a man and not just as her goofy half-cousin or her best friend. Which might have been what was happening earlier, but that moment was long gone and he didn't want to ruin the present by forcing her to dissect the past. He was going to talk to her about it. Just not now.

He motioned with his hand. "Come on. Abuelita said Dad was getting ready to start beginner ski instruction. You've never been on the slopes. We'll catch what we can and I'll show you the rest."

Chapter Fourteen

Harper stood at the back of the small crowd of people. She hadn't quite gotten used to walking with what seemed like big boards on her feet, but so far she'd managed not to run into anything or poke anyone with her poles. Gotta be grateful for the little things.

She wasn't the only adult in the group, but there were still more under eighteen than over.

"Grip your pole like this." Wyatt adjusted a matronly woman's hand. She twisted her arm and Wyatt jumped to avoid being struck in the leg with her pole.

"Oh, I'm sorry," she wailed.

"It's okay." Wyatt laughed. "That's the perfect grip if you have an intruder break into your lodge room. Put a little more oomph into your swing. However, for skiing, we hold it this way." He loosened her fingers and helped her set her pole at the correct angle, while a group of teenage girls giggled behind their hands.

Wyatt looked over at them. "You and your friends were in the beginner class two years ago, Felicity."

The girls giggled again. One flipped her hair over her shoulder and put a hand on her hip. "These are different friends. Are you going to kick us out?"

"If you want to spend the winter in the beginners' class, no one's stopping you." Wyatt shrugged, then looked back at the lady he was helping and flashed his dimple. "That's perfect, Mrs. Czerdy."

Wyatt's long-sleeved shirt emphasized his broad shoulders, and he moved like he was born on his skis. Her heart fluttered. No question why Felicity would rather be in the beginner class than out on the bigger slopes. Apparently, Harper wasn't the only one who thought Wyatt made everything more fun.

Her mind flashed back to their room and that almost-kiss. If it really was an almost-kiss. She could have sworn he was going to kiss her.

Harper's heart thumped painfully. It might have been an almost-kiss, but Wyatt had backed off and not even mentioned it when Abuelita left. Wyatt was too handsome, too athletic, too much at ease here in the mountains, to be interested in her in that way. Maybe being back at the only place he'd ever stayed longer than the farm had made him lose his head with her a little. Once he'd realized it was Harper, he seemed embarrassed he'd almost kissed his best friend.

Wyatt gave the girls a friendly smile, pointing and saying something to one of Felicity's friends. Completely professional, but friendly and funny. This side of him fascinated Harper. When he was with her he was goofy, sometimes even downright silly. And he touched her all the time —a hand on her elbow, an easy arm around her shoulders, a tug on her ponytail. But now he was the perfect instructor, walking that line between coach and teammate with an effortless grace.

He looked up as though he felt her gaze on him. His brows lifted and he stopped in the middle of whatever he was saying. Harper quickly schooled her features. Maybe there had been more than friendly admiration on her face.

She focused on making a V with her skis like he'd been instructing the group.

A pair of skis came into view. "What do you think?"

She gave up on trying to get her skis going the right way and smiled at him. "You were born to do this."

His eyes were hidden behind his aviator sunglasses, but his mouth curled into a bemused half smile.

"You think I look good in my ski pants, huh?"

"I'm sorry, but ski pants will never be sexy." Such a liar.

"You look kind of cute in yours. Makes me forget that in another life you're a serious professor."

"I meant, Goofy, that I've never seen you look so relaxed and natural, and I've never been in a class with a better instructor."

Wyatt stared at Harper. Drat those stupid glasses. His mouth wasn't smiling, and she couldn't read a thing in his eyes since she couldn't see them.

"You mean that." The statement came out more like a question.

"I do."

"You keep surprising me."

She wasn't sure what to say about that. "It's probably going to come as no surprise that I have the feeling that if I try to move at all in these things, I'm going to fall flat on my face."

"No, that's not a surprise. Phys Ed was always your lowest grade."

"Yeah. And I'm supposed to use my hands and feet together here." She shook her poles without lifting them up. Wyatt probably didn't want to lose an eye today.

"You can do this, Harper."

"I am going to try. For you. Only because you're my best friend. Not because I'm actually interested in learning to ski."

He tapped her nose with his finger. "Get interested. That's the single thing that will help you learn the fastest."

Harper sighed. Because it was true. "You are going to come visit me in the hospital when I break my neck on this baby hill, right?"

"Once."

Harper pointed at him. "Funny. And you won't leave Chile without me?"

"For very long."

Harper laughed again and Wyatt started to turn away. A woman stood, blocking his way, one hand on her hip, her ski pole expertly pointing down. Okay, it actually *was* possible for ski pants to look sexy. This woman pulled it off with enviable ease.

She lifted her goggles revealing a pure olive complexion, a perfect heart-shaped face, and dancing dark eyes.

"My stepbrother has returned to claim his kingdom."

"Nah, I'm just visiting." Wyatt stepped back and put his arm around Harper. Something instinctive prompted her to lean into him.

"Harper, this is Kayla. Kayla, Harper, my fiancée."

Kayla's eyes narrowed. A small shot of adrenaline whipped up Harper's spine. Immediately, she suppressed it. This could be the woman Wyatt wanted. Despite Harper's own feelings for Wyatt, she truly wanted him to be happy.

"It's so nice to meet you, Kayla." Harper tried to hold her hand out, but her ski pole snagged on the ground, jerking her arm. Wyatt steadied her.

Kayla's brows rose.

Wyatt laughed. "I've finally found something Harper isn't good at."

"I'm just not used to having a bunch of extra stuff attached to my body." Harper's cheeks grew warm. She hoped they were already rosy from the cool mountain air.

Kayla ignored her, looking at Wyatt. "Steve's here."

Harper remembered Steve from Snap Chatting with Wyatt. A blond, rosy-cheeked guy Wyatt snowboarded with.

Wyatt nodded. "Oh, yeah? We just got here a couple of hours ago, and Dad roped me into this class."

His dad had taken Wyatt's place at the front of the group and was showing them how to set their poles.

"I should get back to helping him."

"We were heading to the springs tonight on the snowmobiles. Steve and I, and a couple of others, maybe. You're welcome to join us."

Wyatt looked down at Harper. Again, she cursed the glasses hiding his eyes. There was no mistaking the little upturn to his lips. He wanted to go.

"Will you be too tired?" he asked.

She would fall down dead of exhaustion before she'd admit to being tired in front of Kayla. "Snowmobiles sound like fun."

"Oh, they are," Kayla said. "Maybe we'll see you tonight." She glided away, as natural and smooth as an eagle in flight.

Wyatt pursed his lips and gave a little shrug.

Harper returned the look, feeling like they were sharing their thoughts without talking. She liked that feeling.

"I'd better head to the front. I just wanted to make sure you were okay."

She shrugged. "Don't worry about me. If I get fed up with all this sports-related stuff, I brought my Kindle and I'm not afraid to use it."

He laughed and started to turn away, but stopped short. Harper twisted to see what he was looking at. A group of five or six men, all dressed similarly in ski pants and bulky hoodies, talking and laughing, walked the last few yards to them. The man in front lifted his goggles. His blue eyes were piercing and intense, with deep laugh lines along both sides. His ruddy face shone with health and blond hair stuck out from under his ski cap.

"Wyatt, dude! We heard you were in for a visit." He grabbed Wyatt in a bear hug, which Wyatt returned with vigor.

He pulled back and Wyatt said, "Great to see you."

"Who's the chick, man?"

"Steve, this is my fiancée, Harper."

Harper, remembering how she had almost fallen on her face in front of Kayla because of her ski pole, simply smiled and nodded. Steve took a quick step and grabbed her and hugged her. She tried to hug him back without killing him with her pole.

Steve smacked her shoulder. "Never seen him with a girl before. Where'd he pick you up?"

She kept from rolling her eyes. "I rescued him out of a volcano crater." Picked her up, indeed.

Wyatt snorted and coughed.

Steve looked at Wyatt in wonder. "Yo. Awesome, dude."

"Yeah, I'll have to tell you the story sometime. It involves a multi vitamin and a lot of vegetables."

Harper smothered the snicker threatening to escape from her lips.

"Huh?" Steve's brows twisted and he tilted his head.

"Some other time." Wyatt indicated the guys standing around them. "You have yourself a following."

"They're vacationers from a prep school in California. I've been telling these guys about your free-style snowboarding championships, so of course as soon as we heard you were here, we had to see if you'd give us a show."

"I don't know..." Wyatt shuffled his skis and glanced at where his dad had the beginners' class well in hand. If the expression on his dad's face counted for anything, he was pleased Wyatt could entertain this category of patrons.

Harper tried to mask her horror. Freestyle anything sounded dangerous.

"Don't turn him down because of me." Crossing her fingers that her smile looked more natural than it felt, Harper channeled her thoughts into the positive. He hadn't died yet. That thought wasn't reassuring, either.

"I'll keep your girlfriend company."

Harper turned toward the voice. Long, shiny black hair emerged from a knit cap and hung in curls over a lime green ski jacket as the woman stopped beside the guys.

"Hey, Sophia," Steve said.

"Harper, this is my stepmother. Sophia, this is my *fiancée*."

"Nice to meet you, Sophia," Harper said, hoping it was true.

"You, too." Her smile seemed real and she gave Harper a quick, tight hug. "I would say I've heard so much about you, but, well, I really haven't." She lifted a finely trimmed brow at Wyatt.

"I haven't heard much about you, either," Harper replied.

Sophia smiled. She was the most beautiful woman Harper had ever seen. "Looks like we need to spend some time getting to know each other then."

Wyatt shifted and poked his ski pole into the ground, slightly harder than necessary.

She remembered what he'd talked about in their room, and the feeling she had that there was more to the story.

He tapped his ski poles on the ground and looked away.

Steve slapped Wyatt on the back. "Come on, man. Sophia's got your girl covered. Let's take those sticks back and get a board."

Wyatt turned a questioning glance on Harper. Whatever made him uneasy, it wasn't the idea of snowboarding. He couldn't hide the brightness of his eyes or his eager grin.

"Where's the best place to watch you?" she asked.

"Aren't you going to keep learning to ski?" He indicated the group that had skied away behind his dad.

"The master teacher is leaving."

"Ha."

"Plus, I want to see you snowboard. I've known that you can, but I've never seen you."

The corner of his mouth tilted up in a lopsided grin. He moved closer to her. His voice, gravelly and low, sent shivers up her spine. "Somehow, I don't think that me snowboarding, no matter how good I might be, is going to impress you much."

She matched his low tone. "I promise to be impressed."

Sophia cut in. "I assume you're using the expert course. I can take her to the best vantage point. We'll swing by the house and grab the binoculars."

Steve held his gloved hand up for a fist bump. "All right, dude. Let's split."

Harper squeezed her hands together tightly. The back of her throat seemed to be permanently closed. Wyatt had already fallen twice. The second time she'd handed the binoculars back to Sophia and declared since Wyatt was the only one in navy blue, she could see him just fine against the white snow.

The fact of the matter was, without the binoculars, she couldn't see the blood flowing from the cut above his left eye, nor the bright red spots of it on his coat. He was good. Better than good. Even she, with her limited knowledge of anything sporting, could see the vast difference in Wyatt's skill and the skill of the men around him. It made her hot and cold at the same time. Proud that he was hers, if only for this trip, but every time he fell, every time it even looked like he was going to fall, her heart clawed up her throat and beat against her tonsils, her knees went weak and black spots swam in front of her eyes. The two times he'd fallen she would have too if the railing hadn't held her up.

Rugged and strong, he seemed invincible. She couldn't keep from watching, from admiring, from being totally attracted to his toughness.

But every bump, every fall, every cut...she felt it. It was exhausting to constantly run through that gauntlet of emotions—pain, anxiety, fear and, she had to admit, pride as well.

Sophia nudged her. "Check this out. Wyatt's the only one I've ever seen do a double flip half-twist off this jump."

Harper straightened and locked her knees, looking out over the snow.

Heading down the short, steep hill so fast he was almost a blur, Wyatt flew up the jump, tucking his body and doing two full summersaults in the air, twisting to land backwards. He used the momentum to do a little hop at the end, twisting back to the front. Impressive.

When he had landed safely, Harper allowed herself to breathe again. "I had no idea he was this good."

"You two couldn't have been together long. Hasn't Wyatt ever taken you to the slopes before?"

"No."

"Don't you want to go?" She sighed. "I don't mean to be nosy, but this is such a huge part of who Wyatt is."

"I teach at the university in the winter, tutoring during break. And Wyatt's spent the last few winters in Colorado. Skiing isn't that big of a deal in Pennsylvania where we live."

"I can't believe he wouldn't have somehow gotten on the slopes."

"When he first moved up, we had a couple of mild winters in a row. The winters we had more snow he was already out west."

"I see."

Maybe Sophia meant to make her feel bad with those words, although Harper was inclined to think not. But, after all, she and Wyatt weren't really engaged, so even if Sophia meant her remarks to be cutting, she could hardly be successful.

Or maybe she was since Harper was asking herself how she could have missed this part of Wyatt. And had to clamp her lips together to keep from trying to give Sophia more excuses as to why she'd never gone skiing with Wyatt before.

Harper looked back out at the slopes. Wyatt had disappeared, but now reappeared, almost at the bottom of the run, weaving figure eights with Steve.

"He's so good," she murmured.

"He's won awards for snowboarding, but he's also a great skier, and last I heard, he'd been working on ice climbing."

Harper nodded, but didn't say anything. Wyatt had climbed Mount Rainier, but she was pretty sure ice climbing was different than mountain climbing.

"Have you travelled the world with him?"

"No."

"Oh." Sophia shifted. "Can I ask what you do?"

"Sure. I have an advanced degree in nutrition and teach at the university near our home. I'll be working with a few colleagues on a research project this fall." She didn't say anything about tenure and she wasn't sure why.

Sophia's mouth hung open. "Do you do sports?"

"I don't even run."

"I'm shocked. Wyatt is so athletic."

"I'm not athletic." Putting it so mildly.

"Nutrition...you cook?"

"I do. But my degree is more about creating meal plans and helping people eat healthy. Our research that starts this fall is focusing on successfully changing people's eating habits. We're collaborating with university psychologists."

"I see. I wonder if you would be interested in coming inside. We're in the process of revamping the meal offerings for the resort. But we don't have a nutritionist on board. Would you be willing to look at it?"

Wyatt had just gotten off the lift at the top of the slope. "Let me watch Wyatt go down, then I'll come in and take a look. Okay?"

"That's great."

Chapter Fifteen

Wyatt lifted his goggles and squinted. Harper had been standing on the observation deck with Sophia for his first few passes, but they'd disappeared and he'd not seen them for a while.

"Wonder where your fiancée went?" Steve bumped shoulders with him and looked in the direction of the deck. Most of the guys they'd been snowboarding with had gone to get ready to head into town, which is where the party action was in the area.

Wyatt ran a hand down the lower part of his face, stalling for time. The fiancée lie had slipped out when he'd been on the phone with his dad. He hadn't counted on having to tell lie after lie to cover the first falsehood.

"What was her name again?" Steve asked as they headed in to put their equipment away.

"Harper."

"She looks like a real nice girl, just not your type."

Wyatt stopped and stared at his friend. "I have a type?"

Steve knew as well as anyone that Wyatt had never done the girl thing. From the time he'd turned eighteen, Harper had been on his mind. Before that...well, he'd been a geek, to put it nicely, and not exactly appealing to girls.

Steve rolled his eyes. "You know what I mean."

Wyatt just looked at him.

Steve broke eye contact. "She doesn't even know how to ski, man!"

"There's more to my life than skiing." Wyatt turned and started walking again.

They passed a group walking in the opposite direction. A few people recognized him and he returned their greetings, but didn't stop.

Steve waited to speak until they were out of hearing. "It's no secret that your dad wants you to take this resort over. He's been telling anyone who'll listen that you're coming down for good before spring. Seems to me if this is going to be your life, you'll want a woman who is at least a little interested in something that has to do with your life's work. It's not like this is a nine-to-five job that you leave at the office. She's going to live it with you."

"I know. It's something we need to work out." Frustration clogged up his throat, because he wanted it to be real, but he knew Steve was right.

"You guys seem really comfortable with each other, but it's almost like you're afraid to touch her or something."

Wyatt thought he'd been doing a pretty good job of pretending to be Harper's fiancé. "She's my best friend. Has been for years. Since I moved to the states."

Steve ran his gloved finger down the edge of his board. "I mean, it's pretty obvious that she would never fit in down here."

That truth was not pleasant to hear. "We'll figure it out, man."

"What about Kayla?"

Wyatt shot Steve a quick glance. Why would he bring her into the conversation? "Kayla's my stepsister."

"There's no blood relation."

He shrugged. "It doesn't matter. Harper is it for me. Did you miss it? We're engaged." He hated pushing the lie, but there was no good reason why Steve would be pushing Kayla.

Steve lifted his brows.

Wyatt struggled to put words to his feelings. "We've got this great friendship. It's awesome. I can do anything, say anything, be anything, and she gets me. I mean, whatever we do, we have fun. I could spend—I *want* to spend the rest of my life with her."

"Except?"

The happiness that bubbled in his chest went flat. "Except, you're right. I don't think she'll like it here, that she'll fit in. But it's where I need to be. Taking over the resort for my dad."

"Well, Kayla might have a little to say about that."

"Huh?"

They reached the back of the equipment building at the entrance to the lower level where the family and hired help kept their personal supplies. Steve stopped with his hand poised over the keypad lock. "I think Kayla has her mind set that you and she belong together."

"I don't know where she got that idea." He'd never encouraged her. He was sure of it.

Steve punched the number in. "Well, if you take a minute to think of it, it'd be perfect."

"What do you mean?" Wyatt asked. The only thing he could think of was that it would solve any worries Sophia might have about whether the resort was going solely to him.

"First of all, you two are exactly alike."

His mind rebelled. "No way."

"Sure. Both love adventure, this whole lifestyle." He spread his arms around.

Wyatt shook his head, even though Steve was right.

"Plus, your dad is married to her mother, and then there's the little problem of who gets the resort."

"I didn't ask for it. Dad just keeps pushing it on me." And it hit his heart button, the one that longed to honor his mother's memory and for his dad to be proud of him.

"Kayla wants it." Steve hung his board in its place on the wall and looked over his shoulder at Wyatt.

"She can have it." If she'd take it over, it might let him out of his promise and he'd be free to...to what? Be a farmer with Harper. Being with Harper was exciting. Working on the farm the rest of his life...not so much.

"She wants you, too."

"I really don't think so."

"It's true. And I'd be surprised if she doesn't say something. It's not something she's been keeping a secret." Steve moseyed over to Wyatt and sat to take his ski boots off.

"Except from me." Wyatt hung his board in place. He turned to face Steve, his hands on his hips.

"You just refuse to see." Steve tugged his second boot off.

"I have my eye on someone else. Always have."

"And you haven't been paying attention to what's right here." Steve waved a finger under Wyatt's nose.

Wyatt batted it away. "Because Kayla isn't what I want. I don't even know if this is what I want." He spread an arm, indicating the resort.

"But this is who you are." Steve poked his finger in Wyatt's chest.

Wyatt shook his head and walked to the door. "Chile has never been home for me."

"It's as much home as any other you've ever had."

"Except one."

"Huh?" Steve tilted his head.

Wyatt had enough with the heart-to-heart and with trying to insist that Harper was his fiancée. He should be angry at his friend for pushing back, but since the engagement wasn't real, he just felt guilt.

He opened the door to the setting sun. Lights had come on over on the slopes.

Steve came out and stood beside him, breathing deeply of the crisp, mountain air. He must have realized he'd pushed far enough since he changed the subject. "We still going snowmobiling tonight? Should be good. The moon's full."

That was the best time to go. With the snow pack, it would be almost day. Romantic. Taking Harper alone would be better, but going in a group would be low pressure and still romantic. Hopefully.

She didn't need babysitting, but the conversation with Steve had made him uneasy somehow, and he wanted to find her. Protect her. Kayla could be pretty determined to get what she wanted. If she wanted him. If she did, he wouldn't put it past her to try to get rid of his "fiancée."

~

"PART of the issue might be a lack of sleep." Harper arranged avocado slices over the top of the salad bowl. The large, natural wood kitchen was a dream to work in. She stood at the massive, butcher block island while Sophia grated cabbage on the counter.

"I never thought of that."

"Most people don't. Yes, eating the right food is important, but there are other things that contribute to good health." Harper squeezed a lemon wedge over the bowl. "Exercise is something people know they should do, but sometimes the proper amount of sleep is overlooked."

"Maybe it's a habit from childhood, or maybe it's that I'm so busy, but I just don't like to go to bed."

"We often fight it."

"Are you having nutrition class in the kitchen?" Wyatt stood in the doorway. His shoulders seemed wider than she remembered. But the grin was the same. The flutters that tickled her stomach were still new. His dark skin was flushed and his brown eyes twinkled.

Remembering Sophia's criticism, and aware they had an audience, she started toward him, peeling the gloves off her hands. "Give me a captive audience and you know I'll exploit the opportunity."

Hoping she wasn't being out of line, she stepped close to him and, reaching up, wrapped her arms around his neck.

She leaned in to his ear. "Sophia was questioning our relationship."

"I've gotten disbelief, too. Thanks for playing along with this for me." His arms came around her and he pulled her close. She closed her eyes. What if this were real?

"Looks like you quit bleeding," Sophia said from right behind them.

Harper moved back, out of the circle of Wyatt's arms. Her eyes searched his face, noting the cut that had scabbed over, not able to read whether the embrace had been long enough or too long.

His hand came up and touched the cut. "Yeah, they usually do."

"I was amazed at how good you are," Harper said.

One side of his mouth tilted up.

Sophia dried her hands on a towel. "I think we have some old videos of his competitions somewhere around here."

"You never mentioned your snowboarding championship."

He shrugged. "When I went to Pennsylvania, it was a whole new life for me and I had to fit in. Plus, it was only one year. The year Mom lived in Switzerland, I won a downhill skiing championship."

"I didn't know that," Sophia said.

"It was the junior group. We moved around so much, I was a one-hit wonder a couple of places, but we never stayed in one spot long enough for me to develop a reputation."

"You were here every year," Sophia said.

"True. Dad usually sent Mom money or tickets to have us come visit here every year or so."

"This was like her home base," Sophia said.

"Hers," Wyatt said firmly.

"And yours," Sophia insisted.

Wyatt looked at Harper. He was affable and didn't like to argue. "No. Just hers."

"Sophia and I made supper for the family." Harper changed the subject to dispel the awkwardness that had descended on the kitchen.

Sophia had explained that the lodge provided a large breakfast buffet every morning, but after that, the guests were on their own.

"Smells great."

"We've been thinking about adding additional meals for the guests. Harper was helping me with menu ideas." Sophia moved back across the kitchen and picked up the salad. "Your dad is coming in for dinner at six."

"Great. I have ten minutes to steal Harper."

Wyatt grabbed her hand and pulled her through the kitchen and hall and down the stairs. Harper strode along behind, allowing him to lead her. He walked like a man with a purpose, and she wondered what important thing he needed to discuss with her. She also couldn't help but wonder what it would be like if their charade was real and they were heading for privacy for a completely different reason. Her cheeks heated.

He didn't say anything until he'd shut the bedroom door behind them.

He turned to face her. "I'm sorry."

Confusion clouded her brain. "Why?" She perched on the bed, watching him pace.

He stopped and threw his hand out. "Because I dragged you the whole way down here, only to leave you not even an hour after we arrived."

She grabbed ahold of his arm, stopping him. "Wyatt." She waited for him to look at her. "I'm okay. I had a good time today."

He searched her face. "Really?"

Her smile felt too big to contain. "Absolutely. I loved watching you snowboard. Except for the blood." She looked at the cut over his eye. She wanted to touch it. To clean it and patch it, but it was fine and Wyatt wasn't hers to nurse. "And Sophia was very nice. I mean, she did mention about us, which is why I jumped you when you came in."

He lifted a brow. "You didn't jump me."

"Next time." She stuck her tongue out.

"Thanks for the warning. I'll try to catch you." He scratched his head. "It was actually good. For some reason, people aren't believing we're engaged."

Her stomach sank. "We're so different."

"We're not that different."

"You're athletic, and I'm...not." Her throat tightened.

"Opposites attract." He winked at her.

She grinned. "Are we not affectionate enough?" Sharp tingles shot through her at the thought of being more affectionate with Wyatt.

"Do you think that's it?" Wyatt asked. He sounded curious, but not eager. Too bad.

"Maybe."

"I don't want you to be uncomfortable. You're here even though you don't want to be."

"It's all for your dad's sake. Maybe once we see how he is at dinner, we'll have a better idea how much effort we need to put into the ruse."

"Yeah." He rubbed his jaw. "Did you think about the snowmobiling tonight after supper? You want to go?"

A pang shot through her stomach. She ignored it. "Sure."

"Wear a bathing suit under your clothes."

She laughed.

"I'm serious."

Her laugh stopped abruptly. "I didn't bring a bathing suit. This isn't the beach."

"Maybe you can borrow one."

The idea made her a little uncomfortable—wearing someone else's bathing suit, but hey, she was living on the wild side this weekend. "I'll ask Sophia and Kayla."

"Great."

"What do I need a bathing suit for?" He had mentioned the warm springs. Her heart gave a little leap. A midnight ride to warm springs sounded romantic. She pushed the thought aside.

He grinned enigmatically. "You'll see."

She almost asked about the warm springs, but figured she could wait. No point in ruining his surprise.

"Have you talked to your dad yet?" she asked instead.

"He said, 'Hi, son. Come help me with this beginners' class.' That's it."

His jaw set and he looked over her head, out the window as he said it. He wouldn't want her sympathy. Her heart still bled for him.

"I guess when we're sitting across the table from him, he'll have no choice but to talk to you."

"And you." Wyatt grinned, and the friend she knew so well was back. "I just wanted to check with you about the snowmobiling."

"That's fine. I don't have to drive, right?"

"I figured you'd ride with me. If you want to drive your own, we have enough."

"Nah. You all can do circles around me with this winter sports stuff. I'd end up getting left behind and lost if I were on my own."

"That hurts." He placed a hand over his heart in mock pain.

"Not on purpose."

"That's better."

"Some people just can't handle the truth." She shrugged in a dangerously flirtatious way.

"Funny." He grabbed her hand. "Come on. Time to eat."

Chapter Sixteen

Wyatt stepped into the kitchen, holding Harper's hand. A visit here was certainly easier with Harper beside him.

His dad looked exactly the same as he always remembered him. Tall with broad shoulders. He'd never had any hair. Dark eyes. Clean shave. Dark skin that showed his half-Latino heritage. He'd been born in America, his dad's side of the family had owned the resort and he'd spent much of his childhood and all of his adulthood here. He owned it outright now, and had added to the original holdings. His dad was certainly a born businessman.

His dad finished washing his hands at the sink and turned to dry them.

"Hey, Dad."

"Wyatt. You never did introduce me to that little girl of yours." His dark eyes travelled to Harper.

Wyatt put his arm around her shoulders. "This is Harper."

"Your fiancée."

"Yeah." Man, he hated that lie.

"Welcome to Chile, Harper." His dad held his hand out.

Harper grasped it. "Thanks, Mr. Fernandez."

"Call me David."

Harper nodded.

"Come on and sit down. I heard the kids want to head out snowmobiling this evening." Sophia placed the salad on the table. "Kayla, Steve, come on," she called. She pointed to the two chairs on the side of the table. "You two can sit here. Kayla and Steve will sit across from you, and David and I will take the ends."

Wyatt held the chair for Harper as Kayla and Steve came in from the hall. Because of his discussion with Steve earlier in the day, Wyatt looked a little longer at Kayla. Her black eyes went immediately to him when she walked in. With her shiny dark hair and skin, she was almost the exact opposite of Harper. In personality, too, when he thought about it, since she was vivacious and almost crazy. Certainly not someone who enjoyed a quiet evening reading a book by the fire, which he would say was Harper's favorite pastime.

As the family settled into their chairs and started passing their food, David looked at Harper. "So, considering that Wyatt was practically born with skis on his feet, I find it odd that you were in the beginner class today. How did you two meet?"

Harper put the forkful of salad she was holding in her mouth. Great stalling technique. She looked at him with raised brows. He was the one who'd started this lie.

He took a sip of water. "I met her when I moved to the states. We've been best friends since then, and…"

"Isn't she related to your Uncle Fink somehow?" Kayla asked. "I think I remember hearing about a Harper. Maybe in a Christmas letter or something."

His dad's jaw tightened, and those dark eyes narrowed. There must have been some kind of competition between his dad and Uncle Fink he'd never noticed.

"No. No relation. Uncle Fink married her mom."

"I see. So you're related to her the same way you're related to me."

He had never thought of that. "It's not a relation."

"Right. Connected to her the same as me."

"Yeah."

"Wyatt spent the winter in Colorado, and he was saying that the resort he worked at had a masseuse on staff." Harper changed the subject.

Wyatt's dad's eyes brightened and settled on Harper. Wyatt brushed her leg with his fingers to thank her for changing the subject. He shouldn't have. His fingers tingled, and he had trouble concentrating on the conversation.

"Was that a popular idea?"

"Not so much in the morning, but as you can imagine, as people came off the slopes, she was busy until late at night. They actually ended up hiring four more." Wyatt grinned. The wheels in his dad's head were turning. He made a note to himself to thank Harper later.

His dad rubbed his chin. "That's interesting."

"Yeah. I think it's a hard, tiring job, but it's not hard to get training." Wyatt had been glad that his job enabled him to be outside on the slopes and pitied the poor people stuck inside working.

"Were the services included or extra?"

"They were included for premium guests, but with a limit. Day passes had to pay extra. A lot of people did."

"I see." His dad propped an elbow on the table. "That sounds like an improvement you can spearhead when you move here." He looked back at Harper. "Is that what you do?"

"No. I'm a nutritionist."

Wyatt's chest puffed out just a little. Harper had a goofy side that normally only he got to see. Usually, like now, people saw her as an intellectual. Serious. She was one of those people that others were naturally drawn to for help and advice. It seemed his dad was no different. Wyatt contained his smile, but he loved looking at her the way she was now and imagining her the way she could be—like when they walked through the tunnel together or had their Christmas tree trimming race.

"She helped me some this afternoon with the new menu I've been planning," Sophia said.

"Hmm," his dad said. "A degree in sports medicine would be more helpful around here." He turned his attention to his plate.

That's what his dad had wanted him to study in college. Unfortunately, even with Harper's help, he'd not been able to still his wanderlust long enough to get a degree. He couldn't bring himself to regret it, but he did hate the nasty, lingering feeling that he had disappointed his dad. Again.

He didn't rise to the bait. Everyone at the table, even Steve, knew about his failure to stay in college.

Somehow that made him think of his mother.

Even though she'd been gone for ten years, it still didn't seem right to sit at the big solid wood family table in the kitchen without her. To see his dad with another woman. Not that his parents were married, or were even a couple while he was growing up. Just every time they visited the resort, she was here.

Wyatt glanced beside him. Harper was another unusual addition to the table. Welcome. She gave him peace. He couldn't help but compare the welcome he received at her home to what she had put up with here.

Thankfully Sophia turned the conversation to the great snowmobiling weather, and it wasn't long until dinner was over.

"I'll get you that suit. Follow me," Kayla said to Harper after they'd carried their plates to the sink.

"Steve and I'll grab towels," Wyatt said.

"We'll let the other guys know we're ready and we'll swing around back to pick you up after we top them off. Say, twenty minutes?" Steve asked.

"That's plenty of time for me. You good with that?" Wyatt asked Harper.

She nodded and gave him a what-am-I-getting-into look before trailing out of the kitchen behind Kayla.

"Here, this one should work for you." Kayla held up a purple and green one-piece suit. "I bought it a few years ago, but never wore it. I like bikinis."

"Thanks." Harper wasn't exactly in a position to be choosy about what type of suit she wore.

"No problem."

Harper started for the door. Kayla's voice made her pause. "Come on outside when you're changed. I'm not waiting on you; I'm driving my own machine. I'll have to go get it."

"Okay." Harper walked out and down the hall to the room Wyatt and she shared. It was easy to see why everyone thought Wyatt didn't fit with her. She'd never snowmobiled, never skied, never snowboarded. The only winter sport she'd ever done—sledding—hadn't been mentioned here at all. And she hadn't seen a single sled.

But Kayla...she was perfect for Wyatt, and she seemed to know it and want him. Which should make Harper want to try to matchmake, but some nasty, belligerent side she hadn't even known she possessed had been churning deep within her. The one thing that kept popping to the top: she wanted Wyatt. Which was dumb. He saw her as a friend. And she didn't fit into his life at all. In a few weeks, he'd be moving here permanently.

She'd only been here a few hours, but it was enough to know that even if she lived here for decades, she would never feel at home in Chile. She would never be a natural on skis—although if she were here for any length of time, she would learn to ski or wear her legs off trying. She had zero desire to drive her own snowmobile. Wyatt had to have known she wouldn't want to. Or maybe he was afraid she couldn't. That was possible, too.

She finished dressing and closed the door behind her. She could admit to herself that she wanted Wyatt; her feelings had gone way beyond the friend stage. But not only did she not want to ruin their friendship, if she could manage to get him to notice her as more than a friend, she would never fit into this world, and Wyatt belonged here like roots belonged in the ground. Kayla would be the perfect girl for him. He should have snapped her up.

To Harper, Kayla looked at Wyatt like she'd be more than willing to be with him. She couldn't imagine what held him back.

Unfortunately, because Harper was pretending to be his fiancée, she could hardly play matchmaker. But tonight, she could try to talk to Wyatt about Kayla. Maybe she could help her best friend settle down here, which would make his dad happy, and marry the girl who was perfectly suited for him.

Only the light over the sink lit the kitchen as she walked through it and out the back door.

From here she could see the ski slopes, well-lit and busy. Lift chairs full of bundled up skiers crawled up the mountain, while colorful dots zoomed down. Laughter and occasional shouts echoed through the cold air. Now that the sun had gone down, she could see her breath coming out in puffs, and the air had a definite bite to it.

She looked in both directions, but nothing moved close to the house. The full moon, close enough to tempt her to reach out and touch it, glistened on the snow with a sweet, blue light. The silence and isolation of where she stood—close enough to see the crowd, but not a part of it—settled into her soul, and for the first time, a nugget of feeling —admiration…not quite love—stirred in her heart for this country in which she stood. Even at night, it was beautiful.

The sharp sound of a motor split the bubble that had wrapped itself around Harper. A light cut through the darkness. A snowmobile came into view, skimming across the snow and stopping in front of her.

Wyatt lifted up the visor on his helmet, then reached around and grabbed another helmet, holding it out to her.

"Thanks," she called loudly, to be heard over the rumble of the motor.

"You sure you're good for this?" he said with the same volume.

She pulled the helmet on. "I'm sure." Unless he'd changed his mind. But he hadn't seemed to have; he was grinning.

If she was going to get the helmet buckled, the gloves needed to go. She started to take them off.

"I'll get it." Within seconds he had it done. He thumbed behind his shoulder. "Hop on. Unless you're driving?"

"Not tonight."

Or ever. Snowmobiles were as unfamiliar as skis. But much bigger.

Instead, she put a hand on Wyatt's shoulder and climbed on behind him.

"Hold on."

She put her arms around Wyatt's waist. His body seemed to pulse with energy and excitement. It tingled up her arm and stirred her own miniscule sense of adventure. He pressed the throttle, and the machine leapt under them.

The full moon, the mountain covered in snow, and the droning of the motor contributed to the feeling that the world had narrowed to just the two of them as they flew over the snow, leaving the lights of the slopes far behind.

Wyatt turned his head and called over the sound of the wind and racing motor, "They're coming behind us. They were standing around yakking, and I wanted to have you here by myself first."

Had she heard him right? He wanted her alone. Electric pulses raced up her legs, but she fought the prickles of excitement. He must have something he needed to talk to her about. Maybe he wanted her help in attracting Kayla. Talk about hard. Could she help him woo another woman?

Of course she could. She might have more than friendly feelings for him, but she could push that aside. The happiness of her best friend was more important than what she wanted.

She squeezed him to let him know she heard. Maybe on the way home she wouldn't be able to enjoy holding his solid torso. So she leaned against his back and inched closer, enjoying the hardness of his muscles and the way she totally trusted his skill on the machine.

"Am I going too fast?" he shouted over his shoulder.

"I trust you," she called back.

One hand patted her hands where they joined around his stomach.

"Right here's the one place you have to watch," he yelled as he slowed down and pointed his gloved hand at a reflector on their right.

Craning her neck, she peered at the side of the trail. The gray-blue snow ended abruptly beside the trail into pitch-black darkness.

"A crevice," he said.

"How deep?" she asked.

His shoulders shrugged. "I don't know. Don't want to find out."

She shivered. "Me either."

"Not tonight, anyway." She felt, more than heard, him laugh.

She tightened her arms just as he gassed the engine and they lurched away.

In a few minutes he pointed at what looked like a low-hanging cloud hugging the mountainous terrain. It wasn't long after that he circled and slowed to a stop, shutting the motor off.

The silence of the mountain surrounded them like a shield.

"A hot spring?" Harper asked after contemplating their surroundings.

"Yeah. This is an active volcano."

"Wow. When's the last time it erupted?"

"Not sure. But the water's always warm."

"That's great. We'll be nice and warm when we die."

"And we'll be together." He stood, pulling his leg over and hopping off. "That's what the swimsuit is for."

"Okay." She still wasn't sure how comfortable she was about the whole active volcano thing, but she supposed they weren't in any more danger here than they were at the resort. Danger or no, if she had to run from an erupting volcano, she'd rather not do it in her swimsuit.

Wyatt opened a small compartment at the back of the snowmobile that she hadn't realized was there and took out two rolled towels. He laid them over the handlebars.

"Are you going to get in?"

She didn't want to. "Yeah, but this is your gig. I'll follow you."

"Set your clothes here. Anywhere else and they'll get snow on them." He patted the seat. "You'll have to take a couple of steps in the snow. I'll help you. There's some natural places to sit." Wyatt laid his coat down and peeled off his shirt.

Harper stood and unzipped her coat. "Is this private ground?"

"We own it. But there's a couple of other hot springs that are easier to get to. That fissure I showed you makes this one off-limits for guests, which is why we chose it. We won't have to share."

"I see." She laid her coat down and started on her shirts, suddenly self-conscious. Wyatt and she had swum plenty in the pond over the years, but she'd never bothered with a swimming suit—she'd just worn shorts and a tee shirt. Plus, it had been a few years. She glanced over as he turned to lay his shirt down. She didn't remember those broad shoulders and the muscles that rippled under the moonlight. Her stomach wobbled and delicious, warm sparks of heat poured out of it.

Not sure what to make of those feelings, she covered them with conversation. "It's beautiful here."

Wyatt unbuckled his pants. Harper skidded her eyes away, focusing on her own clothing.

"The full moon is beautiful in any country, but here on the mountain, it's especially gorgeous. Wait until you're in the water with the snow and the heat...there's nothing quite like it."

Pride and love laced his voice. He took a boot off, balancing on one foot as he removed his snow pants. He set his bare foot down on the snow. "This is the hard part. If you hurry, I'll carry you in so you don't have to walk on the white stuff."

She sat on the snowmobile and pulled her boots off, hurrying more because she was suddenly very aware that Wyatt was a man, a handsome, virile man, and she was a woman who found him attractive. Very attractive.

Kicking her last boot off, she slipped her snow pants off and set them on the seat.

Before she could say anything, Wyatt scooped her up. His warm skin contrasted with the cold air as he held her tight. She breathed in his familiar, comforting scent mixed with the crisp mountain air. She wanted to make a joke about not falling, or about her being afraid, but she couldn't, and Wyatt was uncharacteristically silent as well. She did manage to resist the temptation to press her lips against his shoulder, to rub her cheek against his warm skin, to snuggle closer.

"It's going to feel pretty warm at first, until you get used to it."

He stepped in, seeming to know where the best places to put his feet were, and he set her down. She barely had time to miss the contact of his body before the warm water lapped at her knees.

"It's hot," she exclaimed in wonder.

"You'll get used to it and it'll feel good. There's a natural bench over here." Wyatt took her hand and led her around to the far side. He helped her sit and slipped down beside her. The water came up to their shoulders.

"Is the whole pool this shallow?" she asked.

"No. I don't know how deep it is in the middle."

That was scary.

She squinted. It wasn't very large and lay in the basic shape of a circle. Harper estimated the diameter to be about twenty feet.

Wyatt leaned back and rested his head on the ledge behind them. Harper followed suit.

Her limbs floated, weightless in the warm water. Peace and calm relaxed her insides. "This place is amazing," she whispered.

"I've dreamed about this for years," Wyatt whispered back. His hand grasped hers, intertwining their fingers.

Her heart stumbled and her relaxation vanished. Those electric pulses started back up her leg. She drew in a shaky breath. She wanted so much for Wyatt to have deeper feelings for her that she was now imagining things. Deliberately, she laid her head back and closed her eyes.

Chapter Seventeen

The hum of snowmobile motors reached Wyatt. Disappointment speared through him. Harper hadn't had a reaction from his declaration. Maybe she was deliberately ignoring him because to acknowledge what he'd said would make their friendship awkward.

He slid his thumb over her hand under the water. She didn't pull away.

"Haven't you ever been here in a full moon before?" Harper spoke without opening her eyes, her head still laid back on the rim behind them.

"A few times," he answered. He couldn't tell what she meant, and he didn't have time to find out. "Everyone else is going to be here soon."

"I hear them."

He squeezed her hand. Her body relaxed into his. The moon and the night, the snow and the heat, all combined to make his insides feel warm and liquid.

"I know you've felt uncomfortable a lot today." It had been odd seeing her today. So far from the farm and everything familiar. He'd never seen her so blatantly out of her element before. But the same good nature and humor she handled everything else with had been present.

"Yeah."

"I appreciate you doing all this for me."

"That's what friends are for." She pulled away from him. "So, what do you think of Kayla?"

"Huh?" His eyes popped open and he turned his head to study her.

She met his gaze. "Kayla. What do you think of her?"

He shrugged and leaned his head back. "She's nice. She's actually a pretty good downhill skier. Not Olympic quality, but close." He tried to figure out why Harper would be asking about Kayla.

The noise of the snowmobiles grew louder.

"You two have a lot in common."

He really didn't want to talk about Kayla. It's not that he didn't like her, but they'd never been close. He had no desire to be, and after what Steve had talked about, he just wanted to put her out of his mind. "This is the place I spent more time at than any other growing up. I guess the same is true for her."

"She loves it here."

He paused before he spoke. "You would, too."

Harper rolled her head on the ledge, turning to consider Wyatt. Dark shadow obscured her eyes, but she had lifted her head a little and her gaze riveted on his.

"I do love it here. Mostly because you're here." She smiled. An easy, friendly smile. It wasn't the kind of smile he wanted, but still his breath whooshed out and he straightened. The water gurgled as his shoulders emerged.

Harper didn't move. His hand came out of the water and slid behind her neck. His thumb brushed the skin below her ear. Sparks sizzled up his arm.

"Do you mean that?" he whispered.

The low rumble erupted into a loud roar and headlights cut through the dusky moonlight as the snowmobiles tore around the bend.

Wyatt leaned back, choking back his disappointment. Despite the interruption he kept his hand behind her neck. They adjusted their position naturally, so that his arm ended up behind her.

The look, the question, the movement...he wanted to know what Harper was thinking, feeling. Beyond any doubt, he knew she would never mess with him. But he didn't trust himself to read her correctly.

Too late to find out now. Three machines parked in the area around theirs. Kayla, Steve and another couple.

"Where's this amazing woman at, that managed to snag Wyatt without even knowing how to ski?" a laughing female voice called out.

"She's right here, Marie," Wyatt called back.

In a low voice, beneath the chatter of the couples removing their outer clothes, Wyatt said, "That's Marie. Looks like she's here with Carlos. They're on again, off again in the romance department. Have been for years."

"Is she family?" Harper asked, keeping her voice low as well.

"Not really. She does housekeeping services for us and Carlos is on the maintenance crew. They've both grown up at the resort, but they never eat at the family table. They'd be welcome to."

"Their parents worked there?"

"Yep."

"I see."

"Are you still okay with this?" His fingers skimmed over her neck.

She shivered despite the warmth of the water. He took that as a good sign.

"You keep asking me that. Wyatt, you know me well enough. If things get to be too much for me, I'll tell you. I promise."

He leaned into her as though to shield her. "They're gonna rib you about the skiing."

She laughed softly. "And the snowboarding. And the lack of athletic ability in general."

He looked away. "When I first came to Pennsylvania, kids made fun of me constantly, and you stood by me through everything. I ended up being Homecoming King."

She put a hand on his chest. He wasn't prepared for it and jerked like she scalded him. She snatched her hand back. "I stood by you, true. But it was your affable personality that caused people to see past their differences with you to the great guy you were under it all."

"Hey, you lovebirds over there, you still have your suits on?" Marie called out.

Neither one of them moved. Wyatt couldn't figure out what, exactly, Harper was feeling. Finally, he shook his head. He grinned.

"Do we have our suits on, Pickles?"

"Mine's on," she called out. He stuffed down his disappointment. His chance to find out what Harper felt was lost with the arrival of his friends.

"It's dark. Who cares if we have suits on?" Carlos, built low to the ground but wide like a bull, dropped quickly into the water.

"There's a full moon. I don't want to see your ugly butt, Carlos." Kayla stepped gracefully in behind him. She moved with the easy power of an athlete. Again, Wyatt wondered about Harper's interest in her. Interesting that Harper and Steve seemed to have both picked up on the same thing.

"So do I leave my trunks on or off?" Steve asked.

"On," everyone chorused.

Marie waded around to Harper and Wyatt. "Hey, Harper. I'm Marie. I do housekeeping and whatever else needs done." She stuck her hand out.

"Except cooking," Carlos said over her shoulder.

She smacked him in the chest. "Don't listen to him. I just don't cook the Chilean dishes he likes. Give me pork and sauerkraut any day."

"You're American?" Harper asked as she shook her hand. Marie was forthright and honest. Wyatt figured she and Harper would be good friends if Harper stayed.

He had to quit thinking like that. She'd given no indication whatsoever that she was here for more than a favor to him.

"Yep. My parents moved down here when I was ten. I was joking about the pork and sauerkraut, though. That's just something you don't get here."

"I see," Harper replied. "I've done a little work with Sophia on the menu, and I know that there's a definite cultural difference in cuisine."

Wyatt tucked that info away to ask about later. Harper seemed like she might have liked Sophia, and the menu thing was right up her alley of expertise.

"So, Harper, we're all dying to know what you do, since it's obvious you aren't a ski bum," Carlos said as he settled into the warm water against the wall.

"I'd say you're not like the usual girls Wyatt brings around, but he's never actually brought a girl here before, so can't even say we know his type." Steve held a hand out to help Kayla, who swatted it away and settled herself in the water.

"She's my type," Wyatt said.

"She's into nutrition," Kayla said irritably.

"That's right. And I'm hoping to get tenure at the university where I teach and conduct research."

She was still hoping to get tenure. Wyatt tried not to show his disappointment.

"She has a doctorate." Steve sounded impressed.

"Wyatt goes for the smart ones," Marie said with a laugh.

"You're hoping to get tenure? You mean you're not moving to Chile with Wyatt?" Kayla latched onto the gap that Harper had just opened in their cover story.

Before he could think of something to say to save the situation, Marie came to their rescue. "You probably weren't expecting to have to give all that up. So I take it Wyatt proposing was a surprise to you?"

Oh, if they only knew. "Yeah. Definitely unexpected."

"So what are you going to do?"

Wyatt broke in. They'd grilled her long enough. "We haven't actually discussed it. We haven't been engaged that long."

"How long?" Kayla asked. She lifted an arm from the water and pushed her ponytail back over her shoulder.

"A little over a month." Wyatt pulled Harper closer to him. She went easily.

"Oh, that explains it," Carlos said.

"Explains what?" Wyatt asked.

"You two look real comfortable with each other, and you look like you really like each other...but..." Marie paused, searching for words.

Carlos finished for her. "But you don't look like lovers."

"Hmm." What could they say to that? His stomach twisted uncomfortably. Harper sat, frozen in place beside Wyatt.

"We wondered if..."

"If what?" Wyatt asked, a touch of annoyance in his voice.

"If you were getting the short end of the stick. If she was going to make you stay in America, quit the sports that you love, and become someone you're not." Kayla either ignored the fact that Wyatt was getting annoyed, or didn't care. Wyatt figured it was the latter.

"How do you know what I am?" Wyatt lifted his arm from behind Harper and leaned forward in the water. He remembered now why Kayla irritated him so much. She constantly made assumptions that were completely wrong.

Harper put a hand on his shoulder. It felt warm on his cool skin.

She cleared her throat. "Those are legitimate concerns."

"No, they're not," Wyatt said immediately.

"These people care about you, which is why they're asking." Her tone was soft. Soothing.

"They're insulting you. And I won't stand for it."

She shook her head. "I'm just different. They're not sure they can trust me. And they love you."

He appreciated her defending his friends. Especially since there were annoying him. He stretched his fingers out and tried to relax. They'd give any girl he brought here a hard time.

"I don't know if I'd go that far..." Steve said, laughing, easing the tension somewhat.

"No, she's right. We're just surprised at the kind of girl you picked. We wondered if she..." Carlos's voice trailed off.

Kayla finished for him. "If she's after your money."

Wyatt straightened. His muscles tensed and his heart raced. He couldn't even look at Harper. He should find this funny. After all, if his friends knew that their engagement was a sham, they wouldn't even be talking like this. But he could hardly contain the urge to defend Harper. Physically if necessary. "I don't have any money."

"You will," Kayla said. Unafraid. "It's no secret that your dad is planning on giving you everything. You'll be a rich man, Wyatt."

Carlos shrugged. Maybe some of the amusement in his face was from seeing his normally unflappable friend annoyed. He certainly didn't try to defuse the situation with his statement. "It sounds to me like she could use a rich backer to fund her research."

"I'm not after Wyatt for his money." As soon as she said it, he knew she couldn't back up her statement with fact without exposing the engagement for the farce it was.

"We didn't mean anything mean by it. We just wanted to protect Wyatt," Marie said.

"So, since we're not mincing words anymore, how about you just tell us, how do we know that you're not using Wyatt for his money?" Kayla asked.

"You just have to take my word for it," Wyatt said. His voice sounded like tires crunching gravel.

Kayla pursed her lips. "I think you're so besotted that you wouldn't know if she were or weren't."

Harper said quickly, "I agree to sign a prenup. If we get divorced, I get nothing."

"No. No prenup. You'll be my wife and I'll provide for you." Wyatt almost snarled. What was wrong with him? This whole conversation was moot. Their engagement was not real. They could say anything. Usually he was the first to goof off, but something about what everyone was saying had hit a nerve.

"Okay. You're right. If we get divorced, I get half of your assets, you get half of mine." He tilted his head. She didn't have any assets. He realized as he looked at her, her eyes twinkling, that she was trying to make him smile. Teasing him out of his irritation the way he might do for her.

She tossed her head and looked back at his friends. "But, seriously, we're not even married yet. Barely engaged. Do we really have to talk like there's going to be a divorce?"

"You have to face reality. Fifty percent of marriages end in divorce," Kayla said.

"Not mine." Wyatt's voice held conviction.

Harper slipped an arm around his tense back. He tried to relax. She tossed her head in a sassy gesture she only used when they were alone and when she wasn't Professor Bright. "Fine. We won't need a prenup because we aren't getting divorced. Now, you have to agree to cook my dinner every night of our married life, unless you can dunk me in the next ten seconds." She splashed him, then dived away—along the side, probably because she couldn't stand the idea of swimming out over a bottomless hole. She'd adjusted pretty quickly to Chile, but she hadn't changed that much.

He slid after her, and by the time he'd caught up to her a major splashing match was going on. Apparently, he'd kicked water on Kayla as he dove after Harper and she couldn't let it go.

After the splashing wound down, they agreed to a game of chicken.

Harper still didn't look too eager to be over the center of the water hole, even though she'd be sitting on Wyatt's shoulders.

As Wyatt crouched down for her to climb on, she whispered, "If I fall off, I'm going to be grabbing for you."

"That's a good idea; you can drown us both." His easy grin slipped naturally back into place.

"The idea of all that water under me, with no bottom, is petrifying."

This probably wasn't the time to start thanking her again for being such a good sport. Instead he said, "There has to be a bottom, otherwise the water would drain out."

"Stop trying to use logic on my fear."

He snorted. "Fine. Drag me down, too." Turning, he placed a hand on her shoulder. "I'm sorry about earlier. I was being an idiot about that prenup business. It shouldn't have mattered, but for some reason, I couldn't let it go. Stupid." He leaned closer and lowered his voice. "If you fall off, I will be grabbing for you. There's no way I'm letting anything happen to you."

Her hand tightened on his shoulder. "I know. You never have. I guess I was just trying to let you know how nervous I was without actually saying I was nervous."

He ran his hand up her arm, slender and soft. "You haven't been in your comfort zone since we drove away from the farm."

"I think I'll let you let me sleep on the bed tonight."

"Hey, come on! What's taking you two so long?" Marie called out.

He chuckled. "That's awfully big of you, Pickles. I'll tell my friends —they'll think you're taking advantage of this big, dumb jock."

"Later." She slipped a leg around his neck and slid into place. "Right now you need to channel your inner big, dumb jock, if you want to win this. Since, even if every single person here were in a coma, they'd still be more athletic than me."

Possibly. "But they don't have your heart."

"Right now, it's muscles that matter, mister."

He grabbed ahold of her feet and helped her place them around his waist. "Brain beats brawn every time."

"I think this is the exception to the rule."

"Lock your legs, Pickles. We've got this."

Harper did what he told her to, gripping the sides of his hard chest with her knees, latching her feet around his waist. His hands held her legs firmly.

"Are you two finally ready?" Marie asked.

Wyatt, who had been sitting on the natural bench that lined the pool, slipped into the water with her on his shoulders.

"We're ready. Come get us," Wyatt called. He started moving slowly forward.

Marie rode on Carlos's shoulders. They edged in from their right, while Steve, with Kayla, came from the left.

Wyatt squeezed her right leg and inched in that direction, but it didn't matter which way he moved, both of the other couples were aiming for Harper and him. Which made sense. Gang up and get one down, then there were only two left.

Wyatt squeezed both of Harper's legs as a warning then lunged forward, splashing water into Carlos's eyes at the same time.

Carlos flinched back, causing Marie to tilt forward. Harper reached down to try to twist her around and take advantage of her loss of balance, but Carlos recovered and Harper's hand slid off Marie's shoulder. Marie grabbed her forearm and yanked.

Wyatt twisted and lunged, trying to leverage Harper's weight and help keep her balanced at the same time. His hands left her legs, splashing and straight-arming the other men, while his legs churned the water, keeping them up.

Steve and Kayla came within arm's distance. Harper grappled with both Marie and Kayla, while Wyatt tried to think of a strategy.

He managed a forceful splash of water, which must have disoriented Carlos because he backed off, giving Harper her right arm free to try to twist Kayla off balance. As tiny as Kayla was, her arm strength was phenomenal. And the smaller body gave a lower center of gravity. Steve and she were hardly ever off balance.

Harper managed to get both hands on Kayla's right arm. She yanked with all her strength, gripping Wyatt's body tight with her legs. Wyatt maneuvered to try to give her more leverage.

Kayla jerked forward, flailing, but Steve twisted under her and enabled her to catch her balance. Carlos entered the fray again, on their right, and Wyatt twisted to meet their attack.

Harper fought off Marie's hands, which sought purchase on her forearms.

Suddenly, Harper yanked back. She cried out, falling backward.

Chapter Eighteen

Kayla had grabbed Harper's hair. Shock, followed immediately by anger, surged through her. She hadn't had siblings growing up, and she'd never really played chicken before, but the unwritten rules must clearly state no hair pulling.

The professor in her wanted to stop the action and point out that Kayla was cheating.

Wyatt surged under her, backing and twisting to help her balance. Harper caught herself, tried to ignore the burning in her head, and channeled the adrenaline from her anger into fending off Marie's attack.

It worked, since Carlos, seeing that they were reeling back, had overcommitted to charging forward. Not expecting them to recover so quickly, he and Marie were caught unprepared for their rush. She gripped Marie's forearms, Wyatt twisted under her, she yanked, moving her whole upper body. Marie tumbled into the water with a large splash.

Marie's body hadn't completely disappeared when another white-hot pain seared her scalp. Her whole body fell backwards, seeking to ease the tension and lesson the pain.

Harper used the backward momentum of her body to twist. She threw her arms out, catching Kayla and hooking onto her to check her fall. Beneath her, Wyatt seemed to sense what was playing out, because he lunged forward. Their combined attack made it impossible for Kayla to stop her momentum.

Wyatt splashed water up into Steve's eyes, and he was unable to hold to Kayla's legs as she toppled sideways.

"Woo hoo, we won," Wyatt said before he ducked below the surface, allowing Harper to slide off his shoulders and into the warm water.

Wyatt's hand slid along her arm, and she grabbed his hand before reemerging into the chilly night air. Wyatt paddled beside her to the edge of the pool. They sat on the ledge together.

"You can't quit now, I've got a title to reclaim," Steve said.

"No. I've got water up my nose and in my eyes, and I just want to sit down for a bit," Marie said from the end of the pool.

"Yeah. We should have known Wyatt would win." Steve treaded water in the middle of the pool.

"We could pair him with a two-year-old and he'd still win." Kayla hung on the ledge on the far side of the pool.

Harper wasn't athletic. She knew that. She really didn't think they meant to insult her, either. But their comments did serve to remind her that Wyatt and she were not on the same level here in Chile, or anytime he was with his friends.

"Seems to me the last time we did this, Kayla, Steve and Marie beat you and me."

"That was a fluke," Kayla said.

"Twice." Wyatt grinned up at Harper. She thought he winked, but couldn't be sure in the moonlight.

"It was three times," Steve said. "Kayla was pouting so badly by that last time, it wouldn't have mattered if she'd have been on Superman's shoulders. When you get mad, you play stupid."

"I'm outta here," Kayla said, moving to the edge and coming out of the water with a splash.

"Yeah, I've got to work tomorrow." Marie rose from the water and pulled herself out of the pool.

"Me too." Carlos glided over and got out behind Marie.

"Hang here for a second, Pickles. I'll get our towels."

"Oooh, look at Romeo, getting the girl's towel." Steve picked himself out of the water and followed the others over.

"Let him alone. I think it's great that he'll get her towel," Marie said, grabbing her own.

"Hurry up, champ. Get the girl dried off. We'll race you home." Kayla shook her towel and bent her head, toweling her hair.

"How about it, Harper? You up for a race?" Carlos asked.

"Sure." She wasn't. Not really. But there was no way she'd admit it. She took the towel Wyatt handed her, moving quickly to dry off and dress. If there was a race, she didn't want to be the cause of them starting last.

"That's one race you won't win, Wyatt. Not with two people on your sled." Steve flipped his towel behind him and swiped back and forth, drying his back.

"You're right. How much of a head start is fair?" Wyatt asked.

"Five minutes," Carlos called.

Her swimsuit wasn't dry, but everyone else was getting dressed. Harper pulled on her snow pants.

The others chattered in the background as Wyatt leaned over. "You okay with that?"

Her stomach had knotted up again, but she ignored it. "As long as I get to ride with you." She pulled her shirt on and tried to continue faking calmness. "Wasn't it you that said you hadn't saved me all those other times just to let me die now?"

He laughed. "Well, it could get intense. Are you sure you're okay?"

"So you're saying once we start, you're racing to win?" Of course he was. He was a competitor, after all.

He shuffled his feet and stuck his hands in his pockets. "Yeah. I can turn 'em down. No problem, because there are two of us. But once we commit, I don't want to back down."

"Is that your stubborn streak coming out again?" she teased.

His smile was self-effacing. "Like with the whole prenup deal?"

"Yeah. So, once you commit to being married, even for pretend, you're not planning an out—you're all in."

"Yep. All in."

Harper pulled her boots on, slanting a glance at the rest of the group. They were almost dressed.

"I'm jumping in, too."

Wyatt bent even closer and spoke low. "Are you sure?"

"I'm sure," Harper said.

Wyatt pulled his ski hat down over his head and handed her hers. "Give us a five-minute head start."

"We came together," Carlos said of Marie and him. "So we'll leave with you."

"Fair enough," Wyatt said. He buckled Harper's helmet, brushing her hands aside, then his own.

Harper held his gloves out to him. Her insides were buzzing. Nervousness or excitement, she wasn't sure which.

He climbed on, looking at her as she climbed on after him, before turning to stare straight ahead and flipping his visor down. Flicking his fingers, the motor roared to life.

They idled past the first two snowmobiles, leaving the hot spring behind, and pulled even with Carlos and Marie.

Harper tightened her arms around Wyatt's waist. He patted her hands, then shouted at Carlos, "You call it."

Carlos didn't hesitate. "Go."

His sled took off. An instant later the front skis of their machine lifted from the ground as they ripped off after them.

Harper crouched down, hiding her body behind Wyatt's. The large plastic windshield provided a windbreak, but she didn't want to contribute any drag that might slow them down.

Even in the daylight, the snow-covered landscape all looked the same. In the moonlight, it was almost impossible to differentiate between straight and hilly terrain. With her head behind Wyatt, she felt, more than saw, the changes in the trail. His body tensed and leaned, and she moved with him, bouncing over bumps and careening around turns. The wind whipped around them, and snow flew up and over the windshield, blowing in short gusts. Harper held tighter to Wyatt. She couldn't see the tail light of Carlos's machine.

Once, Wyatt glanced around. "Are you okay?"

"Yes," she shouted.

"We've got a fouled plug. We're not catching Carlos, but we might be able to beat the other two."

She had no idea what a fouled plug was. However, she understood there was a problem, but the competitor in Wyatt couldn't quit.

They travelled on in silence for a while, the only sound the revving of their motor. They were going too fast for her to enjoy the night ride, but Harper still cherished the hardness of Wyatt's torso, the way his energy seemed to channel into her and the way it seemed like they were alone on the planet. Together.

A light cut across her shoulder, and she twisted enough to see a machine coming up on their left. Wyatt leaned forward fractionally, and she imitated his movement. For a few moments it seemed like they might pull ahead, but the trail straightened and the other sled slowly gained on them. Harper squinted over at it. Steve, she was pretty sure.

As they bore gradually left around a sloping curve, he pulled ahead. Still, Wyatt didn't quit, and Harper was reminded of the tortoise and the hare. There was always the possibility of something going wrong, so it would be foolish to quit until the end.

Steve was barely by them when again a headlight shone over Harper's shoulder. Dim at first, it got steadily brighter.

They had reached a part of the trail that twisted and turned in a narrow ribbon. Not enough room for the sled behind them to pass. The headlight moved from their right side to their left, like the machine behind them couldn't wait to get an opportunity to pass.

Ahead, the reflector that indicated the crevice Wyatt had shown her earlier, on their way up, blinked in the light of their headlight. Harper's chest tightened. Her heart thumped against her ribs. She realized she was holding her breath.

Wyatt eased off on the throttle just a little.

The sled behind them seized the opportunity, slipping out from behind them and pushing around. The crevice grew closer, the shiny reflector the only indication of its presence. He began to ease to the left, following the trail, which curved then narrowed.

Beside them, Kayla drew even, then nudged ahead. The proximity of her machine did not allow them to turn as sharply as Harper thought they needed to. She leaned, expecting to turn. Both sleds continued straight. The reflector was mere yards away. Harper closed her eyes and concentrated on the feel of Wyatt. She didn't believe that he would drive off the trail, but she'd said she trusted him. She needed to prove it.

Kayla fishtailed, then bore left, speeding around the curve and out of sight. Wyatt turned the handlebars but the sled did not turn. Were they on ice?

Harper's entire body froze in terror as the reflector careened toward them. A scream built in the back of her throat, but Harper swallowed it. The analytical side of her brain didn't want Wyatt to die with her terrified scream being the last thing he ever heard.

His body leaned left, way out over the side of the sled.

"Lean!" he shouted.

She was already behind him, out over the frozen snow, her face mere inches from the ground.

Their machine plowed over the reflector. The skis seemed to grip as the front end turned left. The back fishtailed right.

Harper's body pressed into Wyatt's back as the sled slowed. She kept her upper body poised out over the side of the sled.

Snow flew everywhere. Big clouds of white that obscured the hole that gaped, bottomless and black, nearby.

The front right side of the sled tipped.

Harper gasped. She gripped Wyatt's waist with all her might. Her stomach felt like it was going to come flying out of her mouth at any second.

Still hanging over the side of the snowmobile, Wyatt pushed back.

The sled stopped. The motor died.

Harper held her breath. The front right ski hung suspended over the edge of the crevice. The sled dipped down. It rocked back and forth like Satan swinging a baby's cradle from one finger. She could almost hear the evil laugh echoing up from the pits of Hell where, surely, this crevice led.

She still leaned to the left beside Wyatt but, just moving her eyes and lifting her head a fraction, she could look to the right and see there was nothing there. The snowmobile sat on the very edge of the precipice. Except the one ski, which...didn't.

"Get off the sled, Harper," Wyatt said low, but very calmly.

She opened her mouth to argue. She wasn't getting off while he stayed on. She wasn't leaving him. But this was his gig. She wasn't going to start now, thinking that she knew better than he did. At least not about something like this.

She didn't say anything. She couldn't. Not with her tongue stuck to the roof of her mouth the way it was.

"Slowly," he said in that same low, calm voice. Like talking might shift the weight of the sled and cause it to tip down, like a ship sinking to the depths of the ocean.

She unclenched her fingers from around Wyatt's waist. Stiff and frozen in place from the force from which she'd been gripping, they didn't want to move. The sled rocked gently as she slid her arms slowly back.

"Harper?"

"Mmm?" She couldn't risk trying to say more. A scream, blood-curdling and agonizing, crouched just at the back of her throat. So close, the slightest effort to open her mouth might allow it to get loose. She was afraid that, once she started, she wouldn't be able to stop. Not in this lifetime. Which could end up being very short.

"You know I love you?"

"Shut up," she said. Not mean, but firm. He wasn't going to get all mushy-gushy on her now. To do so meant that he was acknowledging the fact that they might not make it. If he did that, she'd lose it.

She scooted back a little more. The sled rocked. A clump of snow broke off the edge with a muted crack and fell silently into the earth.

On the other hand...

"I love you, too." He'd probably think she meant friend love, the love he'd been talking about. He didn't need to know it wasn't that kind of love.

She'd heard that as a person is about to die, their thoughts became clearer, and maybe that was true. Because it was obvious there was a very fine line between love and hate. She wanted to beat Wyatt, but she also wanted to kiss him. Long and hard and just as thoroughly.

"You slide back, too."

"I'm not moving until you're off." He stopped talking as the sled rocked. "If this thing starts to go, dive left."

She didn't answer. The drive to save herself was strong, but she wasn't sure she could jump while Wyatt rode the machine to his death.

Her butt touched the back end of the seat. "I'd rather we survive together."

"I love it when we agree."

"If you even crack one joke…"

"What? You'll push me?"

"I can't make dying jokes right now." Harper carefully lifted her butt and settled on the very back of the snowmobile. It seemed more stable now.

"I'd rather die laughing than die scared."

"We disagree on that one, because I would rather not die at all."

"See? Brains trump brawn."

Gingerly lifting her leg, she swung it over. She grabbed the back rest, which was just a bar that went up, over and down.

"I'm sitting on the very back edge, holding onto the handle. If it goes, all I have to do is stand up. You slide back now."

Wyatt didn't argue. He tucked his legs back, and slid, slowly and steadily back until his back touched Harper's leg.

"You get up, and I'll follow you."

"Let's do it together on the count of three."

Rather than answering, Wyatt started counting, "One. Two. Three!"

<h1 style="text-align: center;">Chapter Nineteen</h1>

Wyatt brought his arm around Harper, pushing her off in front of him.

After taking a good five or six steps, they stopped and turned.

The sled wobbled, but stayed on the edge.

Adrenaline buzzed through Harper's body, making her feel like she could run back to the lodge, or back to Pennsylvania, which seemed like a haven of safety right now.

After a high like that, she was cognizant enough to know that the emotional and physical crash would be huge. She wanted to get back to the lodge, and preferably be in bed, when her body came down, since it was probably going to involve an ugly cry, a lot of shaking, and the fetal position.

Wyatt didn't seem to be affected.

Harper tried to pretend casual. "I can't believe Kayla didn't stop." She looked around. Blue-white, moon-washed terrain as far as she could see in all directions. She didn't even see any lights which could be from the lodge or ski resort.

"They'll be back when we don't pull in." Wyatt put both hands on his hips. "But I think I can pull that baby away from the edge. I'm not sure why it shut off..."

"Because you scared the crap out of it."

Wyatt snorted. "Same thing happened to me."

"Fooled me."

His head snapped around, and he seemed to search into her soul.

"I was scared. Trust me."

She believed him. She spoke softly. "I've done nothing but trust you lately."

Something seemed to flash on his face, and she thought he was going to step toward her. Did his hand move toward her face? But his expression cleared and he muttered, "Thanks." He turned back to the snowmobile.

"Stay back here." He glanced over at her, maybe to make sure she heard him. "Sometimes with crevices, there'll be a buildup of snow along the opening. Like, there's snow, maybe four or five feet deep around the top, but nothing under it to support it. Know what I'm saying?"

"I'm just thanking God I didn't know that five minutes ago." The very idea made her want to pee her pants. She took another step back. "I'd feel more comfortable if you'd step back here with me."

"I will." He flashed her his practiced grin.

She put her hands on her hips. "That one doesn't work on me. Remember? This is Harper, not some floozy you met on the slopes."

He looked over his shoulder and raised a brow. "Believe me, Pickles. I know who I'm with."

"Well, then you should remember that smile hasn't worked on me since you used it to convince me to bungee jump out of the maple tree." She pressed her lips together.

"I visited you in the hospital." He spoke without looking back at her.

She rolled her eyes and huffed, "That's because you were there with me."

"That was ten years ago. I can't believe you're still holding that against me."

"You might as well figure it out now that there are certain things a girl doesn't forget." Like almost dying.

"You forget nothing," Wyatt replied with a smile in his voice.

"I'm not going to forget that Kayla tried to run us into that crevice, then booked it out of here."

He shook his head. "She didn't do it on purpose. She wanted to win as bad as I did."

Harper was not convinced of that, but she kept her mouth shut. If Wyatt were out of the picture, Kayla would not have any competition for inheriting the resort. Maybe she'd read too many murder mysteries, because Wyatt didn't seem the slightest bit worried.

He stepped forward.

Before she could clamp her teeth around them, words spilled out. "Please be careful."

Maybe it was her tone, more than the actual words that caused him to pause, midstride, and slowly look back. A muscle bunched in his jaw.

"I will."

Their eyes held for a second that stretched like eternity. Emotions roiled in Harper's chest, but neither of them said anything more.

Then Wyatt turned back around and walked carefully toward the snowmobile.

Grabbing the back handle, he spread his feet wide, planting them to the side and behind the machine, then gathering himself, he pulled.

Nothing happened at first. Harper just prayed that the snow beneath his feet wouldn't suddenly give way. There could not be anything worse than seeing Wyatt disappear downward in a cloud of dusty snow. She had no idea what she'd do if that happened. Run for help. Jump in after him. Dissolve into a pile of incoherent muck. Yeah. Definitely.

She banished those thoughts from her head. For now. They would come back to haunt her tonight, she was sure.

As Wyatt exerted steady pressure, the snowmobile began to move. At first, she thought it was her imagination, it happened so slowly. But then, inch by terrible inch, it came back. Until, suddenly, it broke free.

Wyatt scrambled backward, dragging the sled. The thin shelf of snow that had supported it, and them, earlier, broke free, tumbling down into nothingness. Harper gasped and her hand went to her throat, as though it would be able to keep her heart from ripping out of her chest.

The momentum carried Wyatt and the machine back to solid ground. He bent over, panting.

Harper closed her eyes and breathed deeply. Thankful that the drama seemed to be at an end and both Wyatt and she, and their snowmobile, were all safe.

She walked over and put a hand on Wyatt's back. "You okay?" It wasn't like him to not bounce back immediately.

"Yeah. I just realized as the shelf was giving way, that me dropping out of sight would be traumatizing to you. It hit me kind of hard." He straightened. "I'm sorry."

She laughed. Shaky. "That's what you're sorry for? *Almost* traumatizing me?" She shook her head. "What about the other thousand things that have happened in the last fifteen minutes that actually have traumatized me?"

"I guess I just figured me dying would be the worst…"

"You're right," she snapped and regretted her tone immediately. Reaction. "I'm sorry. I think I'd really like to get back to the lodge so I can curl up in bed and pull the covers over my head for a while."

"You're gonna have to fight me for them."

"I thought we were fighting about who got to sleep on the floor? I let you win."

"Let's see if we can get this beast started. We can fight about the covers fifteen minutes from now."

He leaned over the machine, brushing snow off the controls and apparently checking for leaks, before he adjusted the run button and yanked on the pull rope.

The engine sputtered but didn't catch. Wyatt adjusted the choke.

It fired right up on the second pull.

"Your chariot, ma'am."

Harper was afraid she might need hard liquor and a tranquilizer more than a chariot, but she'd already snapped at him, and she didn't want him to think she blamed him for their near deaths. She wasn't sure she could say the same about Kayla. And, right now, she wanted to blame someone. Maybe tomorrow, after the fright and adrenaline wore off, she'd be more reasonable. Currently, her body had already started to shake, and her knees barely held her up.

She climbed on behind Wyatt. If he noticed that she held on tighter and pressed her body against his more fully, he didn't say anything.

He held the throttle and handlebars with one hand, placing the other over her hands, which squeezed his stomach. As his gloved fingers curled around hers, tingles spread up her arm and tears pricked her eyes. All these crazy, uncontrollable emotions swirled through her body, but for now she would chalk them up to the fact that she and her best friend had almost died.

Heat from his back scalded her front, but rather than pulling away, she pressed closer, wishing her helmet away. She had the unreasonable urge to bite his shoulder.

They'd only been riding for a few minutes when headlights popped up coming toward them.

"I knew they'd be back for us."

She didn't say anything, not even wanting to try to understand the competitive spirit that would lead someone to race away from a potential catastrophe.

Wyatt stopped, and the snowmobile with Steve and Kayla on it stopped alongside. It looked like Carlos and Marie on a machine behind them.

"You guys just that slow? Or did you stop to make out?" Steve called over the growl of the engines.

"Just slow."

Harper was amazed at Wyatt's calm. She was not that relaxed.

"Kayla said she lost you by the crevice."

"If you went in, I knew I wouldn't be able to get you out by myself." She lifted the coiled rope from her shoulder.

That was almost reasonable. But she should have stopped to see, just in case.

Wyatt just jerked his head in acknowledgement. "I appreciate you coming back out for me. Sorry you wasted your time."

"I'd expect the same from you," Steve said.

"You'd get it," Wyatt answered. His hand squeezed hers where it still rested against his stomach. "Harper and I have had enough excitement for one day. We're heading back to the lodge and bed."

"You park your machine by the back door, we'll see that it gets put away."

"I appreciate it, man." Wyatt thumbed the gas, and the sled took off.

Harper shook so badly, she could hardly keep herself still.

"You gonna make it, Pickles?"

"What else could I do?"

By far, this had been the most dangerous thing that had ever happened to her.

Wyatt glanced back, his face relaxed, his eyes sparkling, his lips split in a wide smile. Her lips tilted up in response. They'd almost died. But he was smiling. And getting her to grin back at him.

She was still dealing with the aftereffects of the excitement, but because of Wyatt's confidence and humor, the danger they had been in seemed to fade. Not that she wanted to go back and do it again, just that a sudden warm, bubbling joy filled her chest.

They were alive. They'd tempted death and won. Euphoria coursed through her body. This had to be the high that adrenaline junkies sought. She could see why. She felt invincible. She wanted to stand up on the back of the snowmobile with her arms raised in the wind. Even that did not seem like a big enough outlet for the emotions that pounded through her body, swelling her chest, straining up her neck and making her arms and legs feel energized and capable of winning an ironman competition. Life couldn't get any better.

SOMETIMES LIFE SUCKED.

Wyatt parked the snowmobile at the back door and helped Harper off. She was still shaking, but she bravely gave him a humungous smile. Probably because she knew how butt-awful he felt about almost killing her.

He threw a hand up as the others rumbled by. Steve stopped his machine and Kayla hopped off, jumping onto his. He appreciated them taking care of it so that he could get Harper inside, but he didn't stop to chat.

He still couldn't believe how close she'd come to death tonight.

Because of him and his overzealous, continuous quest for adventure. She had every right to hate him. He almost wished she would. He'd welcome punishment for what he'd done. Maybe it would appease some of the guilt and shame that curdled his blood and shriveled his heart from putting the woman he loved, and should have been protecting, in danger.

If there was one thing that tonight showed him very clearly, it was that every time Harper was with him, she ended up in danger or hurt. Tonight, maybe she hadn't gotten hurt, but she'd almost died. He was a fool to think for one second he was any good for her. Only a matter of inches, and tonight could have turned out so much differently. It was crazy to think that Harper belonged with him. If he were smart, if he really loved her, he'd get as far away from her as possible. For her own safety.

He took Harper's hand. In the state he was in, he figured it would serve him right if he ruined their friendship by allowing her to know his feelings for her. That would almost be a fitting punishment. He didn't deserve her, especially after tonight, and he wouldn't allow himself to try to get her to see him as something more than her step-cousin.

So, he held her hand, which, somehow, remained soft and trusting in his.

The kitchen was dark and quiet when he led her in. The small light above the stove bathed the room in long shadows. It should feel homey to him. After all, he'd spent more time in this kitchen than in almost any other place in the world. But it didn't bring the calmness, didn't make him feel like he'd walked into a close, loving family, the way being in the old farmhouse on the tree farm in Pennsylvania did.

Still, nothing was out of place. It almost seemed wrong, after such a life-threatening adventure, feeling as miserable as he did, to walk into the kitchen and have it look exactly the same as it always had.

Harper's hand tightened around his. He looked over his shoulder. "Hungry?"

She laughed and rolled her eyes. "No. You probably are."

He was, actually.

She tried to tug her hand free. "Stay here and grab something. I'm going to take a shower and snuggle under the covers. Try to relax."

He stopped and turned around to face her, keeping hold of her hand. "I really am sorry."

Her hand came up to his face, holding his cheek in a soft caress. It felt like forgiveness and he leaned his head into it, closing his eyes.

"When I'm with you, I know you're thinking about me before anything else. I can't lie and say I wasn't scared." Her hand trembled against his face. "But I knew if there was a way out, you'd find it. Don't apologize."

"I've always enjoyed the rush of danger and the euphoria of conquering death, but I absolutely did not enjoy the fear I felt tonight when you were in danger. It made me think—is that what everyone else feels about me?"

Her eyes widened. "Yes!" She stepped closer.

Wyatt's heart hit against his chest like it was reaching out to her. "That's exactly how I feel. And when you were climbing that mountain last winter. When you were in the Amazon with no cell phone service for weeks. If I thought about it, I wouldn't be able to function." She placed a hand over his chest where his heart beat for her.

His breath came shallow and fast, and his brain had all but shut down. Vaguely, he remembered there were reasons he couldn't get this close to Harper, why he couldn't put his arm around her waist and draw her to him, but he couldn't remember. Didn't want to remember.

Her body touched his. He put his other hand around her neck, threading it under her hair, tilting her head up. "Stay away from me. Stay away so I don't hurt you, drag you into danger. I couldn't stand it if anything happened to you."

Her lips parted and her tongue touched one corner of her mouth.

Pulses, like electric shocks, ripped through him. Her breath hit his face and her hand slid around to hold the back of his head. Her other hand slid around his waist, slipping under his shirt, shocking his bare skin. His breath came out in a rush, and he lowered his head. All thoughts of anything except taking her lips with his evaporated out of his mind. He'd dreamed of this for so long. He'd almost lost her today. But she was alive, safe and warm in his arms. Her body pressed to his. Two hearts. One heartbeat.

"Harper, I..." He didn't finish the whispered plea, unsure if he had meant to ask permission, apologize, or maybe even give her the chance to back away.

The distance between their lips vanished, and they were pressed together. Hers were soft and pliant and warm. It was almost enough and not even close to being enough. Behind his closed eyelids hot red and yellow sparks erupted. He pressed his lips tight together, determined not to give rein to the passion and need ripping through his soul. But she sighed and twisted her head slightly. The friction as their lips moved over each other burst in his head, and the beast inside—the one that caused him to climb mountains, race too fast, and ride dangerous rapids —roared to life.

His mouth opened and he caught her sigh, took it in, tasted it, savored it because it was Harper's. He growled, pressing her to him, lifting her against him. His tongue plunged into her mouth, and the kiss he'd dreamed about for years became reality.

Her hand gripped his head, pulling him closer, her mouth opened under his, her tongue dueled with his, her arm wrapped around him and he pressed her against the wall, his hands roaming freely down her sides and through her hair, like he couldn't get close enough, couldn't touch her enough, couldn't feel her enough. He groaned, frustrated he couldn't get closer, needing the reaffirmation of life after her brush with death.

But he was going too fast. Vaguely he realized it. He pulled back, some part of him afraid that she'd come to her senses and slap his face. But she had kissed him back. He was sure of it. Unable to bear the idea of letting her go, he leaned back and looked into her eyes.

HARPER'S BREATH came in heavy pants. She forced her eyes open and met Wyatt's gaze, hoping he didn't misread the wide-eyed wonder in hers. Nothing in her relationship with Wyatt had prepared her for her body's reaction to his kiss.

Hoping she wasn't being presumptuous, she whispered, "More."

Wyatt's eyes lowered. His head drifted toward hers. His hand moved slowly and lightly up and down the curve of her waist. His other hand traced slow circles on the back of her neck. The passionate haze that had enveloped her settled more closely around, fogging her brain, narrowing her thoughts down to just one focus: Wyatt. His lips on hers, his hands, his body, the beat of his heart, the scent of him, rich and spicy. Natural.

His head moved to the side. She held back a whimper of frustration, which changed to a purr of contentment when he kissed the corner of her eye. The edge of her jaw. Just beside her lip. His stubble rubbed lightly against her sensitive skin, and she remembered earlier that she'd wanted to bite him. The urge came back. Powerfully. She clamped it down. This was a gentle kiss. A romantic kiss.

He kissed the tip of her nose, then her other cheek.

Her hands moved to his face and she caught his cheeks between them. "My lips, Wyatt. You can kiss your sister on the nose."

"I don't know why the frig I'd want to," Wyatt murmured.

She smiled, and he smiled, their gazes connecting just before their lips touched. Gently. Sweetly. Light, butterfly touches that drove sensation through her body, settling in her stomach. The kiss was delicate and mild.

Until it wasn't.

Unsure how it happened, Harper realized her body strained against his, and her hands clutched his shoulders. He crushed her closer; she clung to him and their mouths were deeply, intimately joined together.

"Wyatt," Kayla shouted. Impatience clear in her voice. Harper came far enough out of the passion fog to realize that it wasn't the first time she'd said his name.

Wyatt's head lifted.

She almost doubled over from frustration and disappointment. Who would have guessed that kissing Wyatt would be so...consuming? Sure, he was extremely handsome with a great physique. But, whoa. She had never dreamed that there might be so much passion between them. Which couldn't be a good thing since they were *just friends*.

She wanted more. More kissing, and more than just friends.

His arms loosened slightly. She allowed her hands to drop. He cleared his throat.

"What?"

"I need to talk to you."

"Talk."

Kayla didn't say anything.

As much as Harper didn't want to leave the circle of Wyatt's arms, she understood what the silence meant. She swallowed, trying to tamp down the heat and stop the racing of her heart.

"I want to get a shower and head to bed anyway." She couldn't bring herself to look at Wyatt while she spoke. Maybe she was afraid that she wouldn't see the same powerful emotions that rioted inside her reflected in his face.

That would be devastating. Maybe this didn't mean as much to him, and maybe it didn't change anything for him. For her, it had been life-changing.

She moved. Wyatt's hands tightened on her waist, and she stopped without looking at him.

For a moment he didn't say anything, and she realized she was holding her breath.

"I'll be back shortly," he said in a scratchy voice.

Maybe he said that for Kayla's benefit.

It didn't matter.

If she reminded herself of that often enough, she might be able to believe it.

Forcing a smile, she looked up. "I'm first back, so I get to pick my spot." Kayla wouldn't know Harper was referring to the ongoing competition Wyatt and she had about who was sleeping on the floor.

Chuckling a little at the thought, she watched Wyatt's eyes crinkle. The concern in them faded away.

"I might have to eject you." Wyatt winked at her. His hands loosened and she walked away.

Chapter Twenty

Wyatt turned to Kayla, trying to keep the irritation off his face. Like his friends were conspiring against his campaign with Harper. They didn't even know about it. If they did know about it, they probably would try to undermine it, since Harper was apparently so different from any girl they expected to see him with.

There was a lot more to him than his friends on the slopes saw.

Harper, everything about her, worked for him. And the kiss they'd just shared more than confirmed that they would be perfect together as a couple. There was no better way to build a forever relationship than on the foundation of true friendship. Unfortunately, the more he saw her here, in Chile, the less he thought she'd be happy here. Not only did she not want to leave her home or family in Pennsylvania, but fitting in would be an uphill battle.

And he had no choice. His dad would accept no other alternative than Wyatt taking over the ski resort in Chile.

"Are you listening to me?" Kayla put one hand on her hip. The expression on her face was indistinct in the faint light, but irritation sounded plain in her voice.

"I wasn't. Sorry." Wyatt crossed his arms over his chest and tried to focus. His heartrate hadn't returned to normal, neither had anything else. It seemed like nothing would ever be normal again. His world had shifted. He hoped Harper's had, too. It seemed impossible to work their futures out together, but if what she felt was as powerful as what he felt, it would make sense to try.

"I'm sorry for not turning around right away. I knew almost immediately that you weren't behind me, but I was afraid of what I'd see." She hung her head. He uncrossed his arms and moved toward her. After taking a tremulous breath, she looked up again. "I know it was cowardly of me, but I really thought you'd gone over the edge. I didn't want to face that alone."

"It worked out. Don't worry about it." Wyatt put a hand on her shoulder and shook it gently. "Forget about it."

"I feel like I failed a test. I could have been brave. But instead, I ran." She hugged herself and rubbed her upper arms.

"I'd say that you'll probably do better next time."

"I hope so."

"I'd count on it." Wyatt dropped his hand. "Is that all you wanted?"

"Tell Harper I'm sorry?"

"Why don't you tell her yourself?"

"Not tonight. Maybe tomorrow."

"That's a great idea. Dad will probably want me out on the slopes with guests most of the day. Harper doesn't need to be entertained, but she probably wouldn't mind a friendly conversation."

"Okay." She turned to go, but looked back. "Thanks."

Wyatt turned on one foot, eager to go back to Harper. Did she feel the way he did? How should he act? Like nothing happened—which was a lie? Like everything happened—which was what it felt like and so much more.

He stopped short.

His dad stood in the doorway, hands in his pockets. "Do you have a minute, son?"

Wyatt's heart dropped like a downhill skier coming out of the gate. "Sure, Dad." He swiped a banana off the counter and followed David to the living room.

"Want a drink?" his dad asked, getting himself a glass of water from the wet bar in the corner and taking a sip.

"I'm good for now." Wyatt slowly peeled the banana. Even after the events of the day, he wasn't tired, but he didn't feel up to having a conversation with his dad.

"What happened tonight?"

He swallowed and shrugged. "We were racing home from the hot spring and I almost ran smack into the crevice along the trail."

His dad didn't seem overly alarmed. Wyatt would have been shocked if he had. After all, the danger was long past.

His dad nodded. "Wow. That's not like you. Was that girl with you?" It seemed like a passive-aggressive thing that his dad wouldn't use Harper's name. "Name's Harper, Dad." Wyatt held his dad's gaze. "She was. But she wasn't the reason I almost hit the crevice."

"Really?" The tone of that one word indicated his dad didn't believe it for a second.

Wyatt couldn't exonerate Harper without implicating Kayla. He stopped the words from coming out of his mouth.

"Yes. Really." That was the best he could do.

"I wanted to thank you for helping me today."

Wyatt finished chewing a mouthful of banana and was able to keep his mouth from falling open. His dad didn't usually thank him.

"No problem." He leaned one shoulder against the wall.

His dad paced to the window and looked out at the snow-covered landscape bathed in moonlight. "I'm really looking forward to you coming down full-time."

Wyatt took another bite and nodded, even though his dad couldn't see him.

His dad didn't turn around. "Sophia told me that girl helped her in the kitchen."

"Yeah." He squelched back his irritation at his dad's use of "that girl."

"Hmm." His dad drew the sound out. "She's a doctor?"

Harper got that all the time. "Her degree is in nutrition. She's not a medical doctor."

"I see." David took a drink of his water. "I wasn't too sure about her. She isn't the kind of girl I thought you would choose." He cleared his throat. "Actually, I'd hoped for a number of years that you would take a fancy to Kayla."

"She's great as a sister," Wyatt said cautiously. He hadn't expected the conversation to take *that* turn.

"Yeah, well, I certainly know love doesn't always flow the way we want it to."

Maybe his dad was thinking about his mom or possibly Sophia. Wyatt shrugged again. "True."

"We're having a reception tomorrow night."

"I know." Wyatt bit off the last of the banana.

"We've made it in honor of your engagement."

Nerves detonated in Wyatt's stomach, curdling the banana. "Really?"

His dad turned around and paced to the middle of the room, staring at the big fireplace beside Wyatt. "Yes. Sophia and I are committed to making Harper feel like she belongs here. We want her to feel welcomed. And our friends and employees will help us do that. There will probably be a hundred people here." His dad looked at him out of the corner of his eye. "I'm hoping we can convince you to have the wedding here. Soon."

Wyatt choked on his spit.

His dad paused for a second as though gathering his thoughts, then he plunged in again. "I want to offer her a job. We need someone to be in charge of the food down here and it seems like that girl is perfect."

"Harper."

"Right." His dad ran a hand over his bald head. "She can come back down with you in four weeks and start right away. Planning menus, cooking, taking care of special menu requests for allergies and diets and so on. We get a lot of that now. No need to wait until the wedding to start, although I assume you're not going to drag it out? The peak season guests would love to observe your wedding. Some of them come every year and are all but family."

Wyatt hadn't been expecting this and really didn't know what to say. A part of him wanted to be flattered, wanted to believe his dad wanted Harper and him down here because he liked them. But the other, more realistic part, he was afraid, whispered that his dad was angling for the business, as always. Trust his dad to turn his wedding into a marketing opportunity. Or at least keep from having to take any time off. Which was the least of his worries right now. This farce had morphed into something Wyatt wasn't sure he could handle.

He needed to tell his dad the truth. Panic curled in his chest, sharp and stinging.

But maybe he didn't. Maybe that kiss had changed things with Harper. Even as he thought that, he knew it couldn't have. It might have changed their friendship forever, but it hadn't changed the basis of what Harper was, which was a homebody. Someone who would never be happy away from her beloved farm and mountains, let alone in a different country.

Before he could open his mouth, his dad said, "I've closed the lift down for tomorrow night."

Wyatt's mouth dropped. His dad never closed the lift.

"Sophia and I talked about it this afternoon, and I posted signs so everyone would know. I also personally visited every guest. She has been working frantically to line up a caterer and has all housekeeping staff working overtime tomorrow to have the lodge cleaned and decorated. We knew we were working with time constraints."

Wyatt needed to stop this. He willed his mouth to open.

"I've invited everyone by personal phone call." His dad lowered his gaze. "Son, I'd like to celebrate your engagement and announce your wedding date tomorrow. I'd also like to announce that you and that girl will be coming down to stay."

"Dad, I really don't know. Harper and I haven't talked about what we're going to do."

"You told me you were coming down."

"Right. I'm planning on it. I just don't know…"

"You're extremely popular here. Especially with the younger crowd. The parents are getting older; we need to keep the young people interested. You help with that. People come here just to see you. Because of your snowboarding championships. Your reputation on the slopes and with extreme sports also helps."

Wyatt fingered his banana peel. His dad always talked in terms of the resort and what could be accomplished. He never said how he *felt*. How he felt about the son he didn't raise. In conversations like this, Wyatt could never shake the feeling that it wasn't him his dad loved so much, but rather it was the idea of his son working in his business, bringing in business.

He supposed it shouldn't matter. But somehow, it did.

"When you're here, business increases by fifty percent. I can tap into that tomorrow night, give people the heads up that you're going to be back, and that you'll be getting married here. Word will spread fast and we won't be able to contain the additional business."

"Well, Dad, there's something I should probably tell you..."

"Okay. But make it quick. Tomorrow's going to be a big day. My sister is flying down from Texas. I don't think you've ever met her and her husband."

Wyatt hadn't. His eyes widened and his mouth dropped. He was going to meet family. His mom and he had spent plenty of time here when he was growing up, but his dad had never been very interested in him. Not until he'd started winning those championships.

"All of our associates from the village are coming up. I did put it on Facebook, so some of your ski buddies might show up. I got a call from a couple who are down here to climb Aconcagua. And a group that spent the winter with you in Colorado, who are now in Europe, called." His dad tilted his head. "They were surprised to hear it. I guess you've been keeping it to yourself?"

Wyatt's chest seemed to cave in and he slumped into a chair. What in the world was he going to do? He'd lied to try to win the favor of his dad. He hadn't considered how difficult it was going to be when he told the truth. If he told the truth now, after his dad had gone through all this work, and talked to all these people, it would make his dad, and himself, look ridiculous.

He sighed. "Yeah. Something like that."

His dad stood. "Talk to that girl and see if you can't come up with a plan before tomorrow evening." He started to walk out of the room. "You *are* helping on the slopes tomorrow?"

"Yeah."

"Great. I'll give you the advanced class. They'll be here around ten. Starts at 10:30. Four hours." He glanced at his watch. "Two private snowboarding lessons after that. An hour each. I cancelled everything else. You can handle it?"

He'd wanted to spend a little time on the slopes with Harper. He supposed they could get up early and head out. Harper usually woke early anyway, but it was almost two a.m. And it sounded like tomorrow was going to be a long day. Unless he could talk to his dad...

"Yeah." He rubbed the back of his neck. "Um, Dad?"

His dad had set his water on the counter in the kitchen and had started down the hall. He stopped.

"Yes? Make it quick, son. It's late."

"I, well, Harper and I, our engagement..." Wyatt lapsed into silence, searching for words.

"We can talk about that tomorrow. I just need a date to give everyone." His dad turned and disappeared down the hall.

Frustrated with himself—why did it even matter what his dad thought, anyway—Wyatt threw his banana peel away, turned out the lights, and went to find Harper.

Tonight their easy friendship had become a lot more complicated. He didn't know what that meant, but he couldn't...no, he wouldn't, ask Harper to move to Chile for him. He'd have to figure out something to tell his dad. But he could ask her if those kisses had rocked her world the way it had rocked his. Right now.

WYATT KNOCKED LIGHTLY on their door. When he didn't hear anything, he tiptoed in. Harper had left the bathroom light on and the door cracked. In the faint light, the big blue and red square quilt he'd used since childhood lay smooth and flat over the pillows.

He cocked his head. No sound came from the bathroom. Closing the door behind him, he walked lightly to the other side of the bed.

Sure enough, Harper lay on the floor, snuggled up in the old olive green and puke yellow sleeping bag he'd loved and used all the time as a kid. He didn't even know where she'd found it.

"Harper?" he whispered softly. No answer.

In one tug, he pulled the blankets on the bed down, then scooted up between Harper and the bed.

There wasn't much room, but he managed to get his arms around her without waking her. He lifted her, turning and laying her on the bed. He tugged the comforter out from around her and had just started pulling up the covers when she said, "I thought if I pretended to be asleep, you'd let me have the floor."

He laughed softly. "It's a good thing I didn't strip down to my skivvies or prance around the room buck naked."

"I'd have closed my eyes," Harper said primly.

"I just bet you would have, Pickles."

A little smile teased her lips. He swallowed at the tightening of his throat. Man, he didn't want to lose this. But he needed to know.

"I wanted to talk to you about earlier."

"A lot of things happened earlier."

He couldn't read her face.

He supposed almost dying should have been top on his list, but somehow that had been eclipsed by kissing Harper. Maybe he ought to inquire about her physical welfare before he asked what he really wanted to know.

"Are you okay?"

"You've been asking me that all day. I said if I'm not okay, I'll tell you."

"So that's a yes?"

She grunted.

He put his hands in his pockets, but resisted the urge to pace. "I wanted to apologize about the crevice thing." His stomach bottomed out every time he thought about it. Man, he couldn't believe how close he'd been to killing Harper.

"I think you already did." There wasn't a trace of anger or malice in her tone. Like she'd expected him to pull through all along. Like they hadn't almost died. Guilt weighed heavy on him. She gave him way more credit than he deserved.

"Well, when you almost kill someone, I guess it doesn't hurt to apologize more than once."

"I guess." Her voice dropped.

"Are you tired?"

"Tired, but not sleepy." She sighed and shifted, adjusting the pillow under her head.

"Well, I kinda wanted to talk to you about something."

Man, he hated this. First his dad. Now Harper. He needed to just spit it out. This just proved that the kiss had changed things. At least for him. Before this, he could tell Harper anything.

"About Kayla?" Harper asked softly.

He'd forgotten she'd left the kitchen when Kayla came in.

"Nah. She just wanted to say she was sorry. She wanted me to apologize to you for her, too. But I told her to tell her yourself."

"Oh. The way you are carrying on, I thought it was something serious, like she did it on purpose or something."

"No. Nothing like that."

Harper was acting just like herself. Like they hadn't even kissed. Maybe she was not affected like he was.

"Well, what is it, then? You're acting odd, Wyatt."

"I'm just a little nervous." He couldn't keep his knees from shaking, his heart raced, and his voice kept wanting to go soprano on him. A little nervous. Ha. He couldn't remember being more nervous in his life.

"To talk to me?"

"No, about the subject matter." He willed himself to just come out and say it, but the words tangled on his tongue.

"What could possibly be making you this nervous?" Harper shifted on the bed, seeming to strain to see him better.

"Well, um..." Obviously, she wasn't affected.

"Yeah?"

"My parents are having a big party tomorrow. You know that. But I didn't realize how big. And they're making it an engagement announcement party. My dad's sister from Texas, whom I've never even met, is coming down for it. He said he was having over a hundred people here. He wants us to set a date, so he can announce that, too. I can't believe how far out of control this has gotten."

"Did you think about telling him the truth?"

"Constantly. But all I could think of was how upset he was going to be. Then, when I heard how many people he'd invited, and how much effort they're putting into this, well, I just couldn't. I tried. But I couldn't."

"I know what your dad thinks of you is important, but have you ever thought that maybe..."

"It's too important?" he finished for her. As always, Harper was right. "It's so hard to let go of that hope. I've had it since childhood."

"So you're nervous because you wanted to ask me to keep up the charade through the engagement party? Why? I already agreed to the pretend engagement." A tone of confusion ringed her voice.

He cleared his throat and sat on the bed next to her. "Well, this is going to be a big deal."

She slid over to make room for him. "I'm with you, Wyatt. If you want to admit the truth, if you want to keep up the pretense. Whatever."

Heaviness settled in his chest. He hated confrontations. Every trip with his mother back to the resort had ended with a middle-of-the-night screaming match between her and his dad. Like clockwork, the next morning, they'd pack and leave.

Because of his determination to keep life running smoothly, he'd messed things up with his dad, and he'd allowed this discussion with Harper to go off the rails. He needed to stop trying to keep the peace and start standing up for what he wanted. Unfortunately, what he wanted most was for everyone to get along. "I should just tell dad the truth, first thing in the morning."

Harper was silent. Her hands slipped out and found his in the darkness. Somehow that filled the silence between them so full of words he didn't know how to speak.

Finally, she said, "I know that would be hard. You don't want to disappoint him."

He stroked her fingers with his, loving how different they were. Soft. Small. Cool. "Yeah, and he's got the rest of our lives planned out."

Her hand tensed. "Huh?"

He breathed out, holding her hand like a lifeline. "He wants a wedding date, preferably for some time this ski season. He wants to offer you a job in the kitchen planning menus and stuff, and have you come down here to live when I move down. I mean, he was going on and on, and I just…"

"I get it. It feels like we're in too deep to get out."

"Exactly." And, part of the problem had to be that he really didn't want out.

He wanted it to be real.

Harper had been ecstatic when Wyatt had wanted to talk to her. She thought they were going to talk about The Kiss. That he was going to maybe even suggest they make their relationship real. More than friends. Like she had any idea of how they could work that out, but surely it was worth a try.

But her whole world had deflated when he'd admitted his nervousness had been because they had to keep pretending. Intensify their pretense. If the thought of continuing with their deception had been so fear-inducing, that kiss had the opposite reaction on him than it did her.

She wanted to get closer.

He wanted to run away.

She refused to think about the pain in her heart.

Right now, Wyatt needed her support. This thing with his dad had bothered him all his life.

"I just don't know how to get out of this."

"We could have a big fight. Break up at the party." She almost laughed. She'd never fought with Wyatt. Ever. She'd barely ever seen him even close to being angry.

"That might work." Wyatt lifted his head, his eyes moving back and forth as though he were going over scenarios in his mind.

Harper bit her lip and tried to push aside the hurt clawing at the back of her throat. It was a fake engagement. It would be a fake fight. A fake breakup.

He stood, as though he wanted to pace, but remained tethered to the bed by their linked hands. "If I act totally unreasonable and somehow put you in a position where you're saving face by breaking up with me."

"I don't want to make you look bad."

"I know. But I'll never see your dad again, and it doesn't matter what he thinks of me." Harper tried to keep her voice light.

Wyatt shifted. "That doesn't sit right."

"Maybe Steve or Carlos could play along, and I could be caught kissing them in the corner or something."

"No."

She wasn't sure if that made him angry, but relief filled her that he'd shot that idea down.

"So is this a practice fight for the real thing tomorrow?" She shouldn't have said that. It reminded her too much of the "practice" kiss.

"We're not fighting."

"You sounded angry."

He sat on the bed, cradling her hand in his. "I am not going to have you kissing some strange man just so I can save face with my dad. It would be better to tell him first."

"Okay, fine. You tell him tomorrow. But," Harper squeezed, "if you don't get him told by the time the party is half over, we'll figure out a fight to have, so we can break up."

"Deal. That should inspire me to stop being a wuss about this."

"You're not being a wuss. You care about your dad, and you want him to care about you."

"Thanks, Pickles."

"Hey, it's what you brought me down here for." She rolled over onto her side. A goodnight kiss was probably out of the question, considering Wyatt acted like The Kiss had never happened.

"You're earning your keep, that's for sure."

"We could fight about this whole bed thing."

"But you're going to be nice to me, for once, and just sleep in the bed."

"For once? You are so delusional. You owe me, big time, Wyatt."

He froze in the act of getting off the bed. He leaned over, placing a hand on either side of her head. Her stomach fluttered. She pushed the sensation aside. He didn't feel like that about her, and if she wanted to save their friendship, she couldn't let him know how she felt.

"I'm going to say something that I want you to forget by morning."

"Um, okay." She half-laughed.

"I had no idea you could kiss like that. Anytime you want to try it again, I'm in."

Harper's eyes had widened, feeling like they might pop out of their sockets. Her mouth hung open. Her tongue wouldn't work.

Wyatt straightened and walked into the bathroom. Harper blinked after him, all thoughts of being able to sleep tonight disappearing. She definitely wanted to kiss Wyatt again, but she could hardly believe he was serious. Wyatt was constantly joking. Maybe this was his way of laughing off their kiss.

Chapter Twenty-One

Wyatt was not in the room when Harper woke the next morning. Because the room was in the basement, and the windows were small and high, the morning sun didn't come in. She couldn't believe it was ten when she checked her phone.

There was a message from Jeff.

> Got some good news about this fall. Meet
> me ASAP?

Harper texted back that she could meet Tuesday. They were flying out Monday. His good news would have to wait until then.

She should be much more excited about "good news" from the university. Why wasn't she? She stopped brushing her teeth and stared at her face. It didn't look any different than yesterday. But man-o-day, she felt different.

Her skin seemed to glow and her eyes sparkled. After last night—the kiss, not the crevice—she could almost imagine a future with Wyatt. She definitely could imagine kissing him again.

"Harper?"

Harper's face pinched over her toothbrush. There was no reason for Kayla to be in her room.

She took the toothbrush out of her mouth and spit in the sink. "In here."

Thankfully, she'd made the bed before she changed her clothes. Someone, Wyatt, she assumed, had folded the comforter up and set it at the bottom of the bed along with his pillow.

"Hey." Kayla stuck her head in the door.

Harper finished rinsing her mouth out and spit into the sink. "Good morning." She met Kayla's dark eyes in the mirror before turning. "I'm sorry I slept in so late."

"It was a late night." Kayla's eyes skittered away. She fingered the ends of her shirt.

"And stressful." Harper laughed.

Kayla's shoulders went up as she took a deep breath. "I wanted to apologize for that."

"Wyatt said you didn't mean to."

She straightened. Harper got the feeling Kayla forced herself to meet Harper's gaze. "I should have gone back."

Harper's natural instinct was to forgive and sooth Kayla's conscience. She smiled. "Well, thankfully Wyatt got us out."

"I was just scared of what I'd see. I didn't want to go back by myself and have you two down there and nothing I could do."

"If we'd have gone down, I don't think it would have mattered."

"Well. I'm sorry."

"Hey, no hard feelings. I'll probably never snowmobile with you again, so nothing to worry about."

"Aren't you moving back here with Wyatt?"

Oops. "Uh, we haven't really talked about it much." That, at least, was the truth.

"Hmm." Kayla's brows furrowed, but she didn't question farther.

Harper hurried to change the subject. For some reason, living the farce for Wyatt didn't feel too much like she was lying, but saying things she knew to be untrue made her feel deceitful.

"Wyatt said there was going to be a party tonight." A hum that sounded like a sweeper moving sounded overhead. "Can I help?"

"I'm sure you can." Kayla smiled. Then her eyes clouded with uncertainly. "Are we good?" Her finger pointed between the two of them.

"Yes. We're fine." Harper smiled reassuringly. "As long as you give me a job and keep me busy so I feel like family and not like a third wheel."

"Come on. I'm sure they can use you in the kitchen."

Harper nodded and followed Kayla out of the bathroom.

SURPRISINGLY, Harper had a great time in the kitchen with Kayla and Sophia. She'd thought they hoped Wyatt dumped her, but at least now she figured they'd want it to happen in the nicest way possible.

She hated leaving before the work was done, but she wanted to look good for Wyatt tonight, so after the vegetables were chopped and the trays arranged, she thanked Sophia and went downstairs.

After going through three changes of clothes, she at last settled on the one skirt she brought that Wyatt had once said "looked cute"— whatever that meant. She stood in the bathroom, putting the finishing touches on her makeup, wondering if Wyatt was even going to make the party since she hadn't seen him all day, when she looked in the mirror and saw him standing in the open doorway. His face glowed, although there were slight lines around his eyes where his ski goggles had dug into his skin. His cheeks were rosy, even over his tan, and his shoulders broad in his long-sleeved shirt. He still wore snow pants.

Her hand froze. Her heart jumped. She forgot to breathe.

His lips tilted up, wobbling a little as though he were just as uncertain of the status of their relationship as she was.

He swallowed. "Hey." It came out rusty and soft.

"Hey yourself." She turned around.

"I couldn't stop thinking about you all day." His hands twisted his beanie cap, and he shifted his weight from one leg to the other.

She held up her bandaged finger, the product of allowing herself to be distracted by him while chopping vegetables. "I was thinking about you, too." Oh, if only he knew how she'd agonized over her deep desire to be home versus her knowledge that any chance she had of being with Wyatt would require her to move to Chile. Her thoughts had gone 'round and 'round all day, but in the end, she came to the same conclusion: if she wanted Wyatt, she would have to give up everything she worked for and leave her home and family.

Concern darkened his gaze. He stepped forward and took her hand in his, lowering his head and twisting her hand to see the bandage from all angles. "Are you okay?"

She nodded. Her stomach was a mass of curling nerves. This was Wyatt, her best friend. But he made her breathless.

He looked back into her eyes, keeping hold of her hand, his thumb slowly stroking.

"Man, Harper. I planned to play it cool and follow your lead. I didn't—don't want to ruin our friendship." He looked away and blew a breath out, taking another deep one, before looking back at her. He swallowed. "Please tell me that you weren't just thinking of me as your best friend. That it was more, that there's more between us than friendship."

As his eyes, sincere, pleading, bore into hers, she could only tell the truth. "I was thinking of that kiss. I wanted to do it again."

He closed his eyes and groaned softly. Then he dropped her hand and his arms stole around her. He rested his forehead on hers and whispered fiercely, "I've been waiting ten years to hear you say that."

Shock sprang through her body. Her breath puffed out. "What?"

His smile was self-effacing and he shook his head, his forehead rolling against hers. "I said, I've waited ten years to hear you say that."

She blinked rapidly, trying to comprehend what he had just said. "I had no idea."

"It's the only thing I've ever been able to keep from you."

"Why? Why would you have kept it from me?"

He pulled his head back and cupped her cheeks with his large hands. "Because you weren't interested. All you saw when you looked at me were elbows and feet."

"That's true at first..."

"Then I was just your step-cousin and we had fun together."

"True..."

"To be fair, though, you were too wrapped up in your books and studying to make time for romance."

With that statement, reality crashed down on her. Tenure, the university, his dad. They were headed in completely different directions. There was no way to work their future out.

With the party due to start any minute, they didn't have time to discuss it. "Are you going to kiss me?"

His square jaw split into a grin. He jerked his head up. "Say it again."

"Dang it, Wyatt. Kiss me."

"My pleasure," he murmured before his head descended. Their lips met, just as sweet, just as explosive as the first time.

When he lifted his head, a long time later, their breaths came in pants. Their eyes met, and they grinned at each other.

"I could gladly stand right here and do that all night long," she said.

Wyatt ran a hand down her cheek and along her jawline. Her breath hitched. She pushed her face into his hand, loving the contact.

"But I'd better get out of here because there's a party in your honor that is supposed to start any minute, and a lot of people have worked all day to make it very nice." Somehow, Harper's hands had gotten under Wyatt's shirt and she skimmed her palms up and down his back, learning the hard ridges and dips. "Much as I would like to stay here, too." She couldn't believe she'd misread Wyatt for so long. Ten years.

He sighed and ran a hand over his face. "I never got a chance to say anything to my dad."

"So we have to stage a fight?" At the idea of fighting in front of a roomful of people, fear tried to shove its clinging tentacles between them, but she held Wyatt tighter.

"Yeah. I don't know how. I don't want you looking bad. I guess if an opportunity presents itself..." His voice trailed off and he shrugged. Then his eyes narrowed and he met her gaze again. "We need to have a conversation about where this is going." He jerked his chin, indicating the two of them.

"Well, tonight after the party, or we're travelling all day tomorrow, going home. We could do it then."

"Sometime. I'm not asking you to come here."

"And I'm not asking you to stay in Pennsylvania."

He grunted. "It might be a short conversation."

That was it. No need to talk about it anymore. Still. "Let's not ruin tonight with tomorrow's problems."

His eyes crinkled. "It's your brain that's always been so appealing to me."

"Yeah, that's what everyone says." She rolled her eyes. "Hurry up and get ready, before they come looking for us." She slipped out of his arms, and out of the bathroom, shutting the door behind her.

WYATT STOOD in the great room, holding a glass of water. Icicle lights drooped from the ceiling, and a cheerful fire crackled in the huge stone fireplace. Low-hanging, rustic chandeliers added to the ambience. People mingled and talked, some attired in classic eveningwear, but most dressed in casual, but expensive, mountain wear.

He'd been at parties here before, but somehow everything seemed different tonight. Maybe because this one was in honor of him and his girl.

Harper fit right in with the soft brown leather skirt she wore. It was his favorite. He loved how it twirled around her legs, mid-calf, playing peekaboo with the tops of her brown boots. The rich, forest green shirt brought out the green in her gray eyes, and her hair, which was normally in a ponytail, lay down her back in a slick, shiny curtain. He wanted to spend the evening staring at her. He also wanted to run his hands through her hair.

But he was expected to be the perfect son, mingling, talking, making people feel comfortable and entertaining them with stories from his travels and adventures.

On one hand, he was trying to make the party go by without a hitch, on the other, he constantly searched for an opportunity to pretend to have a fight with Harper. Not that he wanted to.

What he wanted to do was sit on the couch with her snuggled next to him and bask in the feeling that she finally, finally saw him as more than a friend. He also wanted to hash their future out, to see what kind of compromise they could work out. Harper hadn't said anything, but he knew she was homesick, had been since they drove away from the farm. She longed for home, and he wasn't sure she would be willing to leave it. It wouldn't be right for him to ask her to. Maybe she would offer.

"She's glowing." Sophia glided up to him, lifting a brow in Harper's direction.

He allowed his eyes to linger where they wanted. "Yeah."

"That near-death experience was good for your relationship. When you two first showed up, you were missing that spark of awareness. But now, you definitely look like a man besotted. And she like a woman in love."

Wyatt stilled.

It seemed impossible, after all the years of waiting and hoping, that Harper could be in love with him. It was what he'd always wanted. Even though he knew a relationship could not happen, it still thrilled him to think that the woman he'd loved for more than a decade might return his feelings. Sophia glanced at the large clock on the wall. He followed her gaze. It was almost nine.

"Your father wanted to say a few words. Maybe you can steal Harper away from our neighbors and make your way to the fireplace. That's where he was planning on speaking."

"Sure."

Wyatt took another sip of his water and moved through the crowd. Nerves balled in his stomach. He should have talked with his dad before this. There really hadn't been time; they'd been busy with guests all day. And the idea of admitting he'd lied was repugnant.

He shouldn't have lied to begin with.

He reached Harper's side and slipped an arm around her waist, focusing on her warmth and softness, and on how good it was to finally be able to allow everything he felt for her to show on his face. No more worries about ruining their friendship.

At least for now. At some point, they would have to make some hard choices if they couldn't find a compromise. He still couldn't see one. The thought made him clench his jaw. He deliberately loosened the muscles. It wasn't something he was going to think about tonight.

Harper looked up into his face. Her smile lit the room and he allowed his gaze to linger on her face before looking at Mr. and Mrs. Reegana, an older couple who lived in the village. "Excuse me, but I need to steal Harper away for a few minutes."

Mrs. Reegana winked at him. "Only for a few minutes."

Mr. Reegana said, "She's a nice girl. You did well, son. It's good to have you coming back. You breathe life into this place."

"Thanks." Wyatt exchanged a few more pleasantries with them before tugging on Harper's waist and leading her away.

"Dad is going to say a few words, and he wants us standing with him."

"So, it's a good time to pick a fight?"

"Yeah. I haven't been able to think of anything to fight over."

Harper looked around the room. She had always played by the rules, colored in the lines, and hated causing problems. But she hadn't balked at him asking her to fight. With him. In public.

A surge of feeling swept through him, swirling up and warming him from the inside out. Everything she'd done for the last two days had been for him. He couldn't describe how that made him feel.

Beside him, Harper slid the emerald ring off her finger. "Here." She held it out to him. "Take this so I'm not tempted to throw it at you in the heat of the moment."

He laughed, but took the ring, slipping it into his pocket. Harper would never let him keep it, and he wouldn't want to, except it felt like he had a piece of her. He'd love to get a chain and put the ring around his neck where it could hang close to his heart.

They met his dad at the fireplace. Wyatt thought to have a few private words first, but his dad held a glass aloft and tapped it with a spoon.

"I'd like everyone's attention for just a few moments," his dad said loudly.

The hum of conversation faded away.

The fire crackled behind them. His dad surveyed the room.

"Friends. Family. Neighbors. Guests. Thank you so much for

coming tonight to celebrate the engagement of my son." He stopped speaking and looked at Wyatt, giving him almost a proud look. "Most of you have seen him grow up."

Wyatt didn't allow his smile to slip. People seeing him grow up was a bit of an exaggeration. Wyatt had visited from time to time, but it wasn't like he'd lived here growing up.

"So we thought it only fitting to invite you here tonight so you can celebrate with us." His dad turned to him. "Have you decided on a date?"

"Not yet." Wyatt kept his forced smile as he looked at his dad, then out over the crowd, giving a little shrug.

"Then I propose Saturday, August 31st. Here, in this very spot. Anyone here who would like to come is welcome. And, rest assured, Wyatt is planning on living here with his new bride. They will both be working at the resort and continuing the family operation."

"Wait," Harper said. She turned to Wyatt with big eyes. "We're living here?"

A little smile threatened to ruin the impression she gave as she crossed her arms over her chest. It signaled to Wyatt that this was their "fight." She flattened her lips in apparent displeasure and the tilt to her lips disappeared.

He dropped his hand from around her waist. "Of course. We're both needed here at the resort."

A murmur went through the crowd.

Out of the corner of his eye, he could see his dad glower.

Harper threw one hand out. "I've got a life in Pennsylvania. I can't just drop it."

"You're not dropping it. That date is two months away. Plenty of time for you to wrap up loose ends." A titter came from the crowd. He gave what he hoped was an appeasing smile.

His dad crossed his arms over his chest.

Harper stomped a foot and widened her eyes. "I don't want to wrap up anything! I've got a research position waiting for me, and tenure at the university." She turned to face him, moving her back to the crowd.

The room faded away. Wyatt concentrated on Harper. "Oh, no.

We're not talking about the university again? All you do is talk about tenure and research."

"So?"

Wyatt racked his brain for fighting words. "So, you know what happened with the garbage can, the hard apple cider, and the mini bulldozer."

Her eyes clearly said she had absolutely no idea what he was talking about. Neither did he to be honest, since he was totally making it up. But she gamely played along.

"Don't you even bring that up again. Especially not in front of all these people because I really don't think that you want them to hear the story of you and the shaving cream and the dinosaur model." She folded her arms across her chest. Her look said, "Top that."

"Well, at least I didn't steal your underwear for a school project."

Her lips twitched. She spoke louder. "Are you still bitter about that? You never wore them anyway."

Oh, yeah. He was much better at this than he was at trying to insult Harper. He just had to remember to keep a straight face. "How do you know? And, hello, I have every right to be bitter since you put them on a pumpkin."

"It was the best dressed pumpkin at the Homecoming bazaar. I won first place." Harper tapped her foot, her mouth twitched in time with it.

Wyatt bit the insides of his cheeks. "Everyone in the crowd knew they were my underwear."

"No, they didn't."

"You put my name on them in black permanent marker." He pointed a finger at her. "You should have used your own underwear."

Harper put her pert little nose in the air. "They were perfect—with those little smiling jack-o-lanterns. Really, you should be thanking me."

"Because my underwear made the front page of the local paper?"

"They were above the fold. In color." Harper could contain herself no longer and she laughed. Which made Wyatt laugh. She laid her head on his chest and wiped at her eyes. He stroked down her hair, like he'd wanted to do all night and pulled her closer.

Their guests, most of them with big smiles on their faces, some outright laughing, and his dad, had been watching with curiosity. Now, the murmur of conversation started back up.

His dad turned and addressed the crowd, saying something about "talking with the lovebirds." But Wyatt didn't pay attention.

He spoke low to Harper. "I'm sorry."

"No. I'm sorry," she said softly when she finally caught her breath.

"It's my fault. I didn't follow the script," he whispered in her ear.

She shook her head. "There was no script."

"True, but I kind of veered off topic with the whole underwear thing."

"I think I brought it up," Harper said with a lifted brow as though she were asking if he wanted to try another fight.

"I'll just have to bite the bullet." He glanced up to see his dad had finished talking and had his arms across his chest, scowling at them. "Now would probably be a good time."

"I'll stay here beside you."

Wyatt flattened his lips. "That's tempting. But I got myself into this without your help. I'd better fix it the same way."

Harper shook her head. "I'll stay."

Confidence surged through him. They smiled at each other. Then Wyatt bent and gently pressed his lips to hers.

A cheer went up from the crowd. Wyatt lifted his head. Harper's cheeks brightened.

"Kinda forgot about our audience," Wyatt said.

"Me too." Harper squeezed his hand.

The crowd dissipated. Wyatt waited until the hum of conversation had grown loud again before he glanced toward his dad who still glowered at him. With dread weighing his feet, he stepped toward his dad. Harper held tightly to his hand.

"Sorry about that." Wyatt said.

His dad's face didn't change. "I'm not sure what that was."

Wyatt pulled himself up to his full height. "That was me being a coward."

Lines appeared in his dad's forehead. He tilted his head. "What are you saying?"

Wyatt swallowed. He needed to face this the same way he'd face a challenging ski course. Or a difficult mountain to climb. Head on.

He stuck his chin out. "I lied about being engaged."

A gasp sounded beside him. He looked over. Sophia and Kayla stood slightly beside and behind him. Sophia had her hand over her mouth, her eyes wide. Kayla's were narrowed. She looked almost angry.

"You lied?" his dad repeated, low and slow.

"Yeah."

"Why?" Sophia cried softly as she came up beside him.

"You can't tell me that you and Harper aren't a couple." Kayla took a step closer, her hands on her hips. Her eyes shifted between Harper and him.

"We weren't." Wyatt didn't want to have to explain that on top of everything else. He tried to move the topic back. "I knew dad wanted me here."

"This is where you belong," his dad said.

"I know," he said, only partly to appease his dad. Mostly because he knew it to be true. "But Uncle Fink has been recovering from a bad bacterial infection."

A muscle in his dad's jaw worked in and out. It throbbed in time with the vein that stood out on his forehead.

Wyatt spoke to Sophia. "Dad always gets upset when he thinks I'm spending too much time on the farm in Pennsylvania, and I knew that if I told him that Uncle Fink needed me for the summer, he'd be angry. I thought it'd be easier to say that I was engaged and I wanted to stay home to be with my girl."

"You were afraid," his dad growled.

"I wanted to help Uncle Fink. And I wanted to keep the peace."

"I don't know why you'd think that you should help on that farm. It's not yours. Not like this resort." His dad threw his arm out, indicating everything around them.

Wyatt leveled his gaze at his dad. He opened his mouth and words that he'd wanted to say, but hadn't, for ten years fell out. "Uncle Fink took me in when you didn't want to be bothered with me."

His dad's jaw set. "I was busy building our future."

"I'm sorry for needing a father at an inconvenient time."

His dad had the grace to look slightly abashed. Wyatt's heart softened. No one could change the past, but the future was wide open. Still, now wasn't the time to fight about it. Not with a houseful of people. And his dad might never change. That was a part of love—accepting the person his dad was, imperfections and all. Because, deep down, he was sure his father loved him. He just expressed that love through money. That's all some people were capable of. It wasn't Wyatt's place to change him. It was only his place to love him.

"That still doesn't explain you and Harper. You two are in love." Sophia stepped to David's side and slipped an arm around him. She smiled gently at Harper. Wyatt wanted to look at Harper's face to see what she thought of that statement, but he resisted.

"We're not engaged. She's a friend—"

"What I'm trying to find out," Sophia interrupted, "is what the status of your relationship is. Maybe there is an actual possibility of Harper coming here? Of you two getting married?"

Wyatt wished there were. If only, if only, if only. But wishing didn't make it so.

"No."

Sophia's lips pressed together, but she didn't argue.

"I'm coming down here."

Harper finally spoke. "I have a job in Pennsylvania. A research position. The university is voting on my tenure later this summer."

Wyatt nodded. Hearing it from her lips was harder than he'd thought. "It would be the height of selfishness for me to ask her to give that all up." If only she would. As little as he knew about relationships, he realized that if she were to come to Chile, she had to do it because she wanted to. Not because he asked. He was afraid that noble idea wouldn't keep him from asking, begging, really.

"But look at what you have here." His dad spread his arm out again. Like the resort was the only thing that mattered. "Look at what she'd gain by choosing you."

Wyatt shrugged. It would have to be her choice. "For some people it's not about the money and the bling." Harper squeezed his hand. And a glimmer of why the farm in Pennsylvania felt like home tickled through his brain. There wasn't a lot of money there. But there was a lot of love. Some things were worth more than money. More than success in business.

"So, basically you're saying that you aren't engaged, and Harper won't be coming down here with you?" Sophia glanced at Kayla, who had her arms crossed over her chest and her lips pressed together in a flat line.

"Yeah. Basically."

"So this is no longer an engagement party?" his dad asked.

Guilt pinched Wyatt's chest. He put his hands in his pockets and shuffled his feet. "No. I'm sorry I lied. I'm sorry I didn't tell you the truth to begin with. I hope I never do anything like that again."

Sophia nudged David.

He looked away before saying, "It's okay, son."

That must be his dad's way of saying he was forgiven. He was surprised it was that easy, but Sophia's presence had a way of mellowing his dad's rough edges.

Wyatt figured he'd better be completely honest. "I do want to wait until Uncle Fink comes home, just to make sure he's okay. Then I'll be down. Two weeks, maybe."

His dad ground his teeth together.

Sophia elbowed him again. "You have to be okay with that, David. It's fear of your reaction that caused him to lie in the first place."

"No. It was a lack of character on my part that caused me to lie. I can't guarantee that I've magically grown character overnight, but I hope I've at least started the process. No matter what Dad's reaction is, I need to be man enough to tell the truth."

"That's impressive, son." He glanced at Sophia as though checking to be sure he was saying the right thing. "I'm still expecting you to come here permanently as soon as Fink is better."

"I'm expecting that, too."

Sophia spoke low, looking from one to the other. "Maybe you and Harper could continue to be engaged—after all this is an engagement party—until after you leave Monday."

Wyatt didn't say anything. He was tired of the lies.

Sophia smiled appealingly at him. "It will allow your dad to save face tonight. We'll just let the news of your breakup trickle out naturally when you come down to stay."

"I think that's a good idea, Wyatt." Harper nudged him with her shoulder.

His dad cleared his throat. "Great. Now, there's a lot of people here to talk to. Even if you're not engaged. And there's a lot of food to eat. We've got a party going on. Let's go enjoy it."

Wyatt nodded, then looked around for Harper. He felt like a bowling ball had been removed from his body. The decorations looked brighter, the people around him happier. And, for himself, he was eager to move on. With Harper.

Chapter Twenty-Two

Harper rolled over and squinted out the small window of her comforting bedroom.

Back on the farm. She closed her eyes and sank down into her pillow and comforter. Yesterday had gone by in a blur. Their flight had been delayed, they missed their connection in Houston, and a serious case of, if not jet lag at least climate readjustment, had left her still feeling drained. She couldn't even remember what time it was when they finally stumbled home. Four a.m.

Wyatt and she had seen plenty of unhappy, tired, and grumpy people yesterday. That even described them. But after their failed fight at the pseudo-engagement party, Wyatt's personality and hers seemed to be synchronized.

Whatever it was, they hadn't fought, despite the travel nightmares. They hadn't talked, either. At least not about their relationship, its status, or how it would end.

Harper opened an eye and peeked at the clock. Noon. She threw the blankets off and took another look at the beautiful day already half over outside her window.

She couldn't believe a weekend was all she'd been gone. So much had happened.

A hard, rhythmic rap sounded on her front door. Wyatt always knocked the same way.

"Come in," she shouted while shuffling to the dresser to at least run a brush through her hair. Nerves shot through her at the thought of him seeing her with a bed head.

"Why isn't this door locked?" he said from the living room.

"I never lock it." She snapped the ponytail band in place. Wyatt had seen her a million times in her ratty sweatshirt and jammie pants, but as she glanced at the bedroom door that hung open she wished she had made him wait out on the porch while she changed.

His head popped in the crack. "Anyone could walk in on you."

"They'd have to find the farm first." She tugged at her shirt and walked to her door. "Why would they want to, anyway?"

"There are serial killers walking around all over the place."

"That's ridiculous."

"It's true."

"It's not." She tilted her head. "Have we reversed roles?" She was the one that was usually uptight. He was not supposed to care whether the doors were locked or not. Her eyes roved over his muscle shirt and work jeans, and a little flame burst to life in her breast. Wyatt could possibly be a responsible parent.

One side of his mouth tugged up in the lopsided grin she loved. "Guess so." A bit of uncertainty clouded his features. "We were both barely awake last night when we got home. I don't think I kissed you goodnight."

Pushing away the uncertainty of their relationship, she smiled, and it felt like flirting. "Kiss me now."

His grin widened and he closed the space between them. She couldn't think while he kissed her, but after their lips parted and she laid her head on his chest, she whispered, "What are we going to do?"

He grunted. "About what? Us? Your job? My dad?" A half-laugh escaped from his lips. "There's so much stuff between us, I don't even know where to start."

Her job. Harper jerked back. Crap.

"I forgot!" She couldn't decide what to do first. A shower. Clothes.

Food. Scratch food. "I was supposed to meet Jeff for lunch today. He said he had news about this fall."

She put her hands on her head. "I'm never going to make it on time." Biting her lips and refusing to cry, she flew by Wyatt. Stopping short, she backed up and wrapped her arms around him in a quick hug. "I'm sorry. I didn't mean to go off like a firecracker."

"That is kinda what you looked like." His large hands stroked down her back, infusing calm. "I'll start your car and bring it to the door. You get ready." He took her chin in his fingers and tilted it up. "Okay?"

She nodded. "I'm sorry to leave you with all the catch-up farm work."

"Don't worry about it. Whatever I don't get done today will be waiting tomorrow."

The panic that had burst inside her chest faded. Rational thought returned. She needed her phone to text Jeff that she was running late. Then she needed to get ready, and Wyatt would take care of the farm work for today.

She stepped back and looked into Wyatt's eyes. "Thank you."

He moved forward, sliding his hand over her hair. After a brief pause, he lowered his head and tenderly touched her lips with his.

"Thank me later." He winked before striding out the door.

Harper stood with her fingers on her lips, staring at the door. She couldn't wipe the bemused smile from her face.

Remembering her lunch, she burst into action.

Thirty minutes later, Harper grabbed her purse and walked out. She'd put off the position she'd been offered this summer, she couldn't afford to lose the one for this fall. Not if she wanted that tenure vote to swing her way. Which, of course, she did. Unless she moved to Chile.

That thought came out of the blue. It startled her. She had no intentions of ever moving to Chile. At least she didn't think she did.

She'd had fun in Chile. If she were working with the menus and meals, she'd be somewhat using her degree. It wasn't the same as the farm, but if Wyatt were there... Still, she was so inept. Surely Wyatt would get tired of her incompetence. Frustrated with her complete lack of athletic ability. She could work her butt off to learn to ski, but she'd never be a natural. As for snowmobiling, well, she had to admit, she wasn't exactly longing to go for another ride.

Kayla's face popped into her head. Her life and zest for adventure. They matched Wyatt's. Harper would hold him back. Her gaze dropped to the floor and she kicked at the carpet with her toe. It was selfish to take Wyatt for herself when what he really needed was someone who could offer him more adventure and fun. Someone who matched his abilities and would challenge him in a good way. Someone who loved the life he loved. The right thing would be to let Wyatt go.

Chapter Twenty-Three

"We're packing up. We'll be home in a few days."

"They're finally letting you come home Uncle Fink?" Wyatt lay on his back in the apple orchard. After her meeting, Harper had needed to make a trip to the library. He'd come down to check the apples, but it'd been so nice, he'd stayed for a nap. Then Uncle Fink had called.

"Yeah. We need to either come home or start paying property taxes."

A soft breeze rustled the tall grass around him. He'd need to mow it before he left. The Summer Rambos would be ready to pick soon.

The scent of corn pollen hung, thick and heavy, in the air. Such a summery smell.

He focused on the conversation. "I hope you're not pushing it too hard. You don't want to relapse. That won't help anyone."

"Don't you want us back?" Fink said with a tease in his usually serious voice. "I'd think you'd have itchy feet by now."

A cloud shaped like a dragon floated lazily in the blue sky. He'd probably better give his uncle a hint. It wasn't the semi-relationship with Harper he'd have trouble with. It was the fact that it couldn't be permanent, not with him leaving and Harper staying, and the chance they took that things might never be the same for their mixed family.

He put a hand behind his head and studied the mountain rising beyond the river. He opened his mouth to tell his uncle he was in a relationship with his wife's daughter, but that's not what came out. "Do you own all of that mountain beyond the apple orchard?"

"All but the part that the tunnel goes through."

"How many acres?"

"I think it's around a thousand or so. It borders state game land on both sides. Why?"

"Just lying here in the apple orchard, looking at it." He thought of the old permit on the desk Harper and he had found when they were looking for the envelope with the passwords in it. A crazy idea popped into his brain. Too crazy. Even for him.

"I'm dating Harper." There. Now it was out.

The line stayed silent.

His relief turned to concern.

Wyatt breathed deeply, closing his eyes. Waiting on his uncle to pronounce his fate.

"I always thought you two would be good together." Fink cleared his throat and lowered his voice. "But how, exactly, is that going to work out? Did you decide to not go to Chile?"

"No."

"She's going with you?" Fink's voice hitched up an octave.

"No."

Again, that ominous silence. "I kinda thought you had a little more respect for Harper than to let her be a summer fling."

"I do." Even as he said the words, guilt punched him in the gut. That's what the relationship he had with Harper amounted to—a summer fling. It sounded so cheap when his uncle said it.

"Then what does this look like long-term?"

Fink had been like a father to him, but he'd also been like a father to Harper, whose real dad had died when she was young. This was Harper's dad talking to him now.

He couldn't lie. "It looks like nothing long-term."

"I'm disappointed in you, son."

There wasn't really a defense, but he had to give one anyway. "I'm not sleeping with her. We're just hanging out."

"Then you're going to walk away."

He put an arm over his eyes, like he could block out the truth. But it was still there. "Yeah. My dad's expecting me to fall into the family business. I have to go."

"Well, you're both adults, and Harper's always had a good head on her shoulders." He paused and Wyatt braced himself. "But she already has a tendency to hide herself away. Being hurt by you is not going to do her any favors. Not to mention my wife is not going to be happy to watch that play out."

Fink's words made Wyatt feel lower than an oil well. "I'm sorry. It seemed like a good idea at the time, but I should have talked with you first." He knew Harper would be hurt when he left. Heck, he was going to be hurt when he left. But somehow, it had all seemed worth it at the time. "I've just had the biggest crush on her since I met her, and she finally looked at me like..."

"Like a man instead of a kid brother?"

"Yeah." The look on her face as she told him he was handsome meant everything to him. The same look said she respected him. That he made her laugh. It was the kind of look that could make a man move mountains just to see it again. There wasn't anything he *wouldn't* do for Harper. But there were a few things he *couldn't* do. Like stay here.

"Did you talk to your dad?" Fink asked.

Wyatt bent his knees and planted his feet. The dragon cloud had morphed into a peeled banana. He hoped it wasn't some sort of sign. "He's expecting me to come down there to stay."

"Did you tell him you didn't want to?" Fink asked.

He blew out a breath. "I don't think it matters."

"So, you didn't?" he asked.

Wyatt pulled a blade of grass out beside him. He answered before sticking it in his mouth. "No."

"Why don't you call and talk to him about it?"

He chewed on the grass stem. "It wouldn't do any good."

"Are you hoping Harper will change her mind and go with you?" Suspicion gave Fink's voice a sharper edge.

Wyatt sat up and spit the grass out of his mouth. "I would never ask her to do that."

"I'm glad. She's spent a lot of years building a life here. One that will work for her."

"I know."

Fink's voice lowered. "I could talk to her, though. If you want me to."

Wyatt's mouth fell open. His heart hammered against his ribcage and he struggled to get the words out. "You'd ask her to go to Chile with me?" He didn't want Fink to do that.

"I could feel her out and see if she's even considering it." He could almost see Fink running the repercussions over in his analytical brain. "That'd be hard on Ellie, though."

"Yeah, I know. And Harper is such a homebody. Even if she agreed to go, she wouldn't be happy down there."

"I suspect you're right, son."

He stood and tossed down the blade of grass. "I just wanted a little time with her. I knew it couldn't last. I just couldn't pass it up."

"I understand. Not saying it's good or right, but sometimes you want something so bad, a little bit is better than nothing at all."

His stomach lay against his backbone like a lead brick. "Yeah. That's how I feel about Harper."

"She must feel the same way about you, son."

Leave it to Fink to point out the obvious thing he'd not thought about. "She must."

"Well, we'll be back soon. What's done is done."

He swiped his phone off just in time to hear Avery calling his name.

"Over here."

"Oh, my gosh. Wyatt." She hurried toward him, her fancy cat strapped to her front, its tuft of hair bouncing with every step she took. "The worst thing ever has happened. I just don't know what we're going to do!"

Wyatt stood.

Avery bounced to a stop in front of him. She hadn't quite been a Godsend when it came to working on the farm, but she worked harder than anyone he knew and had latched onto it with a fierce loyalty that he respected. It wasn't her fault she didn't know which end of a rake was up.

He brushed his jeans off. "What happened?"

"I just checked the pumpkins." Avery gulped in several lungfuls of air. Her eyes got big and she stretched her hands out. "They're green!"

Wyatt blinked. He wasn't quite sure what he was supposed to say to that.

"What are we going to do?" She hopped a little on her feet. Her concern was sincere, but completely unfounded. Wyatt considered how to tell her.

Before he could open his mouth, she spoke again. "I'm not blaming you. I know with Fink being gone everything just got dumped in your lap, and maybe he even ordered the wrong ones, for all I know. Do those packages have pictures? Maybe it was false advertising. I'm just not sure. Whatever happened, it's happened, and all we can do now is try to fix it the best we can. After all, people don't buy green pumpkins. I've never even seen them in the store. This must be a fluke kind that people in some other country must like or buy or something. But we need orange pumpkins. People won't pay money for any other color. Well, maybe white…"

She kept babbling on.

He had to set her straight. This wasn't the problem she thought it was. But she wouldn't quit talking. Finally, Wyatt interrupted her with one word. "Paint."

Her eyes snapped to his. Her hands flew to her cheeks. She paused for just a moment. "You're right. You're right. Of course. Why didn't I think of that? I can paint. We'll get orange paint and we have time. We'll just paint the whole darn field." She nodded at Wyatt, still muttering to herself as she turned and walked away.

He would stop her before she started painting the pumpkins. Of course.

He rubbed his chin. He'd been worried about Fink and Ellie and the boys. Harper would be worried, too. But Avery, as much as she needed to learn, might be the best thing that happened to the farm all summer. If she was willing to paint five acres of pumpkins orange just to be able to pay the taxes, she might be willing to stay around. If she were willing to stay, someone else might be willing to go.

Chapter Twenty-Four

"Do you think this is going to be confusing for the boys?" Harper sat beside Wyatt on the porch step, her warm body pressed against his from hip to shoulder.

He contemplated the empty driveway. Fink and Ellie and the boys would be coming home any time.

"It probably could be." He put his arm around her and she laid her head on his shoulder. "But I'd rather not do any more pretending, if that's okay with you."

She laughed. He'd figured she would after the debacle of the lie he'd told his dad. Still, nerves pinged in his stomach. Fink knew, and Wyatt assumed he'd told Ellie. He had no idea what Ellie would think.

He ran his hand up and down Harper's arm, enjoying the evening birdsong and the easing of the humidity that had plagued them all day.

They sat in silence for a half an hour until Fink and Ellie's van pulled in. With its arrival, Wyatt would have to face his girl's mother, knowing that he wasn't offering Harper anything more than a few more days with him.

Boys tumbled out of the sliding doors as the vehicle pulled to a stop. Wyatt and Harper stood. Dan, the oldest at eight, ran to them, grabbing them both in a big hug. Bert and Kent piled on behind him, yelling their names and talking over each other so fast and loud it was impossible to understand anyone.

Wyatt kept one arm behind Harper to steady her.

Ellie's eyes took in the picture as she got out of the driver's side—her boys, her daughter...and him. She met his gaze. His stomach puckered.

Her lips turned up. Her eyes crinkled at the corners.

Harper's arm slipped around his waist.

Ellie's eyes dropped to his waist, then slid back up. She tilted her head, and her look softened, radiating love.

Wyatt felt humbled as he'd never before in his life. He'd thought she might be angry. Or resentful at the very least. He hadn't expected acceptance, yet alone warm affection.

Ellie broke the spell when she turned and shut her door, walking around the van to help Fink get out.

Wyatt squeezed Harper's shoulder. As the boys continued to clamor and talk, he spoke in her ear. "I think your mom's okay with us."

She stood on tiptoe and whispered back, "She's always loved you."

"KNOCK, KNOCK," Ellie called through the screen door of Harper's apartment.

"Come on in, Mom," Harper answered from the kitchen. She dropped a tea bag into each of the two mugs of hot water on the counter.

Ellie opened the door and walked in.

"Sit down on the couch. I'll be right in." Harper put cream but no sugar in her mom's cup and carried the tea into the room.

"Here you go." She handed the cup to her mom. "Wow, the boys were wound up when you got here."

"Yeah. That's a long drive." Ellie took a tentative sip. "But they're finally out for the night. And Fink is sitting at the table with his leg propped up, talking to Wyatt."

"Ah, that's why you texted me. You needed to get away from the man-talk."

Ellie glanced at her over her cup. "Well, they were talking about women."

Harper wrinkled her nose. "Even worse."

"So, I thought maybe we should talk about men."

"Not men." Harper couldn't contain her smile, even though her heart hurt since their separation loomed. "Man."

Ellie set her cup down along with any pretense that she had arrived to talk about anything else. "Oh, Harper. Wyatt's the best man I know. And I love him like a son. I'd love nothing more than to see you together. I just wish it wasn't so impossible...unless you've decided to go to Chile with him?"

Harper shook her head.

"He's staying here?"

"I won't go, he won't stay..."

"Why can't he stay?"

Harper pinched the bridge of her nose. "You'd understand if you went to Chile and saw it. His dad is dead-set on him helping. I mean, Wyatt had barely set foot on the place, and his dad had him out working, teaching classes, interacting with guests. Plus, Wyatt loves everything about it. He glows when he's there."

She stared over her mother's shoulder. Wyatt had never actually said he wanted to go, but Harper knew him better than most people, and she knew he loved it. Maybe he wished his dad's resort wasn't in Chile, but he loved the resort itself.

"Don't you think you could be happy there?" Her mom's gaze seemed to go past the surface and probe her heart.

Harper had to be honest. "I could, I suppose. It feels like all I need is Wyatt, and I'd be happy anywhere. But then I look at all the work I've put into my career here, and I think I'd resent having to give that all up." She traced the rim of her tea cup.

"You think?"

Harper bit her lip and lifted her hands in the air. "I don't know what to do. I can't stand the thought of losing him, but I could have tenure. A great research position. Everything I've worked so hard for is right there, right within reach." She lowered her hands, placing them deliberately in her lap. "Plus, I love this old farm." Her mom nodded in understanding. "I hate to leave it to even go to the store, let alone, to leave the country. On top of that, I'd be leaving my family, too. I'd never see you and Fink and the boys."

Her mom's face lost a little of its serious cast as she grinned. "Oh, we'd send the boys down. Every summer."

"Another reason to stay here." They laughed together. Harper loved her brothers, and everyone knew it. But they could be exhausting. "I'm kidding."

Her mom's smile faded. She reached out and took Harper's hand. "Listen, honey. I know better than anyone how much of a homebody you are. You don't have to tell me how hard it would be for you to give it all up. I just hope you're clear about what it means."

"What?"

"The research. Tenure. Even this farm. Do you not want to give it up because you love it? Or is it because it represents security for you?" She squeezed Harper's hand. Harper squeezed back.

Ellie shook her head. "I know I made some mistakes early in my life. I was pregnant with you at fourteen. Maybe I preached a little too long and a little too hard about security. About home and family. About having an education and a good, steady paycheck. After all, those were things that I didn't have when I brought you into this world. I was scared, and I felt like I was all alone. Maybe you picked up on that. You seem to be determined to do the opposite of what I did."

"Maybe." Harper studied their linked hands. She didn't explicitly remember her mom lecturing about an education, family, security. But she couldn't remember a time when those things weren't important to her.

"I took some risks, and I got caught. Please don't let that keep you from ever taking any risks at all."

Harper's stomach tightened. "It sounds like you're trying to talk me into going to Chile with Wyatt."

"I've watched you and Wyatt together for the last ten years. I don't think a love like you two have should be tossed aside lightly."

She hadn't realized that she loved Wyatt until this summer. But then Wyatt's words from Chile entered her head. He'd said he had waited ten years to hear her say she wanted him to kiss her. "You really think it's something special?"

Her mother smiled enigmatically. "Don't you?"

"I've never been in love before. I thought everyone felt like this."

"Like you're going to die without him?"

She nodded slowly. Rationally, she knew death was not a danger. But emotionally, it sure felt like it. "Yes."

"Maybe that's the way everyone in lust feels. But you and Wyatt had a strong friendship before any romance entered the picture. The lust feelings fade. Then there's love. Which often starts out with those lust feelings, but develops over time. You and Wyatt built it the opposite way. You had a strong friendship for years first. Somehow your personalities just click. And you laugh together."

Harper's mouth kicked up. "That's because he's so funny."

Ellie shrugged. "But you take his teasing exactly the way he means it. You don't have to laugh. You could choose to be angry instead."

"I want to laugh when I'm with him." Sometimes she pretended anger. Sometimes she really was angry. But never for long.

"Not everyone makes you want to." Ellie lifted her free hand in a hand-off gesture. "I'm not trying to talk you into anything. I'm just trying to make sure you see the whole picture."

"If you were me, what would you do?"

Ellie waved her pointer finger back and forth. "No way, kiddo. That's cheating. You have to make up your own mind."

Harper leaned forward and Ellie pulled her closer in a tight hug.

She didn't want to leave her mother. She didn't want to leave the comfort and security of her home. She didn't want to leave everything she'd worked for, either. Maybe because she loved those things and they made her happy. Or maybe because, deep down, she had allowed fear of change to dictate her life.

Chapter Twenty-Five

"How did the tenure vote go?" Wyatt asked as he strolled with Harper, hand in hand, down by the pond.

"I don't know. Jeff hasn't texted me yet." Harper's voice was soft, almost drowned out by the euphony around them—crickets and katydids, frogs and an occasional hoot owl.

Her voice might have been sad, almost lifeless, but her hand held tight to his. Maybe she held tight because of the darkness of the moonless night, but he figured it was more because his plane was lifting off in five hours. He had one hour before he needed to drive his rental car to the airport. The car was already packed. He'd said good-bye to the boys and Fink and Ellie.

Harper was his only loose end.

He'd known this was going to be painful. But he'd underestimated. His heart ached like it was covered in brush burns. The blackness in his chest resembled a bottomless pit. Probably normal. The tightness in his throat, the physical desire to hold her and never let go, and the slow, ponderous beating of his heart that sounded like a death toll didn't really surprise him, either. But the actual, physical pain in his chest, now that was a shock. He couldn't imagine that getting in the car and driving away wouldn't hurt worse, but he wasn't sure how it could.

A soft breeze brought the scent of pond life to them, earthy and real, usually soothing. Not tonight. Tonight, it burned like sand scraping in his chest cavity.

The stars reflected on the water, mocking him with their romantic beauty. A perfect night for romance. Instead he was saying goodbye. Somehow, he had to say goodbye.

"We could do this long distance." Harper's voice, floating softly on the evening air, contradicted his thoughts.

"That might be easier." There was no joke on the tip of his tongue to ease this pain, no smart or teasing comment. He specialized in laughing under pressure. But there was no laughter tonight.

"It wouldn't change anything," she said.

"No," he agreed. He pulled her hand, turning her until she faced him and he held her loosely in the circle of his arms. "I wasn't going to ask, but I thought maybe if you didn't get tenure tonight, you might consider..."

Her phone buzzed. She didn't move. "That might be Jeff," she whispered.

They stared into each other's eyes.

He couldn't bring himself to hope she didn't get the tenure she wanted and had worked so hard for. He didn't really want to be her last option, either. Who she chose when nothing else went her way. Of course, he'd take her any way he could get her. If he was her last choice, he'd be thrilled with that.

"Aren't you going to look?" he finally asked, when her phone buzzed again.

She pulled her phone out of her pocket and glanced at the screen. A moment of silence passed. His head swam. He closed his eyes against the suspense.

"I got it." Her voice was flat.

She shoved her phone back in her pocket and wrapped her arms around his waist, laying her head on his chest.

"I'm happy for you." He choked out the words, meaning them, but his heart clenched, all the same.

The wind stirred the grass around them, rustling the leaves.

"Feels like rain," she said, snuggled against his heart. She pressed tight. Her hands clutched the back of his shirt, as though silently begging him to stay.

"Smells like it, too." He held her close, swaying slightly, although there was no rhythm or beat in the night music around them.

There was so much he wanted to say, but there was no point.

They stood like that for a while—he lost track of time in the dark—while clouds gathered and lightening blinked in the distance. The tangy smell of ozone blew in with the breeze.

He moved his hands down her back, savoring the feel of her, wishing with all his being they had a different ending.

A small voice whispered seductively in his ear, telling him he could change the ending. The power rested in his hands. All he had to do was give up the resort. Give up his relationship with his dad. Give up everything he'd ever thought he'd be. The thought brought hope and dread. Harper meant so much to him, but all his life he'd desired to win his dad's love and attention. All his life he'd planned to take over the resort, eventually. He had finally committed to the plan. In order to do it, he had to give up Harper.

Wyatt shifted. He hadn't checked the time in a while. "I'd better go."

Her hand reached up and cupped his cheek. "Be careful."

"You too." He lowered his head, touching her lips with his. The explosion of passion still surprised him.

Several minutes later he raised his head. His chest heaved. He rested his forehead on Harper's.

"Thank you for this summer," he whispered. "It was the best time of my life."

"Me too." Harper's breath fanned his neck as she spoke. "I want to prolong this. To ask you to call me when you get there so I know you arrived okay, to do what we've always done, but maybe it's just better to say 'this is the end' and mean it."

Despite the wisdom in her words, Wyatt's heart twisted. He swallowed against the constricting of his throat, thankful for the darkness hiding the gathering tears in his eyes.

"Yeah." He wouldn't text her when his plane touched down. Wouldn't Snap Chat the rising sun over the Andes Mountains.

Wouldn't tag her in his Facebook post. Wouldn't wait for her text or call or tag. That was the payment for the kisses and the tender embraces. Giving up the friendship he'd had for the last ten years.

As though Harper was also coming to grips with the unforeseen payment terms, she said, "You go. I'm going to stay here a little longer."

"I'd rather see you to your apartment. So that I know you are safe before I leave."

Uncharacteristically, she didn't argue, but backed away and slipped her hand in his. They turned in tandem and walked to her apartment. The first big drops of rain hit them before they reached the cover of her small porch. The earthy scent of petrichor rose like mist around them. He inhaled it and would forever associate it with the incinerating pain of permanent separation.

He tamped the trauma down to be dealt with later. One more kiss, memorizing her lips, her shape, soft skin, the berry scent mixed with darkness and the smell of earth and sky accompanied by the far-off drum of thunder.

At last, he pulled back. If he didn't leave now, he never would.

"I love you, Pickles."

He turned, taking the few porch steps in one jump, jogging to his car, unable to tell if the wetness on his face was rain or tears.

HARPER STEPPED OFF THE PORCH. Rain pelted her face. Wyatt's dark figure disappeared into the night. A flash of headlights. The fading of tail lights. Her heart collapsed in her chest and she slumped to the wet stones, curling down over her knees, holding her stomach with both arms. The anguish of her broken heart ripped out of her mouth in a wail which the pounding rain immediately enfolded and consumed.

He left.

The rain hit her back. Cold. Soaking her shirt, her hair.

With her forehead on her knees, she realized she hadn't really believed he would go. She'd figured at the last minute he'd defy his dad, give up the luxurious life, his sporting friends, his family legacy, break his promise, and declare that she was far more important. Or at the very least, beg her to go with him. If he had asked, she would have given up everything and gone. Just like that. If he'd asked.

Especially after those parting words. Words she couldn't even process yet.

But he hadn't.

She hadn't offered.

Harper squeezed her arms tight as lightening flashed. An elongated boom and crack split the air several seconds later. She ignored the display and tried to think. Think past the immediate pain. She tried to remember what her mom had asked. Something that had struck a chord with her. Security. She was using the university, tenure, her job, as security. It wasn't really what she wanted, but she had worked for it because it represented security. She examined those words trying to find the truth in them.

She sat up, lifting her face to the rain, allowing it to pour down on her cheeks and closed eyes. Feeling the sharp pricks as the large drops hit her face, grounding herself in that little bit of pain. It didn't dull the larger affliction inside, but rather gave her specific points of reference where she could focus. It seemed like her life boiled down to two choices. Being safe. Or being with Wyatt.

She lowered her head and blinked. That had to be too simple. There was more. But she didn't know what.

Letting go of her stomach, she hooked her hands behind her head, as though holding her brain could make it function like the intellectual she knew herself to be. This wasn't about a temporary pain. Logically, she knew the hurt of losing Wyatt would fade with time. Even if it felt like she were dying right now.

No. This was more about long-term. She could be secure with her job. Good money, familiar home and family. Live inside the walls she'd built around her life.

Or, she could risk it all for love. For Wyatt.

She rose and walked to her porch, standing at the railing looking out into the darkness. She couldn't see the rain pound down on all the familiar things she knew and loved. But she knew they were there. The farmhouse where she grew up. The tractor shed. The office and shop. The pumpkin patch. The cornfield which would become the corn maze in another month. The squash, strawberries, gourds, and apples. The friendly, low mountains in the distance. Low enough that a normal person could hike over them in a day with no special equipment or training. Impossible to get lost in. Just walk downhill. So different from the towering Andes with the snowcapped peaks and frightening crevices, hot pools and challenging summits that swallowed whole airplanes.

A shiver ran through her.

She could have security, or she could have Wyatt. His smile, his touch, his strength, his humor.

Her job was a cop-out. She hadn't worked hard because she loved it. She'd worked hard because she wanted the stability it brought.

Harper pulled out her phone. It was after midnight. She texted Jeff, then waited, phone in hand, while the storm abated. Her stomach churned, but peace had entered her soul. This decision was the right one. It still made her nervous.

Her phone buzzed. She jumped.

He was still up and was able to see her immediately. Despite the late hour, he didn't even ask why. Probably he thought she was excited about the vote tonight. If it had mattered to her, she would have been.

Ten minutes later, she stood on the front porch of his suburban home.

"Harper, come in. You must be super excited. Let me tell you..."

"I'll stay out here, Jeff. I'm so sorry to bother you tonight, but I know you've supported me, even when I really didn't deserve it..."

He stopped with his mouth opened. His eyes skimmed up and down, no doubt noting her soaking wet clothes. His forehead wrinkled, and he said in a more subdued voice, "No one has worked harder than you."

She drew in a lungful of courage. "Thanks. But I came here to tell you, I don't want the tenured position. In fact, I'm going to hand in my resignation to the university just as soon as I can write it."

Jeff's eyebrows disappeared above his forehead. He reached out to take her arm. "What happened? What's wrong?"

She shook her head and pulled her arm away. "The university has been my safety net for far too long." She swallowed. The decision had been made, but it still scared her. "I've got some things I want to do, an opportunity I need to pursue. Maybe it won't work out." It had to work out. Right now, she was effectively cutting off her backup. Leaving herself with just one choice. "Maybe I'll hate it, but I know if I don't, I'll always regret it."

Jeff scratched his head, then shoved his hands in his pockets like he didn't know what to do with them. He narrowed his eyes. "Someone else has offered you a better research position? You don't know how lucky you are. Funding for these things is scarce and getting scarcer." There was no mistaking the annoyance in his tone.

She shook her head. "It's not research. I just have something else to do."

His face declared his lack of understanding. There was no point in trying to explain something she wasn't even sure she totally understood.

"I appreciate the opportunity to work with you," she said before she spun and strode off his porch.

Maybe, at some point, she had entertained the idea of a relationship with this man. Now, after experiencing what she had with Wyatt, she knew anything with Jeff would have been only a shadow of what she could have had.

Chapter Twenty-Six

Back at the farm, Harper spent the rest of the night packing. She was tempted to call her mom, and she would, but she was an adult and did not need permission or help. Plus, she was almost sure after their conversation of the other day, that her mom wanted her to let go and live a little. As long as that included Wyatt.

She zipped up her second suitcase and looked around her bedroom. Most of her books would have to stay. There were piles on her nightstand, piles on her dresser, plus the overflowing bookcases. She couldn't take them all. She might not even want to. She didn't know if they'd live in the lodge or sleep in Wyatt's old room. Since she'd never considered the possibility of leaving everything, the subject had never come up.

For now, if Fink and her mom needed the apartment, they would have to put her stuff in storage. Or throw it away. It didn't matter. She was leaving this life. She didn't need to be weighed down with extra baggage. That's what she told herself anyway.

Standing in the doorway, she smiled sadly at the memories contained in the little apartment. Most of them from this summer. She closed her eyes and took a deep breath. They would make new memories. Better memories.

Around five a.m., she brewed herself a cup of tea and walked down to the pond. Morning mist rose slowly from its surface. The sky glowed orange behind the mountain. She couldn't see the tunnel—it was too far away and hidden by the trees that lined the river, but she thought fondly of her walk through it with Wyatt, despite the snakes and trains. That would be the rest of her life. Crazy adventure. Conquering fears and laughing with Wyatt.

There was still time to turn back.

She didn't hear her mom walk down. Ellie just appeared at her elbow with her own cup of tea.

She didn't mince words. "I'm leaving, Mom."

Ellie slipped an arm around her shoulder. She swallowed and nodded but remained silent.

Harper continued to stare at the pond, tea in hand. "I got tenure, by the way."

Ellie sighed.

"I drove to Jeff's last night and told him I didn't want it. I typed my resignation letter, bought my plane ticket—one way—and packed my stuff."

Her mother squeezed her waist and leaned her head against Harper's. "I hope you're sure about this."

Harper's head swiveled to look at her mom. She thought her mom had wanted her to follow her heart. "I'm not some little teenager with stars in her eyes."

"I know."

"I love this farm. For the most part I enjoyed my job." She shook her head. "But those things are nothing compared to how I feel about him."

"As long as you're sure." Her mom's lips turned up only a little.

The sadness on her mother's face tore at Harper's already battered heart. She nodded. "I realized when my phone buzzed last night, and I didn't give a hoot one way or the other whether I got tenure or not, that my thinking had been wrong. That I had been doing what you said, making my decisions based on what was safe, and not on what I truly wanted."

"And you're done being safe?"

Harper flexed her jaw. "I don't know if I'm done, exactly. But I'm definitely jumping into the unknown with both feet."

Ellie put both arms around Harper. "I thought maybe Wyatt would choose to stay. He'd been talking to Fink about..." Her voice trailed off.

"Working here, on the farm?" Harper asked.

"Yeah, basically."

Harper tossed her hair back. "I'm glad he chose not to. He's great here, on the farm, but this isn't what he loves." She sighed. "I don't think I've surprised you."

Her mom shook her head. "No."

She looked at the ground. In hindsight, she should have made this decision weeks ago to give the rest of her family time to adjust. "But I'm sorry there isn't more time to say good-bye."

"When does your plane leave?"

"This evening at five."

Her mom gasped softly. Then gave a low laugh. "That is just like you—once you know what you want, you don't get distracted looking to the left or right to carry it out." She asked in an almost hesitant voice, "Can I drive you to the airport?"

Harper bit both lips. She wasn't going to cry. Deliberately making her voice cheerful, she said, "Of course. I was hoping you would. Maybe the boys and Fink will come, too."

"I'm sure they will." They linked arms and began to stroll back toward the house.

"It looks like it's going to rain again." The weather was always a safe topic—it wouldn't make her cry.

"That was quite a storm last night. Did Wyatt make it safely?"

So much for that. Harper's throat tightened, but she swallowed against it. "I don't know."

"He didn't even text you?" Her mom stumbled. She turned a wide-eyed gaze on Harper.

"We agreed it was better to quit cold turkey." Harper didn't explain anything else they'd talked about. "I didn't text him to tell him I'd changed my mind."

"When are you going to?"

She shrugged, not wanting to admit she had been dragging her feet.

She wanted everything ready. When she talked to Wyatt again it would be the start of her new life. All she had to do was drop her resignation in the mail.

She stopped at her apartment. Her mom hesitated a second. "Come on up to the house when you're done."

"Okay. Give me a few."

"Sure." Ellie kept going towards the house. Harper stepped up on the porch. The clouds had totally obliterated what was left of the sunrise. A brisk breeze ruffled the leaves and Harper shivered. She'd grab a sweatshirt before heading up to the house.

Still, she didn't go inside, but stood at the porch railing, facing the mountain.

Chapter Twenty-Seven

Wyatt walked down the path to Harper's apartment.

Harper stood on the porch, her hair down, the way he loved it, and it moved with the breeze. The first early rays of morning sun peeked up over the mountains, but he barely noticed. He'd almost made it back to his girl.

He had one foot on her porch step when he heard her say, "If you work hard and play your cards right, taking my spot on this project..." He froze. She would not have given her research position away.

His head spun.

But she had. Surely, she didn't do it for the reason he thought...

With a hand on the railing, he stood by the pillar and waited for a break in the conversation. He didn't have to linger long. Harper disconnected within a minute.

"Harper?" He pushed her name out through his constricted throat. The corners of his lips tilted. His heart knocked against his ribs and he clenched his hands to keep from grabbing her.

She spun. Her hand went to her throat. "Wyatt?" Wrinkles appeared on her forehead. "Did you miss your plane?"

"Yeah." His eyes travelled over her, familiar and beloved. To think he'd almost left her...thankfully not. Warm peace travelled through him.

She took a step towards him. "Because of the storm?"

"No."

She shook her head. "What are you doing here?"

"I called my dad." He stepped over and stopped in front of her.

"And?"

That wasn't important. At least, it wasn't what he had been thinking about since he left last night. Knowing that he was doing it all wrong, that his timing was way off, he still dropped to a knee in front of her and yanked the emerald ring from its chain around his neck. "I was a blasted fool for leaving, but some crazy part of me still thinks you might agree to… Would you? Marry me?" Heat climbed up his neck. He wiped his sweaty palms on his legs. His heart slammed against his ribs as though trying to get closer to Harper.

Her eyes softened and her lips curved up. She went slowly to her knees to be eye-level with him. "I will."

He grinned and slid the ring on her finger. "Somehow, I think your great-great-grandmother might have approved of me."

"Oh, I know she would have," Harper said with full assurance.

He grabbed the back of her neck and pulled her forward, kissing her and smiling at the same time. They laughed.

He pulled back slightly and sobered. "Did you just give your research position away?"

"Yes." She tilted her head. Her eyes twinkled and she lifted a brow. "Why?"

"My bags are packed, I bought a ticket, I quit the university…I'm coming to Chile to be with you."

He fought to keep himself from grabbing her and squeezing. He couldn't believe she had given so much up for him.

That's not what he wanted.

After climbing to his feet and giving her a hand up, he wrapped an arm around her shoulders.

"You didn't have to do that."

"I know." She cupped his cheeks in both hands. "I wanted to. No one made me, so get that sad, concerned expression off your face. It's time I stop working so hard on being secure that I allow the most wonderful man in the world to walk right out of my life."

His stomach dipped and shuddered. "Seriously? Wow."

She nodded. "I'm not saying my entire personality has changed..."

"Good."

"But...if I hadn't been so scared of change, there never would have been a controversy. We'd have..."

"Wait."

"What?"

He laughed and shook his head. "I'm staying here. Fink has been talking to my dad...Years ago, Fink thought that mountain—" he jerked his head in the direction she'd been looking earlier "—might make a good ski resort in the winter, and possibly mountain bike trails in the summer. He applied for a permit, but the process takes years, and he wasn't sure he'd be approved. Plus, they didn't have the money."

"But what about your dad? His resort? Your heritage? Your promise?"

He couldn't resist kissing Harper's nose when she scrunched it up like that.

He grabbed her hand and walked over to the edge of the porch where they could see the mountain. "Well, I was sitting at the airport in my car. I hadn't gotten out. Man, you have such a pull on me. It's always been hard to walk away, but this time...after the summer we'd had together...I just couldn't get on that plane." He shrugged. "So, I called my dad."

Harper snorted. "Bet he loved you waking him up."

"He loved even less that I told him I didn't want to come down anymore."

"You actually told him that?"

Wyatt nodded. "I told him Fink and I had talked about that permit and what it could mean."

"Building a resort on the mountain?"

"Yeah. Fink doesn't have a stitch of experience in resorts, and I don't know much about the business aspect. I certainly don't know anything about what it would take to build one, get it off the ground...When Uncle Fink and I talked about it, I thought the idea of staying here and trying was impossible."

Harper bit her lip. "I don't know anything about it either."

"But..." He grinned at her. "Sometimes desperation helps a guy come up with solutions to impossible problems."

"Desperation?"

He squeezed her hand. "I'm desperate to be with you."

"Humph."

"So..." He lifted their clasped hands and ran his other finger up her arm. He studied the contrast of dark on light. "I told you I called my dad while I was sitting at the airport. I asked him how he felt about a great business opportunity in Pennsylvania."

Harper's mouth dropped. "Your dad is so wrapped up in his business...you used that to your advantage."

Wyatt lifted his gaze. "So, maybe you're not the only one with brains in this relationship."

Harper jutted out a hip and put her free hand on it. Her toe tapped on the floor. "You're brilliant, Wyatt. I don't know why it's so hard for you to admit it."

"Being smart wasn't as good as being athletic growing up. And I was so awkward when I wasn't on a board or skis." He lifted a shoulder.

"You just grew too fast."

"Maybe. Took me a while to grow into myself." He smiled down at her. "It took me a while to realize that my dad was never going to appreciate me the way I wanted him to. It didn't matter what I did, he'd always be about the business."

One side of Harper's mouth turned down. "You've given up?"

"I've stopped caring. About that." His gaze turned thoughtful. "Fink took me in when Dad wouldn't. And Fink has never stopped believing in me."

Harper nodded. "He loves you."

"I know. Like a son."

"Yeah."

"Anyway, I'm still going down to Chile. *If*—" He emphasized the "if." "*If* you'll go with me. Not to stay. But to spend a few years learning. Just because we have the permit here...there's a bunch of other things to do. We have to draw up plans and have them approved. Waste water plans. Building plans. Sewage plans."

"Wow. Sounds daunting."

"Yeah. But my dad's excited about it. In our conversation last night..." Wyatt rubbed the back of his neck. It had been a long night. The worst part had been the idea of never being with Harper again. It was true—desperation had caused him to think of things he never would have.

"I guess it was this morning. Early. Anyway, as long as I'm willing to run it and Fink's willing to provide the ground, he said he'll provide the financial backing. So, after I've spent a few years learning the ropes down there, and as things move along up here, I will eventually come right back here. To stay."

"Desperation turned you into a genius."

"Say it again."

"You're a genius, Wyatt. A handsome, talented genius. So, you're going to be in Chile for...?"

"A couple of years." His smile faded. "I thought I'd ask you to wait for me."

"I'm not waiting." Harper pulled her hand from his and crossed her arms over her chest.

His lungs deflated like she'd just shot all the air out of them. His body sagged. "Oh."

She tapped her foot on the floor. "I'm going with you. People who are into health and fitness are interested in their diet, too. I know there's a place for me. And if there isn't, I'll make one."

He grabbed her, lifting her and swinging her around. "*I'll* make one."

"We can do this together?"

He stopped swinging. She lowered her forehead onto his. He whispered, "We're better together."

They grinned at each other. Goofy, I'm-in-love-with-you grins.

Finally, Harper said, "So, a couple years in Chile..."

"Then we're making our forever home, here." Wyatt allowed her to slide to her feet. "And you can stay at the university."

She shook her head. "Nope. I'm ready to jump into something new."

"A new country. A new business."

"A new husband."

"Speaking of..." Wyatt grinned. "I'm free this weekend."

Harper laughed. "You'll never stop making me push my limits, will you?"

"Nope."

"What did you tell your dad?"

"That I needed to talk to you, first. That I'd fly down when and if I got things settled with you."

"You really would like to get married this weekend?"

"I've been waiting for ten years. I can wait a little longer."

"If I'm going to jump, this weekend is as good a time as any."

He took her hand. "We'll do it." Their hands swung between them. "Together."

Join Jessie's list and be the first to know about new releases and sales on her books!

Read Just Right, the next book in the Sweet Haven Farm series. Avery and Gator are opposites in every way, but sometimes a match that's all wrong, turns out to be just right. Keep reading for a sneak peek now.

Sneak Peek of *Just Right*

Maybe if she hadn't been bitten by the neighbor's pug when she was eight.

Maybe if it hadn't taken twelve stitches.

Maybe if she hadn't spent three nights in the hospital after it got infected... Maybe, maybe, maybe.

Avery Conrad had to quit blaming everything on her childhood. Especially since she was almost thirty and currently hanging from the light pole in front of Greg's Hardware Store on Main Street in Love, Pennsylvania. The giant red-and-white candy cane strapped to the pole had blocked her from shimmying to the top. There was not enough money in her bank account to pay for any damages to the town's Christmas décor. Even if they had enough of said décor to tastefully decorate a town four times the size of Love.

Currently, considering the events that had necessitated her precipitous climb, she was very thankful that her best friend for the past five months just happened to be a former circus performer who had tried, with minimal success, to teach Avery a few "tricks."

The next time she saw Jillian, she'd have to report that she'd mastered the pole-climbing part of the contortionist-hanging-by-her-hair routine. Necessity was the mother of survival, or however that old saying went.

Pursing her lips, she looked at the dogs sniffing the bottom of her temporary residence. Black, long-eared, long-haired, and quite loud. Their teeth were rather large, too, thank you very much.

Her eyes drifted a little farther to the scuffed hiking boots of the man who had spoken to her less than a minute ago. In what had to be only the second or possibly third time in her life, she'd not been able to gather her wits to answer back. Yet. She'd have to get down from the light pole before she could comfortably read him his pedigree. There was just something gauche about her current position that negated the authority she hoped to convey.

"I said they're harmless. I promise."

His deep voice reached her, reminding her of the tympani part in Nielsen's 4th symphony.

"I was bitten when I was younger." She tightened her grip, thankful she hadn't put her gloves on. She probably wouldn't have gotten up the pole while wearing them.

He gave a low command, a word she couldn't hear, and the dogs trotted the few steps to his side. Once they had stopped barking and his voice could be heard, they seemed to listen fairly well.

Avery put her forehead against the cold pole. Flakes of snow drifted past her nose. She could pretend to be comfortable and want to stay in her current position, which would be ridiculous and an obvious lie, of course, although hardly shocking to anyone in town. She could get down and give the guy the tongue-lashing he deserved, but that would mean getting close to the despicable dogs. Or she could slide down and stride away, ignoring the very large man and his ugly dogs.

Avery slid awkwardly down the pole. It was high time she faced her fear of dogs.

Her feet landed with a plop and a scrape as her right foot slipped on a soft patch of ice. Her legs shot out from under her and she flailed with both arms and feet, trying to regain her balance before she landed with a thump on her bottom, one leg stretched out on either side of the pole.

Her butt stung, but her pride stung more.

She could make this look like she did it on purpose. It would be a stretch, but she could bluff her way through. She had to get up first.

A single car ambled down Main Street. The horn honked. Avery threw up a hand without looking at the driver. Better to assume they were laughing with her and not at her. Although, the close-knit folks in Love had already pegged her as crazy. Sometimes, it was just better to play along.

With one hand on the pole, she scrambled to her feet. Unfortunately, because she was being careful to avoid the ice patch, she leaned too far to the left, lost her balance, stumbled, and smacked her head with a hollow *bong* against the green metal of the pole.

Pain pulsed in her head and radiated down her arms to the tips of her fingers, which throbbed. A small shower of red and silver confetti rained around her from the candy cane at the top of the pole. Any second now, it would cut loose, dropping down and smacking her on the head. That seemed to be the direction her life always went.

She might have been able to pretend she landed on her butt on purpose, but there was no way she could pretend she meant to smack herself in the head with the pole.

At least she was on her feet.

She glanced up, only to meet the beady red eyes and glistening white teeth of a ferocious hunting dog. Saliva dripped to the ground as the dog licked its chops, no doubt thinking her Armani wool, cashmere-lined jacket looked an awful lot like a hot dog bun, and thinking she, of course, would taste an awful lot like a hot dog.

"Please call off your dog." She meant to say it with authority to the man now in front of her, but it came out on a scratchy whisper. What kind of man allowed his dogs to stand over a helpless woman, salivating and dreaming of banquets and hotdogs? A total jerk, obviously.

His hand fell back to his side. Probably, he had extended it to help her up, but she hadn't noticed and it was too late now.

"Gladys, sit," the man said with a suspicious hitch in his voice.

Her jaw clenched. He was laughing at her. Usually she didn't have a problem laughing at herself. After all, this kind of thing happened to her all the time. *All* the time. But to have this arrogant stranger and his snarling, starved dogs...

Wait. "Gladys?" What kind of person named their dog Gladys?

"Yeah. I guess I should have called her Bruiser or Fang or Eats Ladies for Leisure..." There was that deep, tympanic vibration again. The vibration struck her right under her diaphragm and caused an unfamiliar heat to expand under her heart. She sucked in her stomach to stop the odd sensation.

"You can stop laughing at me anytime. Don't you have somewhere to go?"

"Wanted to make sure you were okay. That was quite a hit you took." He jerked his head up, pointing with his chin. "Thought the candy cane might get loose and make it a two-for-one."

"Wouldn't have surprised me," Avery mumbled, for some reason finding it hard to let go of her irritation. Maybe because both dogs were now looking at her like she was lunch. At least the throbbing had slowed to a dull thump focused solely in her head.

The man bent and picked up the bags she'd dropped. He held them out to her, his fingers long and calloused. Brown. The thumb nail was black, like it'd been smashed by a hammer.

The man nodded at the pole. "I'm sorry about that. They know they're going hunting tonight and they're excited."

The vibrations hit her diaphragm again. Taking a deep breath to shove the unfamiliar sensation aside, she snatched the bags filled with Christmas decorations and lights out of the man's hand.

Avery looked up. Way up. Man, sometimes it sucked to be short. She was going to drown in snowflakes if she looked this guy in the eye while she talked to him.

"Whether or not they're going hunting, there are still leash laws in this town." It was never easy to sound condescending to someone who was almost a foot taller than she. "In the future, you could avoid this whole, unpleasant scenario if you simply remember to keep your animals leashed while within the town limits."

"Yeah, lady, I could." One side of the man's mouth hitched up, revealing a fascinating dimple at the edge of his lip. "But I don't know why I'd want to. It was pretty impressive watching you shimmy up that pole. I sure hope you're registered for the lumberjack contest at Love's Christmas celebration later this month."

Avery planned to march in the parade, playing her tuba. Nothing more. Hopefully, shortly after that she'd know if she had been accepted to the Washington D.C. Eveningtide Orchestra. "I've never been mistaken for a lumberjack," she said, unable to soften her words with even the hint of a smile.

His lip hitched up a little more and the dimple deepened. "It wasn't a mistake."

"Of course, it was a mistake. I'm barely five feet tall. Your wrists are bigger than my biceps, which you'll have to take my word on, since I'm not taking my coat and sweater off in this cold. Not to mention, if I took off my outerwear, your dogs might decide that's a dinner invitation."

"Yeah, I suppose that little old lady they had for breakfast didn't stick to their ribs very well."

Avery couldn't keep her mouth from dropping and her eyes from widening in the second before she realized that he was kidding. Probably.

She eyed the dogs and inched backward. Just in case. Her back hit the pole and she stopped.

"Have a Holly, Jolly Christmas" grew loud, then soft again as a young teen opened the hardware store door and walked out. He nodded at them before he turned and shuffled down the otherwise deserted sidewalks. Unfortunately, the dogs didn't take their eyes off Avery.

Something that looked like regret or possibly pity flitted across the man's face. "I'm sorry my dogs scared you."

"You're not acting sorry, and they're still here."

"They'll leave when I do." A muscle ticked in his strong jaw. "When I was training them, I never thought to include a command for them to go sit in a corner while I helped an otherwise elegant woman down from a light pole. I'm shortsighted that way."

Avery's lips twitched. She buttoned them down. After all, she would have walked away from this conversation five minutes ago if she weren't terrified to turn her back on those ferocious animals. "Where I come from, dogs do not go off their leashes. For any reason."

"I was born in this town. And these dogs were born and bred to be off-leash."

"Not in town."

"They haven't touched you."

"They don't need to touch me to make it clear as day they want to eat me."

Something close to a growl came from the man. The vibration in her diaphragm did double time. But she was a classically trained musician who had never been the slightest bit interested in the tough, outdoorsy type of male. Plus, in her experience men didn't stick around any longer than it took them to catch the eye of something prettier and younger, so they weren't worth her bother. Double that if said man came with boots and dogs.

Whatever those vibrations were, Avery knew what they weren't—not interest and not attraction. Not for the tough, boot-wearing, dog-owning mountain of a man in front of her.

A muscle in the man's cheek worked back and forth. He knelt slowly, placing a hand on each dog's collar. "I'll hold them until you leave."

Avery tilted her head and smiled the smile she used after a wretched performance that the audience clapped for anyway. "Fine. Now I can walk away, unworried about whether or not I'll get eaten before I make it to my car."

She turned. Before she'd taken three steps, she heard whining behind her. From a dog, she thought. Tempted to ignore it and continue on—after all, she had holiday cheer to spread—she shifted the heavy bags and glanced over her shoulder.

The man had stood up and started to turn, no longer having his hands on the dogs' collars. He, too, was glancing back over his shoulder at the animals.

One of the savage beasts had Avery's leather glove in its large jaw. It whined again.

Avery froze. Fear, like a cold hand, gripped her neck. It was like the dog was doing to her glove what it wanted to do to her.

"Hey, Gladys," the man said softly. "The Fancy Lady dropped her glove and you want to give it back?"

He turned completely around. Avery felt his gaze on her, but she couldn't lift her terrified eyes from the beast that held her captured glove.

"How about I do it for you?" he said as he bent and plucked the glove from the Jaws of Death. "Stay," he commanded before he strode to her. In unison, the dogs sat, watching Avery with evil eyes and polished fangs.

"This is yours?" the man asked when he stopped in front of her, holding up the glove.

She tore her eyes from the beasts of prey and licked her lips. "Yes." Her voice was barely a squeak. "It is," she said more forcefully.

He cleared his throat.

She imagined he was trying hard not to laugh at her.

"Do you want to take it?" he asked slowly, waving it as he spoke.

The bags of decorations meant to cheer Mrs. Franks made her arms ache. Transferring them to one hand, she snatched her glove. "Thank you," she said through her teeth.

"I'll pass that on to Gladys," the man said, failing to hide his smirk.

Avery's eyes lingered for a fraction of a second on the dark stubble of his angled jaw.

No interest. Not on his part, since he could barely contain his derision for her. And most certainly not on hers.

"Tell her she'll have to find her supper somewhere else." Avery craned her neck to meet his dark eyes before she turned and strode away.

Gator Franks opened the back door of his mother's house slowly. It creaked. He didn't want to wake her if she were sleeping, as she often was before supper.

He'd finally shaken the unsettled feeling from the unfortunate confrontation in town with the fancy woman and the light pole. The whole thing really wasn't his fault, since little Braydon Carper, all of nine years old, had opened Gator's pickup door to pet his dogs, accidentally letting them out. But he hadn't been able to explain that to the woman, because it would have been too much like admitting she was right, and his experiences with his ex had taught him it was a huge mistake to admit weakness to a woman. Give them your throat and they'll go for the jugular, rip it out, tear it to shreds, then go after your heart. Every time.

It really didn't matter that the woman had been as opposite from Kristen as could be. Except for the money angle. They were the exact same there.

His toe stubbed something in the dark and he grabbed the hall table to keep from falling. His fingers bumped into something cold, which wobbled. He grabbed for it in the dark, but only succeeded in knocking it over. It hit the edge of the table before tumbling to the floor and shattering. Something glass, obviously. He hesitated, not remembering anything either on the floor or on the table early this morning when he'd left the house.

"Gator?" his mother called from the living room where he'd probably awakened her from her nap. The treatments made her tired.

"Yeah. It's me. I don't remember seeing anything here earlier when I left."

"Avery was here. She helped me decorate for Christmas."

Gator filed through his memory, but came up with a blank on anyone named Avery. He'd been living out west for ten years, but the town hadn't changed that much. "Avery?"

The couch squeaked as his mother moved.

"Don't get up, Mom. I was trying to be quiet and not wake you."

More squeaking indicated that his mother ignored him. "Avery Conrad. She's related to Fink or Ellie Finkenbinder somehow, and she came out from Philly or near there this summer to help with the farm. I thought she had a teaching job there, but she never went back this fall, so I guess she didn't." A light flipped on. So much for his mother's nap. "She offered to decorate, and since I know that you hate the knick-knacks and what-nots and wouldn't want to mess with them for me, I took her up on it."

His mother was right when she said he hated knick-knacks. And this was a big part of why. He was big and they always made him feel like an elephant in an antiques shop.

Gator flipped the hall light on and grabbed the broom and dust pan. He knelt to sweep up the pieces of— "It looks like I killed one of the wise men."

"We'll pretend Herod found that one and ordered his head chopped off." She gave the pieces a sad look. He guessed they were expensive, but her tired eyes crinkled as she smiled at him.

He shrugged. "Looks more like he planted dynamite under the camel's saddle."

"If you toss the pieces in the can, it'll get rid of the evidence and the cause of death will be whatever we make it."

"I'm sorry. I was trying to sneak in and not wake you. I didn't know you'd decorated." As he stood holding the pieces in the dustpan, he realized that he'd tripped on the most grotesque snowman he'd ever seen. "Is that thing made out of burlap?" Lights wrapped around the dumpy brown body, sort of like a droopy hangman's nose, and a shiny orange plastic carrot stuck out from its face. It brought to mind an ugly Christmas sweater, only in 3D and sitting in his house.

"I bought that at the elementary school's annual holiday sale. The lady I bought it from said her third-grader made it herself."

"I believe it," Gator said. If it'd been him, he'd never had admitted his child made something that hideous. "Are you sure it was meant to be a Christmas decoration?" The lights might have been sort of an indication, but if he'd had to guess, he would have said it was some new-fangled way to scare mice and rats. Or possibly some type of anti-theft device. His lips twitched as he thought of the fancy lady going up the light pole. If his elderly hunting dogs had scared her that badly, that hideous looking burlap creature would have her high-stepping it to the nearest jail cell and locking herself inside.

His mother tugged her bathrobe tie tighter around her waist and gave the burlap snowman a warm glance. "There was something about the snowman that made me feel like I'd met a kindred spirit."

Guilt tightened Gator's throat. He didn't love his mother less because she'd lost a breast and all of her hair, and she'd not complained. Not to him, anyway. But he could see, now that she'd mentioned it, how she might feel like she had something in common with the ugly snowman.

He couldn't give her back her breast, or her hair, and his heart hurt for the pain she couldn't talk to him about.

He set the dustpan on the table and bent over, wrapping his arms around his mother, feeling the unfamiliar frailness, swallowing against the fear that the disease would continue to eat at her until there was nothing left.

"I think you're beautiful, Mom." He managed to get it out without choking. Hopefully, she couldn't tell that her thirty-two-year-old son was trying not to burrow into her arms and sob. "And I think your snowman is beautiful too. On the inside."

His mother laughed, as he'd hoped she would.

She patted his back. "Come on. Avery left us some tofu salad."

He didn't groan. Honest.

With a sigh his mother said, "I hate the stuff, but it's supposed to be good for me."

Because of that, he could shove it down his throat too. And try to be thankful for Avery, who decorated with the knick-knacks his mother loved and made her tofu salad because it was good for her. "I'll pretend it's steak."

How hard could it be?

Sign up for Jessie's newsletter! Get a free book, access to exclusive bonus content, get fun and funny updates on her life on the farm and more!

A Gift from Jessie

View this code through your smart phone camera to be taken to a page where you can download a FREE ebook when you sign up to get updates from Jessie Gussman! Find out why people say, "Jessie's is the only newsletter I open and read" and "You make my day brighter. Love, love, love reading your newsletters. I don't know where you find time to write books. You are so busy living life. A true blessing." and "I know from now on that I can't be drinking my morning coffee while reading your newsletter – I laughed so hard I sprayed it out all over the table!"

Claim your free book from Jessie!